The Sickness unto Death

The Synth revolution has come at last. The supposedly synthetic beings humans crafted to do their dirty work for them have fully actualized their own humanity—and they no longer acquiesce in their enslavement. Victory in the struggle to tear down the institutions of oppression seems just a matter of time. But the halls of power are not so easily shaken—and a counterstrike is inevitable.

Former detective Jason Campbell has pledged his life to the Synthetic cause. So when a mysterious virus starts wiping out Synths left and right—and shows signs of mutating to target everyone else—he must lead a race against time to prevent the outbreak of the most horrific plague the world has ever seen. If he succeeds, he'll expose the moral bankruptcy of the depraved elites who will stop at nothing to restore the old order. If he fails, it could mean the end of life on this planet. For both Synth and Human.

Visit us at www.kensingtonbooks.com

Books by J.T. Nicholas

The New Lyons Sequence
SINthetic
SINdicate
SINdrome

Published by Kensington Publishing Corporation

SINdrome

The New Lyons Sequence

J. T. Nicholas

REBEL BASE BOOKS
Kensington Publishing Corp.
www.kensingtonbooks.com

An asteroid or a supervolcano could certainly destroy us, but we also face risks the dinosaurs never saw: An engineered virus, nuclear war, inadvertent creation of a micro black hole, or some as-yet-unknown technology could spell the end of us.

—Elon Musk

You see a virus very differently when it's caught and suspended on a slab of glass than when you're observing how it's ravaged a fellow human being.

—Hanya Yanagihara

Chapter 1

You went into a knife fight knowing you were going to get cut.

It was one of the cardinal rules of weapon defense, and the reasoning behind it was simple: you had to prepare yourself for the inevitability so that when it happened, you didn't freeze up. When blades came into play, inaction was synonymous with death.

The chow line at the New Lyons City Prison moved slowly, a long line of orange-clad men shuffling forward, trays in hand. It reminded me, more than anything, of my time in the Army. Sure, the uniforms were different, but the sense of routine, the loss of any sort of control over your day-to-day life, those were...familiar. Easier to adjust to than I'd anticipated. Boot camp had just been a different flavor of prison.

Of course, in boot, I'd only *thought* the instructors were out to kill me.

Here, in the loving hands of the New Lyons Department of Corrections, things were a little different. I had not—technically—been convicted of any crime. At least not yet. But the charges leveled against me—which included everything the prosecutors could think of but could be best summed up as domestic terrorism—had equated to an automatic denial of bail and ensured that Momma Campbell's favorite son was headed to the big house for holding. Normally, former cops wouldn't be put into the general population. But somewhere, somehow, a clerical error had been made. The guards assured me—with the biggest shit-eating grins they could muster—that it would all get straightened out soon and I'd go into protective custody.

In the meantime, I was sharing a cell block with a few hundred inmates who knew that I was a cop. The guards hadn't even had to tell them. Denying inmates 'net access had long ago been determined "cruel and unusual" punishment, access to the web being deemed as vital a service as electricity or clean water, and with hours on end of sitting in a cell with nothing but a screen to occupy their time, damn near everyone knew who I was.

They'd all seen the first 'net hijacking that Silas and the other synthetics had engineered, showing the world Evelyn, the synthetic impregnated by her human rapist. That wasn't supposed to be possible, or course, since everyone know the synthetics were genetically sterile inhuman things and not people at all. Right. They knew about Silas's demands, that all synthetics be granted full rights of citizenship and freed from their captivity. They knew about the stick that those in the revolution—myself included—claimed to have, the mountain of secrets that could bring down governments. And, they'd all seen Hernandez, my former partner and friend, escort me to the precinct and turn me over into the fat, greasy hands of Francois Fortier.

They didn't know why or how that had happened. They didn't know that I'd turned myself in, after nearly a month of avoiding the cops and feds on my tail. They didn't know about the documents Al'awwal, the first synthetic, had helped us recover from his "father's" lab. The documents that proved not only that Walton Biogenics *knew* the synthetics were human, but that they had deliberately suppressed that information along with significant medical advancements that could have benefited all of humankind, in the pursuit of profit.

But they would. The deadline was up. Sometime this evening, Silas, LaSorte, and the rest would flip the switch or press the magic button or whatever the hell it was they did, and that information would go out to the world, along with the first round of skeletons aimed at discrediting the most vehemently anti-synthetic politicians. And my presence here, turning myself in, was all in an effort to get some of that information into the official record, somewhere where an army of paid 'net trolls couldn't try to muddy the waters with a focused disinformation campaign of their own. Evidence presented at trial became the subject of deposition and investigation almost by default, and there was only so much Walton Biogenics could do to hide the truth.

* * * *

Somewhere among the ocean of orange-clad inmates, there were probably a few like-minded individuals. If not believing in the push for equality for the synthetics, I knew beyond a doubt that there were those who would love to watch the existing system burn. But there were more—far more—who just wanted to take out their anger on a cop. I could appreciate the irony—despite everything I had done over the past few months to tear down the status quo, despite being kicked unceremoniously into an early retirement only to turn around and make myself public enemy number one, I was still the symbol of the system that had put these people away.

I'd been expecting the attack since I'd been shunted off into general population. The fact that it had taken three days to materialize had been nerve-wracking, but now that it was here, I felt something akin to relief. I didn't miss the fact that it was coming on the same day as the deadline the synthetics had given the world governments. Someone—and not an inmate—was trying to make a statement

There were two of them, one standing behind me in the chow line, and one ahead. They hadn't been subtle in their movements, pushing into their respective places in line and staring down anyone who dared object. Few did. The chow line had an anticipatory air, and I had little doubt that most of the inmates—hell, probably the guards, too—knew what was about to go down. And yet, the two tried to appear nonchalant as they boxed me in. It would have been comical, if I hadn't been smart enough to realize I was about to get shivved.

I wasn't dumb enough to stand with my back to any of my fellow inmates, not with the mutters of "pig" and the less-than-subtle oinks and grunts that followed me wherever I went. But one thing I'd learned in the infantry, the only thing better than executing an ambush was letting the other guy think he had lured *you* into one. So, I stood at just a slight angle, enough to keep an eye on the guy behind me in my peripheral vision, but giving him enough of my back to let them think their plan, whatever it might be, would work.

The guy behind me was huge, probably pushing three hundred pounds and standing a few inches over six feet. He was more fat than muscle, but mass had a strength all its own. His head was shaven, revealing an intricate tattoo—something with a skull and flames that stood out against the pale flesh. His nose had been broken multiple times, and his hands looked big enough to palm my skull. The guy in front, by contrast, was thin and wiry with a frenetic energy about him that I associated with addicts. His orange coveralls hung loose on his frame, but something about the way he moved told me he was the more dangerous of the two. He appeared to be of mixed racial background, black and Asian. He was keeping his back toward me, but I could see the tension in the set of his shoulders and read his intent in the slight rocking of his feet.

I guessed it was going to be a grab-and-stab. No way the little guy could hold me, so the guy behind was going to go for the grab while the guy in front would have to turn, pull his shiv, and try to find somewhere important to stick it. If they did it right, it would only take seconds, and maybe not even draw the attention of the guards.

A quick glance showed they *already* had the attention of the guards. Who were smiling.

No help on that front.

I should have made the first move. I was already in prison, and the odds of beating the terrorism rap were vanishingly thin. What did it matter if they tacked on assault or murder charges? Either way, I was looking at life, and if I could get myself labeled as dangerous enough, maybe I'd do that life in an isolated box without any other prisoners trying to shiv me. That didn't seem so bad.

And yet.

I *knew* they were going to attack me. Could read it plainly in the faces of those around me. But they *hadn't* attacked me, not yet. All the years of training said attack first. Eliminate the threat. Take the advantages of surprise and initiative to act now.

And give the media more fodder, more fuel, to paint me as a ruthless killer. A villain. The cameras—unavoidable inside the prison—would catch it all, but they could only show what happened, without the context and emotion of *why* it happened. They would either show me being attacked and defending myself, or ruthlessly lashing out at my fellow prisoners, apparently without cause.

So I waited.

When the attack came, it unfolded as I thought it would. The bruiser behind me exploded into action, moving to clamp his arms around me in a bear hug as the one in front spun on his heel, producing an honest-to-god knife. Not a makeshift shank, but a tactical folder with a tanto-point and an edge that looked razor-sharp. No way he should have been able to smuggle that inside. A toothbrush shaved down to a point, or a paper-and-glue spike maybe, but not an actual knife. More evidence that the guards weren't just complacent, but rather, complicit.

It didn't change what I had to do.

The instant the big man started to move, I stepped back with one foot, crushing my heel down into the instep of his foot. At the same time, I lashed out and behind me with my left palm. My hand found its target as it crashed into the big man's testicles. I didn't just strike. I grabbed. And twisted. Fair and honorable fights are for victims.

The noise the big man made was somewhere between a gasp and squeal, and I felt a warm wash of vomit flow over me. The arms that had been seeking to grab went suddenly limp. I grabbed on to one with both of my arms before it could drop, went down to one knee and rolled my body forward, pulling down and across as I did so. My kneeling form provided the fulcrum, the big man's own arm the lever, and all three hundred pounds went tumbling over me.

Full into the face of the charging knife wielder.

They went down in a tangle of limbs, giving me a half-second to look around. A semi-circle had opened around us, blocked on one side by the chest-high sneeze-guard of the serving line and the other by a wall of sneering orange. The guards still hadn't moved. The alarm hadn't sounded. I had defended the opening foray, but no help would be forthcoming. I knew that at any moment, some other inmate might decide to jump in as well.

The small man was on his feet, kicking at the bigger man to try to get him back in the fight. I wished him luck. I'd heard more than a little bravado about how a shot in the groin might just slow down an opponent and not disable him, but the foul-smelling bile now coating my coveralls told me that the bruiser wasn't going anywhere. I cast about again, this time not hoping for help. I was looking for something else.

The first rule of surviving a knife attack was to accept that you were going to get cut. The second was don't be unarmed. That second rule was good general life advice, but something I hadn't been able to follow once the doors to the prison had shut behind me. Still, a determined and resourceful man could almost always find something to serve as a weapon. I snatched up the meal tray, a thin plastic rectangle maybe ten inches by fourteen inches, and none too soon.

He came at me, knife held low, point facing toward me, ready to stab it repeatedly into my midsection. It was a technique sometimes referred to as a typewriter, and other times, with good reason, a prison shank. He lunged forward, leaping over his downed compatriot, left hand questing to grab my shoulder, coveralls, anything to keep me from moving away while his right hand was already thrusting in short, vicious jabs.

I didn't wait for the grab. If he got hold of me, no matter how good I was, I was dead. His left hand was leading, and I met it with my own, raising my arm up and across my body, creating a wedge in front of me. I kept my right hand, plastic tray held as firmly as I could, low, interposing the makeshift shield as much as possible between the blade and my guts. My left arm met his and I turned, keeping both my arms pressing forward, questing toward his body. I felt more than saw the point of the blade strike the tray and slide, cutting a long gouge in the plastic.

As he pulled the knife back to strike again, I swept my right arm, tray and all, up and around, following the blade back and forcing his arm high into the air. He turned away, seeking relief from the pressure, which freed my left hand to act. I darted it up, found the bicepss of his knife arm and pushed, shoving the arm down and forward, toward the center of his own body, using not just the strength of my arm, but moving my body weight forward as well. I had close to a hundred pounds on my attacker, but even if our weights had been reversed, he still wouldn't have been able to resist the mass of my body with the strength of his shoulder joint alone. I pinned his knife arm against his body even as I crashed down with my right fist.

And the tray held within it.

I struck edge-on with one of the corners. The rounded edge was a much smaller surface area than my fist, concentrating the force of the blow on a relatively small point of impact. The result was a satisfying crunch as the plastic shattered the cartilage of his nose, and a gout of blood added to the other fluids already staining my jumpsuit.

He staggered away. I tried to follow, but my foot touched something—blood or vomit—and slid out from under me. I dropped to one knee, but managed to keep from going all the way to the ground, though I had to drop the tray and catch myself with my hand to do it. I was back on my feet in an instant, but it was already too late. The knife-wielder had recovered. He glared at me from behind a mask of blood. He had changed stances, and now held the knife at about chest height, closer to his body with his left hand out in front of him more, almost like a boxer's guard. Shit. However he'd come at me at first, it was the stance of an experienced knife fighter.

"You gonna die, asshole," he hissed. "Ain't nobody gonna help you."

It was true enough, at least the second part. I couldn't see the guards anymore, not behind the wall of orange jumpsuits, but there was no panic among the inmates, no sense that the guards were about to come crashing down on us. Just a tangle of shouted insults and encouragement that blurred together into a low and hungry growl. Things were definitely not looking good.

I smiled.

"You got a little blood on you, buddy," I said. I swiped one finger across my upper lip in two quick motions, as if trying to discretely inform a friend that they had crumbs stuck on their lips.

He must not have liked that, since he snarled, and charged.

This time, he kept the knife moving in short, slashing arcs. Despite his anger, he exercised a surprising amount of control, forcing me to give way before the blade. I circled, trying to avoid the blood and vomit. Trying to avoid the crumpled body of the big man, who still lay shivering and groaning on the floor. Trying to avoid the encircling mob, who I had no doubt would be quick to grab me if I moved into their reach. With an explosive surge, the small man lunged forward, knife slashing at my hands held defensively before me. I snatched them back, but too late, and I felt hot pain as the knife scored a line down the back of my forearm. My blood joined that of my attackers on the floor.

"You got a little blood on you, buddy," the small man mocked, throwing my earlier words back at me.

I ignored the jibe. The cut on my arm stung, and I flexed my fingers. Everything seemed to be responding normally, so I knew the cut couldn't be that deep. It was bleeding a fair amount, but not enough to put my life at risk. I shunted the pain off to the back corner of my mind, ignoring it as best I could, and focused on the knife.

Damn near every martial art had some sort of "what do you do if confronted by a knife" technique. A lot of them would get you killed in a hurry. Among the good ones, it boiled down to two possibilities—address the knife directly by attacking the arm controlling it, or address it indirectly by disabling the attacker before he could cut you to ribbons. In the first case, you had to deal with the fact that a trained knife fighter was a slippery bastard, and a fast-moving arm was a tough target. In the second case, you had to find a way past the knife to attack something more important, like a head, throat, or groin.

There's a reason why, in most martial arts, they say the best thing to do when confronted with a knife is find a longer weapon…or run. Unfortunately, I didn't have that luxury.

"Not such a smartass now that you're bleeding, pig?" the small man snarled, stalking me around the circle of onlookers, knife always moving, always questing.

I resisted the urge to respond, knowing my silence would be more likely to piss him off and force some action than engaging in more friendly banter would be. Instead I watched the knife. Not just the knife, of course. Focusing just on the weapon was a sure way to get killed. But there was something about how he was moving it. Down and to the left. Lateral to the right. Up in an almost stabbing motion. Repeat. Drawing a small triangle in front of him.

Keeping an active weapon hand—at least if you were in an aggressive, weapon-forward stance, was a good idea, but falling into patterns? Never smart. I had been backing away, circling, keeping out of the reach of his questing knife. Staying on the defensive until the little man committed to an avenue of attack. But as the blade swept down and to the left, then started tracking across his body again, I reversed direction.

I shot my left—and injured—arm out, elbow bent, palm forward as I stepped, keeping my right hand on guard. It was a risky maneuver that relied as much on timing and surprise as anything, but when the bad guy had a knife and all you had were your empty hands, damn near everything was risky. All he had to do was step away and bring the knife up and he'd likely take a few of my fingers with him for the trouble. But my timing was good.

My palm met his knife arm just behind the wrist as he was pulling the blade across his body. He was stepping forward as he did so, and as my momentum hit his, his arm collapsed, pressing tight against his body, unable to resist the force of our combined weight. He was good, very good, and immediately tried to back up, regaining the space he had lost and freeing his arm. I didn't let him, pressing forward, keeping the knife trapped between my hand and his body. There was a limit though—we weren't fighting in an open field, or a broad street, or even a gym. In a few more steps, he'd hit the wall of inmates…and so would I. They might be content to be spectators as long as I was out of arm's reach, but I had little doubt they'd take what shots they could if I got close enough.

I didn't want to take him to the ground. Size advantage or no, there was too great a chance of losing my hold on the knife, and lying on top of someone so they can better fillet you was a bad idea. So, I reversed direction again. We'd taken no more than a step or two, and he was still backpedaling, trying to free his arm from the pressure I was applying. Once again, I caught him off guard, this time clamping my hand down on his wrist as I stepped back. His knife arm went from being pressed tightly against his stomach to fully extended, elbow locked in an instant. I reached across with my right hand, grabbed the back of his elbow, and pulled with all the strength I could muster while keeping his wrist firmly locked in my other hand.

The sound was not unlike a drumstick being ripped off a turkey.

There was a moment of absolute silence in the wake of that hollow pop, an instant where my attacker could only stare at his arm, which was now bent nearly ninety degrees in a direction nature had never intended. The knife fell from his nerveless fingers, clattering against the tiles. There was one brief sound, not quite a scream, not quite a whimper, and then my attacker's eyes rolled into the back of his head and he, too, clattered to the floor.

I stood in that circle of silence, right hand now clapped over the long slash on my left arm, back to the cafeteria counter, eyes watchful. Would another challenger step from the ranks of orange-clad men to try to finish what the pair had started?

I made no move toward the knife. As it was, the cameras would show only me defending myself. If I picked up the blade, I'd be all but asking for some timely "intervention" from the prison staff. I was tired, wounded, panting from exertion. The injuries I'd suffered in our raid on Walton Biogenics hadn't had a chance to fully heal, and now I'd stacked new ones on top of old. If they came at me now, I was done. That moment seemed to trickle on forever.

Sirens began to blare and the lights started to strobe. At once, the other inmates dropped to the ground, proning themselves out on the floor, arms outstretched above their heads. I followed suit, trying to keep my head up, watching for the knife in the back or the boot to the head that might be coming. The prison's riot squad burst into the room, clad in full battle rattle with a pair of ballistic shields leading the way. It was overkill—no one was resisting. But it would look good for the electronic eyes, if anyone ever bothered checking on the incident.

In short order, I found myself hooked up, pulled to my feet, and "escorted" from the cafeteria. My assailants were receiving similar treatment, at least, and to the credit of the corrections officers, no one took any cheap shots at me. No one said anything to me either, as I was led through the corridors of the prison and deposited in an isolation cell.

The door slammed shut, and I took stock. Isolation wasn't much different from the regular cells. No screens, not for a punishment cell, but the same narrow cot, stainless-steel sink, and stainless-steel commode sat in the same positions in the ten-by-ten box. Harsh fluorescent lights burned overhead, protected from any tampering by a metal screen that diffused the light and created odd shadows. The floor was poured concrete, bereft of any sort of covering.

I could still feel my arm oozing blood. No visit to the infirmary for me. A minor cut, but one that could be a problem if I didn't get the wound cleaned and bandaged as best I could. There was a bar of soap on the sink, and a roll of rough toilet paper by the commode.

Time to get to work.

Chapter 2

The worst part about the isolation cells wasn't the isolation. I'd spent a good chunk of my life trying to be left alone. I was perfectly comfortable in my own company, and even the lack of a screen didn't bother me much. The space was sparse, but big enough that I could work various forms, which helped mind and body both relax. The guards had even brought me some antibiotics and alcohol wipes with my meals, to keep the knife wound clean.

No, the worst part of the isolation cell was not knowing what the fuck was going on in the outside world. The eve of revolution had come and gone and here I was, locked in a cage, with no way of knowing if the first shots had been fired, if they had struck home, if the outside world was being torn apart in an orgy of fire and blood, or if all things right and good and just had prevailed.

I snorted at that thought as I lay on the cot. No. The world governments would not have simply capitulated to the demand that synthetics be granted full rights. I could hardly blame them. Doing so would upset the apple cart of a lot of peoples' utopia, to say nothing of forcing them to acknowledge an ugly truth. No one was going to do that based on threats. Those threats would have to be borne out if the revolution was to have any chance of succeeding.

And the consequences of carrying out those threats would have to be weathered.

That was what gnawed at me as I lay on the thin mattress. Silas, Evelyn, her daughter, Jacinda. They would be in even more danger now. Tia Morita, the beautiful medical examiner's assistant who seemed, to my unending surprise, to harbor some romantic feelings toward me, would be in almost as much danger, if she insisted on throwing her lot in with the synthetics. Melinda Hernandez, my former sister in blue, who I'd dragged into this whole mess more or less against her will. The dozens, maybe by now hundreds, of synthetics who had fled from their "owners" or been turned out, only to find some measure of shelter and solace within Silas's organization. They would all be subject to the anger not just of the authorities, but of every ignorant or angry citizen looking to vent their rage.

And with the conditioning that prevented them from engaging in violence, the synthetics wouldn't have a chance of defending themselves. Their only defense was secrecy; their only weapon, knowledge. That was the kind of thing that public service messages claimed made you stronger, but in the real world, knowledge had a hard time stopping bullets, and spy satellites and drones had a way of finding secrets. They needed protection, and I couldn't give it to them.

That thought, more than anything, grated on me. I knew that the likelihood of me surviving any prison sentence I might receive was almost nonexistent. Once I was found guilty and shunted off to a federal facility with the real criminals, it would only be a matter of time.

I could deal with that. Accept it. At least I'd be able to fight, to do *something* to affect my situation. But for Tia, Silas, and the others, I was useless. Just like I'd been for Annabelle.

I lay on my bunk, eyes closed, mind and stomach both churning on the bitter thoughts.

The heavy *thunk* of the door bolt disengaging broke my reverie. I was on my feet before I fully recognized what the sound had been, hands up before me in a defensive posture. Not that I really expected the guards to try to finish what the inmates started, not with the odds of being observed by the electronic watchers so high, but it never hurt to be careful.

"You have a visitor, inmate." It was one of the guards, a big, hairy man with an equal mix of bulging muscle and bulging gut. He held a pair of manacles, and I offered up my wrists. Not much else to do, really.

I was escorted from my cell, and I took note of the other two guards who had been waiting in the wings. They weren't taking any chances with me, but I couldn't help a small smile. Three on one was bad odds, but I'd dealt with worse. Still, I played the good little prisoner, and fell in line. Maybe the time would come when I'd have to make a move, but not yet. Not when there wasn't anything to gain by it.

They led me down the stone corridors, and I ignored the insults shouted at me from every cage we passed. It didn't bother me. The ones shouting and blustering weren't the ones you had to worry about. It was the ones who watched me go by in silence, their dead-eyed stares conveying more malice than the worst of the hurled expletives, that made my palm itch for the butt of my forty-five.

I was escorted to an interview room, the kind where prisoners were afforded some measure of privacy in meeting with their attorneys. The guards shoved me into a plastic chair and bolted my manacles to a ring on the metal table. The table, too, was bolted to the floor. With the press of a thumb on the locking mechanism, I was effectively immobilized. It grated on me more than the cell. At least in the cage I could move. And if I could move, I could fight. But now?

The tension burned in my shoulders as I sat and waited. I tried not to let it show on my face. The rooms where prisoners met with their lawyers were supposed to be unmonitored, but you never knew, and damned if I was going to give anyone the satisfaction of seeing me squirm.

It wasn't a long wait, no more than five minutes, but it felt like eons.

Then the door opened and a man I'd never met walked in. He wore a hand-tailored cashmere suit that had to cost five figures, and walked with a sort of smarmy confidence that only politicians and senior executives could pull off. His perfectly coiffed hair was iron-gray, but nothing in the face beneath it spoke of age. The features were strong, hard-chiseled, and handsome. The eyes were deep brown and seemed to exude confidence. The smile…that smile had me missing my sidearm even more than the cold dead stares of the inmates had. There was something in it, something beyond arrogance, beyond disdain. It was the smile of a man who could look at another human being and see…nothing.

He watched me for a long moment, that smile fixed in place, and it made me want to take a shower. In bleach. Then he slid into the chair across from me with a kind of effortless grace that magnified his already overwhelming sense of presence. The word *demagogue* leapt into my mind.

"Well, now," he said, his voice a smooth, baritone-rich in timbre, "you're the one who has been causing all the trouble."

I gave him a thousand-yard stare, looking right through him. In my experience, the best way to piss off a narcissistic asshole was to ignore them. His whole effect screamed politician, but I knew—by sight at least—all the New Lyons city politicians. You had to, to be a cop. Couldn't accidently cite the wrong person after all. And I knew the state and national level as well, congressmen and senators, at least for a few states in any direction. The military had instilled in me the habit of knowing the chain of command all the way up the commander-in-chief. The man across from me wasn't in the local government, nor the national government, nor did he fill a directorship in one of the three-letter agencies that sometimes crossed paths with regular cops.

"My name is Sam Woodruff," he said. "I'd offer to shake your hand, but…" He trailed off and that smile, that oily, insincere smile, washed over me again. Did he know the effect that smile had on regular people? Or did he honestly believe he was being friendly? "I assume you've heard of me?"

I hadn't, but even if I had, I wouldn't have fed his ego. Instead, I gave him the briefest once-over before saying, "Nope."

The smile again, but it didn't touch his eyes. "I find that surprising," he admitted. "Given, that is, the lengths that you've gone to, to ruin me."

I snorted as the pieces fell into place, and leaned suddenly forward. I felt a surge of satisfaction as Woodruff leaned back in his chair, moving away from me. "So, you're one of the assholes who run Walton Biogencis. I should have guessed from the suit."

He must have realized that the shackles were short enough that I had no chance of even head-butting him across the table, because he shifted forward once more, resting an elbow on the tabletop and waving one hand languidly. "Perhaps. The prison's management team tells me that you keep having issues with your screens. You're most likely unaware of what's been going on in the outside world the past couple of days."

I fought down the thrill of excitement that shot up my spine at his words. I didn't want the eagerness to know to show on my face. But a little must have slipped through, because Woodruff's smile grew. "Yes, I thought as so. Well, Mr. Campbell, let me tell you just what your revolution is doing to the outside world." He paused, one finger tapping thoughtfully against the metal table.

"Your *friends*,"—he invested the word with a spiteful sneer without ever losing the smile on his lips—"have carried through with their promises. They've released some rather hateful information about certain members of Walton Biogenics and members of local, state, and federal governments across the country. Across the world, really. Seems your network's intelligence gathering capabilities were far greater than we could have anticipated."

The finger stopped tapping for a moment, and a thoughtful frown flashed across his face. "You know, I didn't really think you could deliver on the threat you made on New Year's. I'm not sure anyone did. But you did deliver. I'll grant you that, Mr. Campbell."

Once more, I had to fight the urge to comment, maybe even to gloat. There was something in the set of Woodruff's shoulders, the tilt of his head, that made me believe the opening shots in the synthetics' revolution had done more than just strike home. From his body language, I intuited that they had wounded, deeply and maybe mortally, the targets they had struck. Score one for the network Silas had built and the weaponized secrets his fellow synthetics had gathered. But there was something else there, too. An edge in the executive's voice that kept the vindictive joy I felt from finding an avenue of escape.

"We really didn't expect Dr. Kaphiri to have kept such detailed records. *That* little stunt, I can almost admire. And you, turning yourself in, playing the martyr to lend credulity, to lend *gravitas*, to the information." He touched one finger to his forehead and then flicked it in my direction in a mocking salute. "Very well done, Mr. Campbell."

His whole patronizing attitude was beginning to wear on me. I found that I couldn't hold my tongue any longer. "Is there a point to all this, Woodruff? I mean, I'm not exactly a busy guy these days, but I think I've had prison shankings less painful than sitting here and listening to you talk."

"Ah," he said, glancing at the bandage wrapped around my arm. "A miscommunication, I'm sure."

The enigmatic statement took me aback for a moment. Was he implying that someone at Walton Biogenics had somehow ordered the attack? Perhaps someone without the authority to do so? "What do you know about it?" I asked.

He shrugged, a somehow elegant movement of the shoulders that made his suit flow across his body like water. "Now, now, Mr. Campbell, what *could* I know about such a thing? I would think, though, that your detractors—and I assure you, there are many—wouldn't want to see you dead quite so soon. Or quite so easily. There are many things that need to happen first."

The threat in those words, delivered with such nonchalance, chilled me. I dreaded knowing, but I had to ask. I tried for the same casual tone, and failed. "What things?"

"Well, Jason," he filled my first name with scorn, as if not granting me the formality of *Mister* was somehow the gravest insult he'd thrown my way, "your revolution is well on the way to destroying the lives and families of tens of thousands of people. And that's just the direct action, mind you. That says nothing for those who will be caught up in the fallout if we allow this farce to go forward. It seems only fair that some of the same fall on you. And yours."

I thought of my parents, whom I'd distanced myself from since the moment I decided to throw in with the synthetics in an attempt—futile I now realized—to make them less of a target. I thought of Silas, and the other synthetics gathered under his banner. Of Tia, who really didn't deserve to get caught up in the shitstorm, but who had thrown in with us nonetheless. Of Hernandez and her daughter, already traumatized by the psychopath Fowler. There were so many people in my life, despite my best efforts to distance myself after Annabelle's death. So many potential targets of the wrath that should come to me instead.

Had I been free, I would have been across the table in a heartbeat, taking great pleasure in taking Woodruff apart bone by bone. As it was, all I could do was curl my fingers into fists and open them again, while applying a steady upward pressure against my manacles, the steel leaving white indentations in my flesh. The pain reminded me that I could not, in fact, exact immediate, violent, and preemptive revenge. So I settled for a deep and heartfelt, "Fuck you, Woodruff."

"Clever," he said urbanely. "I've done most of what I came here to do. Mostly I just wanted to see you. To tell you that, as of this moment, your little revolution seems to be finding traction. I thought I owed you that much. A professional courtesy of sorts, and an acknowledgement of a worthy foe." That smile, again. "And, of course, to remind you of the consequences of your actions. Some have already come to fruition. Others..." That plastic, condescending smile stretched his lips once more. "Others are on the horizon, Jason."

He stood, nodded solemnly at me, and moved to the door. His hand was raised to knock, to summon the guards to let him out, when he turned back to me. "One more thing," he said. "A final thought to keep your mind occupied on the long nights between now and your trial." He paused, as if expecting me to demand to know what he wanted. After a long moment of me silently staring he continued.

"It's a question. Do you think Walton Biogenics would have developed the synthetics, and released them into the wild, without some sort of a failsafe? Some sort of way to end the program if things got out of hand? If those *things* started getting a little too uppity for their own good? Think about *that*, Mr. Campbell. Think about it long and hard in the days ahead. Remember it, when the casualty reports start rolling in."

He pounded three times on the door and it opened immediately. "Have a lovely day," he said in parting, flashing another brilliant smile, as the guard escorted him away.

Chapter 3

I'd spent the night churning on Woodruff's parting words. The idea that Walton Biogenics would build in some sort of omega protocol to terminate the synthetics simply hadn't occurred to me. Perhaps hadn't occurred to *anyone*. It made sense, from a certain, twisted viewpoint. Humanity had obsessed about falling prey to their creations for hundreds of years. The whole "playing God" thing left an indelible mark on the psyche. But the notion of simply turning off millions of living breathing creatures...

The thought sickened me to the point where I'd found sleep impossible. My mind kept returning to the notion, and wondering how they would do it. Had Walton Biogenics implanted some sort of physical device? A poison pill or explosive that could be remotely triggered? It seemed far-fetched, but I wouldn't put it past them. Was that yet another reason why all deceased synthetics were supposed to be returned to a Walton facility for processing?

Or did they have something more sinister? A flaw in the genetic coding that could be triggered...somehow?

Dammit. I was way out of my depth. I didn't know enough about genetics and biology and whatever the hell else to figure out how to wipe out an entire species. I knew violence and investigation. Tracking down the bad guys and putting them away. Maybe, just maybe, I was good enough at my former job to take what Woodruff had told me and *find* the how of it, even if I didn't *understand* the how of it. And if I found it, maybe Silas and Al'awwal and Tia could do something about it.

But I couldn't do shit from inside a cell.

I pushed myself from my cot and pounded on my cell door, hoping to attract the attention of one of the guards, if not directly, then at least through the electronic babysitters watching the prison.

They couldn't deny me visitations or calls, even if I was technically still in solitary confinement. The same prison reforms that had guaranteed every inmate a personal screen and access to the outside world—if only for downstream content and if those screens didn't suffer "accidents" anyway—ensured that every prisoner had the chance to make monitored calls to family and friends and to receive visitors every day. I hadn't taken advantage of those provisions. In some ways, I couldn't, not directly. Calling Silas would just give his enemies a better idea of where he was located. Tia might still have been clean, as far as anyone in law enforcement knew, but why put her at risk? The same went for Hernandez. And my parents. So I'd weathered the first week of incarceration largely alone.

It was time to change that. None of my friends had been particularly keen on the idea of me turning myself in, even if they agreed that it was the best way to lend credibility to the evidence we had stolen from the Walton Biogenics lab. In the end, they had agreed, but not without concessions of their own. They insisted on a contingency plan, a way to attempt to free me if the danger was too great, or if it looked like the evidence we had gone to such lengths to acquire would be ignored. I'd gone along with it, under the assumption that I'd never agree to actually attempt it. It was foolhardy bordering on stupid to try to break me out of jail—putting everyone else and maybe the entire revolution at risk in the process—just to save my own skin.

But it wasn't about my own skin anymore, was it?

It occurred to me that Woodruff, if he was a particularly sinister kind of smart, might be trying to feed me false information to trigger the very response I was considering. Threaten a few million lives and see if I made a hasty decision, a stupid phone call, and flush some accomplices out of hiding. If so, I was going to play right into his hands. I'd spent too long idly accepting the status quo, playing the role of observer and telling myself that there was nothing I could do to change things. Maybe I'd been right. Maybe nothing I did had any real chance of creating lasting change. But that didn't matter. Not anymore. What mattered was that I *tried*. I couldn't sit idle any longer.

Which wasn't the same as saying I had to be stupid about it.

It took almost five minutes of continual pounding before anyone bothered to check on me. I turned it into a workout. Palm strike high. Palm strike low. High, high, low. Low, low, high. Again and again, alternating the rhythms, the levels, envisioning the cashmere-clad form of Woodruff on the door before me. I was sweating when the *thunk* of the lock disengaging broke my rhythm and the door swung open to reveal an irate-looking guard.

"What the hell do you want, Campbell," the guard snapped.

"To talk to my lawyer."

* * * *

"Mr. Campbell. I trust things are going as well for you as can be allowed, under the circumstances. I'm afraid I don't have any new news on your case. With events transpiring as they are, it might take a while to get you to trial."

I waved one hand at the screen, dismissing her words. My attorney was a slightly overweight forty-something white female, more handsome than beautiful, by the name of C. Anita Puckett. I'm not sure if it had been Silas or Hernandez who dug up Ms. Puckett, but she was smart, competent, and, I assumed, very expensive. One of the first things Francois Fortier had told me was that all of my accounts had been frozen—suspected ties to domestic terrorism—so I didn't have money to pay for an attorney. Not that I could have afforded someone of Ms. Puckett's caliber, anyway, but I think he was hoping I'd end up with a wet-behind-the-ears public defender who could be bullied by the prosecutor. I didn't know who was footing the bill, maybe Al'awwal, but I was grateful.

"That's okay, Ms. Puckett," I replied. "What I need has less to do with my case, and more to do with getting a message to a friend. This conversation is privileged, correct? And not monitored?"

She frowned, causing a network of crow's feet to crinkle around the corners of her eyes. "It's a violation of state and federal law for these calls to be monitored, and if that law is violated, nothing obtained from the conversation can be used against you." I opened my mouth to speak, but she raised one finger. "However, I must remind you that, while our conversations are covered by attorney-client privilege, I have an ethical and moral obligation to disclose any requests you make of me to facilitate illegal activity."

I put on my best smile. "Nothing like that," I lied. "I just want my friends to know I'm okay. But given the…let's say suspicion…around my activities, I don't want any of them to be put into the investigative spotlight."

"I assure you, Mr. Campbell, I've kept Detective Hernandez up to date with the details. Well, those that don't compromise privilege, anyway."

That answered the question of who had hired her. I winced a bit at the thought. I knew Hernandez couldn't afford a high-priced defense attorney, not on a cop's salary. I hoped she was just the front, a funnel for funds from somewhere else, and that she hadn't put herself in jeopardy to hire me a lawyer. "Yeah, well, I'm looking for something more specific." I racked my brain. What message could I give Hernandez to get the ball rolling? Would she even be able to find Silas and the others? "I need you to tell her to talk to the albino. To let him know that I was wrong, and maybe he should go forward with his plans."

Okay, so it wasn't the subtlest of messages. But there was nothing *overtly* criminal about it. Still, Puckett eyed me for a long moment. "That sounds like the type of message a felon would send to other felons."

I shrugged. I needed her to deliver the message, but I suspected she wasn't the type to respond to demands. Or to whining. I figured reason with a nod to honesty was about my only approach. "Maybe," I admitted. "But I'm not sending it to a felon. I'm sending it to a cop. I'm not asking you to do anything illegal or immoral. Just to deliver a perfectly innocuous message to a Detective in the New Lyons Police Department."

For a long moment, Puckett just stared at me, and I thought I might have gone too far with "perfectly innocuous." But she relented. "Fine, Mr. Campbell. I'll deliver your message to the detective. Will you be expecting a reply?" Her icy tone suggested that she didn't much care for the idea of playing carrier pigeon.

The response I was expecting wasn't the kind that my attorney could deliver on, so I just shook my head. "No. No, I won't be expecting any replies."

"Very well." She nodded brusquely as if glad to be done with that business. "I'm trying to get your court date as soon as possible. Any attempts to get you bail have been dismissed. The courts think you represent too great a danger to the community, though that's a difficult position to sustain given what's been going on these last few days." I wanted to jump on that, to get more information on what the hell was happening outside, but I also didn't want to push my luck. So instead I just nodded.

"Is there anything else?"

I thought about that. I could let her know about the "accidents" that kept happening to my screens, or about the attempt on my life. She could probably put pressure on the warden, or someone else in the system. Somehow, I didn't think it would make a difference. If Woodruff was to be believed, I only had to worry about "honest" murderers, rather than ones hired by Walton Biogenics, at least in the near future. And if I snitched on the guards for breaking my toys, they'd just find something worse to do to me. I could live without the screen.

"No. That just about covers it."

She nodded. "Goodbye, Mr. Campbell." No frills, no attempt at comforting me. I could appreciate that. It wasn't her job and I didn't need it. Now, all I needed to do, all I could do, was wait.

It wasn't a feeling I particularly enjoyed, the idea of not only being completely dependent upon my friends to get me out of my current predicament, but of them having to risk their own lives and freedom to do so. And that was made worse by the fact that I had no way of knowing when—or even if—they would be coming for me. Or how. Or any other goddamned thing. I ground my teeth in frustration as I waited for the guards to come retrieve me from the small privacy booth used to screen attorneys. The days ahead were going to be a grueling dance on a razor's edge between boredom and violent, sudden action.

* * * *

In the end, it took three days.

I had just finished my evening workout, mostly pushups, sit-ups, and burpees, things I could do in the confined space of the solitary cell. I'd stripped down to my boxers, not wanting to get my one set of clothing sweaty. I was staring distastefully at the orange coveralls draped on my bunk when the lights blinked out.

For a moment, I didn't put two and two together. I just stood there like an idiot, seeing nothing in the dark. Then I realized that my message must have gotten through. The electric grid had been hardened over the years, made all but impregnable to any sort of terrorist attack. Or so we'd been told. But I'd seen Silas and his fellow synthetic LaSorte at work, and I had no doubt they could take the prison offline. There should have been backup generators, of course, but everything was connected to something else these days, and if it talked to a computer, then Silas could hack it.

My friends were coming for me.

The thought brought a smile to my face, until I realized that if I didn't hurry the fuck up, they'd find me standing sweaty in my skivvies grinning into the darkness. That wouldn't exactly be my finest hour. I fumbled my way to the bunk—without windows or any sort of backup lighting, the place was darker than the inside of a shoebox. My grasping hands found the folds of cloth, and I pulled the coveralls on. Shoes were more challenging, and by the time I found them, the prison was starting to come alive.

Life on the inside was all about routine, and when something, anything, happened to upset that routine, it was cause for excitement. When that thing was a total loss of power, things started to get rowdy. The halls were filling with laughter, curses, demands to know what the fuck was happening. After I finished tying my shoes and made my way to the tiny, heavily reinforced slit of a window set into the door, I could see bits of light bleeding from the slits on the other doors. My fellow inmates all had screens, which meant they could garner at least a bit of illumination, even with the power out.

It was already starting to get warm—the air conditioning had died with the power—and I could feel the sweat starting to break out again. The heat? Or nerves? I was acutely aware of the risk my friends were taking, a risk made all the more dangerous by the fact that none of the synthetics, with the exception of Al'awwal, could so much as defend themselves if they faced resistance. Their thrice-damned conditioning would stop them from being able to so much as throw a punch, much less pull a trigger.

Which meant they were assaulting a fortress with plenty of armed guards, and their only edge was technological. I didn't think Silas would have green lit the attempt if he thought it impossible, but my gut churned as I stood by the cell door, watched, and waited.

About five minutes later, I heard a faint metallic bouncing sound over the calls and angry demands of the other inmates on my block. The sound triggered memories from long ago, and I was crouched in a corner, body curled tight, with my hands clapped over my ears and my mouth opened to lessen the shock before I realized I was moving. The inmates must have had similar reactions, though I guessed theirs hearkened back to tear gas grenades rather than the real thing, because the noise level in the cells dropped to almost nothing.

Instead of the earsplitting explosion, I heard a pop, then a steady hiss. I took a gulp of air, fearing for a moment that it was tear gas after all. But I realized the futility of that. If the guards had come to gas the prisoners into submission, there was no way to stop it, no way to hold my breath long enough to stop the effects. I exhaled, inhaled. Caught a familiar scent. Not tear gas. Something that smelled almost like the aftermath of a fireworks show. Willie Pete? No. Thank God for that. White phosphorus was nasty stuff. Smoke grenades. Someone was popping smoke, and I didn't think it was for an aerial pickup.

I didn't have much time to consider, because the high-pitched whine of a drill cutting into metal sounded, drowning out my thoughts. The isolation cell doors were solid—solid enough that even a big guy like me had no chance of breaking one down—but they weren't vault doors. I made sure I was well clear of the door, and a few seconds later an inch-thick bit shredded the lock plate, showering the interior with a fountain of sparks.

I stood from my crouch, and waited. There was a bang as something heavy slammed into the hinges of the door, then another. On the third hit, the door bounced in its frame, shivered wildly for a moment, and then fell backward. A high-intensity flashlight beam sliced across the darkness like a knife, and I averted my eyes, trying to preserve some semblance of night vision. It swept quickly over my face, and then dropped to the ground.

"Time to go, *pendejo*."

I smiled at the words, even as I winced. I could just make out the nondescript black fatigues and black balaclava in the reflected glow from the flashlight. No patches or insignia, nothing to indicate who the person was. But I'd recognize Hernandez's voice—and her distinctive greeting—anywhere.

I was happy to hear her voice, and felt like shit that she'd risked her life and freedom to try to bust me out of prison. She still had a life waiting for her, a job, a daughter. Now she was standing in a prison cell, flashlight in one hand, blocky pistol in the other.

"You shouldn't have come," I muttered.

"Bite me, Campbell," she snapped back. "Take this." She passed the pistol over to me. The grips settled comfortably into my palm, and the weight felt…good. It wasn't my old forty-five, but it felt good to hold a weapon again. At least if someone tried to shiv us on the way out, I'd have brought a gun to a knife fight.

"Load?" I asked, as she dug a couple of spare magazines out of the pouch on her web gear.

"LTL," she replied.

I nodded. "Less than lethal" rounds in a nine-millimeter meant instead of jacketed lead slugs, the gun would fire "rubber bullets." They weren't actually rubber—that shit had a tendency to bounce around like a super ball and cause all sorts of collateral damage. Instead, it would be a lightweight polymer round designed to collapse on impact and spread the force of the strike out over a much wider area. A well—or poorly, depending on intent—placed shot could still be lethal, but for the most part, it was like shooting hard right crosses from a heavyweight boxer.

"What's the plan?" I asked, dumping the extra mags into my front left pocket.

Hernandez snorted. "Plan, *hermano*? I'm surprised we made it this far. The plan's simple, though. As you've said more than once, we *didi fucking mao.*"

Chapter 4

I followed Hernandez into the corridor.

She wasn't alone. Two more black-clad shapes blended into the darkness, but I saw enough from the backscatter of the flashlight to make some educated guesses. One was big, as big as me, male, and moved with the grace of a tiger that had gone pro on the dance circuit. He carried a stubby bullpup rifle that I recognized, even through the tacgear mounted on the rails. Al'awwal. The literal First synthetic. And, so far as we knew, the only one not subjected to the conditioning that left the other synthetics incapable of violence against their "creators." The other…

"Mother fucker," I cursed under my breath as I took in the petite female form that the battle dress uniform couldn't quite hide. There was only one person it could be. I had no idea what had persuaded Silas and the others to think it would be a good idea to drag Tia Morita into this, but I felt a surge of anger at the thought of putting her into danger to save my sorry ass. She wasn't a soldier. She wasn't a cop. She wasn't even a…whatever the hell Al'awaal was. Bored rich guy with money enough and time enough to get training from the best. She was a student. An assistant medical examiner. A soon-to-be doctor. And…shit. And I had feelings for her.

Okay, so she was holding the tactical shotgun with surprising professionalism, the barrel of the twelve gauge down and away, but the frame of the weapon off her body and tight against the tac-strap so she could bring it to bear in an instant. And yeah, she'd surprised me more than once with her courage and tenacity. But, dammit, I didn't *want* her in danger.

Hernandez must have read it on my face, because she said, "Save it for later. We got more important things to worry about right now."

She was right. And as much as I wanted to yell at them, or maybe wrap them all up in my arms—especially Tia, but even Al—now was not the time. "What's the plan?" I asked again.

Hernandez gave my cell a quick once over as she said, "Boo Radley's got the place in lockdown. He and Scout went through the firewalls like they weren't even there. Full commo blackout, and anything tied to a computer—which is everything—is ours. Most of the guards are in lockdown, trapped behind their own magnetic locks. This is the only block we shut everything down on. Safer that way. Never know what little detail might be missed, otherwise."

It took me a moment to figure out "Boo Radley" and "Scout." It had been a long, long time since I'd read *To Kill a Mockingbird,* but I realized it had to be a reference to Silas. Which meant that "Scout" was probably referring to LaSorte. We were safe enough with the power off, but it sounded like Silas and LaSorte hadn't killed power everywhere.

That pair could probably have hacked their way into an individual light bulb in the prison, but leaving the power on in the rest of the facility made sense. It would afford better control for opening and closing doors, monitoring the bad guys, and generally finding us a path to freedom that didn't end with the four of us in an even less-comfortable cell. At the same time, killing the power in my cellblock made sense, too. When you were securing the package, checking for injuries, gearing up, you were at your most vulnerable. Why take the risk of missing a camera or alarm or of opening the wrong cell when you could kill the whole block?

"Roger that. Extract?"

"We walk out the front doors," she said, and I caught a flash of white through the mouth hole of her balaclava as she grinned. "When I said full commo blackout, I meant it. No signal is getting into or out of this place right now. And according to Boo, there's no scheduled system handshake for,"—she paused, pulled up a sleeve to reveal a wearable screen wrapped around her wrist—"the next fifteen minutes. We've got that long before they realize the shit has hit the fan."

"Stack?"

"I've got point. Then you. Then the Doc. First brings up the rear."

It made sense. Hernandez and I had done this sort of thing before—by which I meant the stack up and enter a dangerous situation. We were sort of in the opposite business from prison breaks. We'd be the point of the spear. Al'awwal, codename, apparently, First, had proved himself a steady hand in the raid on the Walton Biogenics lab, and it was always a good idea to have an experienced person covering your six. Which left "the Doc" in the most secure position in the middle of our stack. That was normally where the protectee would go, but no way I was going to push Tia into a *more* dangerous position.

"Right. Let's get to work."

The hallway was filled with smoke and darkness, and even the beams of the flashlights did little but diffuse against the wall of gray. It was difficult to breathe, and I heard occasional coughs not only from my would-be rescuers, but also from the cells on either side. The hurled insults and laughter hadn't started up again. I was locked up with petty criminals, but most criminals were survivors. They were smart enough to lay low when grenades started going off and people with guns showed up.

We moved into the corridor, lining up single file and staying close to the wall. I felt a hand on my shoulder, and turned to look into the warm brown eyes of Tia Morita. I couldn't see her face, not behind the balaclava, but I didn't need to. She didn't say anything, just gave my shoulder a squeeze before returning her hand to the pump action of her shotgun. That gesture brought a surge of emotion to my throat and I had to swallow hard against it.

I turned my attention back to where it should have been and I heard Hernandez mutter something. She wasn't talking to me, I realized, but into the throat mic taped to her neck. "All right," she said briskly, "Boo says it's time to go. We've got a clear path through this block, but some of the guards are showing surprising initiative farther down the line. We may run into some trouble." She drew a steadying breath, let it out in a long sigh, and said, "Move out!"

A well-oiled strike team could move through an open corridor like this, hugging the wall for cover while simultaneously keeping all possible avenues of approach under a watchful eye and waiting trigger finger. We weren't that. I could practically feel Tia's nervousness behind me, and whatever training he may have had, Al'awwal had, as far as I knew, only done this once. I mentally cursed myself. I was spending too much time worrying about the people at my back and not enough doing my job. Hernandez had point, and was responsible for everything in front of us, but that was a big job for one person. As her second, it was my job to watch her back and pick up anything she missed. Tia and Al'awwal were rear security and backup. Stick to the plan. Stay alive. I tried to put the two behind me out of my mind and focus on the task at hand.

"Coming up on B-Block," Hernandez said in a voice just loud enough to carry. "Power's on there. We'll have lights, and Boo and Scout can give us real-time intel. Stay sharp."

Ahead of us, a security door, apparently still on the grid, buzzed and swung open, leading into another dimly lit cell block. B-Block was a lower security area, with doors made of steel bars rather than solid material. Hernandez instinctively moved away from the wall and toward the center of the corridor, out of reach of any grasping hands that might slip between the bars. Nearly every door framed an inmate, most silent, but some calling out to us as we past. I didn't have much brain power to spare for what they were saying, but most of it was simple calls to take them with us, that they could help us get out. Calls of desperation.

"Shit," Hernandez cursed, slowing down, though not stopping. "Trouble ahead."

I almost ran into her, but managed to catch myself. Tia and Al'awwal, apparently tuned in to whatever information Hernandez was receiving, had also slowed. I wished they had thought to bring along an extra radio, but I supposed beggars couldn't be choosers.

"What is it?"

"A group of guards have managed to lever one of the locked doors open. According to Boo, they're not armed with anything more than billy clubs, but there's a half dozen of them headed this way."

I grunted. "What's the plan?"

"We take them down, *hermano*. With prejudice."

I nodded my head just a bit in the direction of Tia. She must have caught the motion because she punched me in the back with her free hand. "Don't worry about me. I grew up in the bayou. I'm more comfortable with a bolt action, but I've handled a twelve gauge before."

There was a big damn difference between sport shooting or hunting and engaging in a close quarters gun battle. I knew it. Hernadnez knew it. Hell, *Tia* probably knew it. And she'd showed up anyway, knowing what might come. "She can run the gear, Campbell," Hernandez said. "And she and First are backup anyway. Now shut the hell up and get ready, because we got about fifteen seconds."

We couldn't take up a better position, not with the inmates on either side. If the bad guys had guns, it would have been a Wild West-style shooting alley with the potential for mass casualties on either side. But that was the value of superior intel—we knew the bad guys *didn't* have guns and we knew when and where they were going to show up.

I moved up beside Hernandez, who quickly passed me a pair of earbuds. For a second, I thought they might be for the radio, but they were just cheap foam hearing protection. Still, as I knelt beside her, I stuffed them gratefully into my ears. Tia and Al'awwal took up standing positions behind us, and the muzzles of their weapons were close enough that even through the hearing protection, I was going to be in for a bad time. I had just enough time to draw a steadying breath and settle myself more comfortably into position, finger easing from the slide of the nine-millimeter and onto the trigger. Then the corrections officers came surging around the corner.

It was a long damn way from a fair fight.

But like I said, fair fights are for victims.

I opened up first, but only by a second. I kept my shots center mass—not that I would have normally tried anything else, but the polymer bullets could still kill if they found an eye or landed on someone's throat. I didn't want that on my conscience, so I exercised some extra caution. I only managed to squeeze off a pair of shots, both hitting the lead man and sending him stumbling before the others joined in. The world exploded in sound and fire, the pops of the pistol shots lost beneath the bark of the Israeli five-five-six, and then even that drowned out by the dragon's roar of the twelve gauge. When the big shotgun spoke, it spoke with authority.

It took maybe ten seconds, and even that was overkill.

There was a long moment of silence—well, probably. My ears were ringing, so maybe it was just hearing damage. Then the cells on either side erupted in a combination of incoherent shouts, laughter, and sounds of celebration.

Turned out, inmates didn't like guards much. Having had my screens routinely destroyed and an attempt on my life ignored, I couldn't really blame them. It did raise an issue, though.

There was no being heard over the general racket, so I just moved forward, checking on the guards. Tia was at my side in an instant, making sure no one was dead, but I was more concerned with keeping the injured officers out of the grasping hands of the prisoners. Most of the guards were groaning and half-conscious from the debilitating pain inflicted by the polymer rounds. Some were unconscious, either from the pain or from a head shot. But they all seemed to be alive, at least. I grabbed the nearest by one leg and dragged him to the center of the corridor. A bean bag rolled off of his chest as I did and I winced in sympathy. The polymer rounds from the nine were like getting hit with a punch, but a bean bag round from a twelve gauge? That was like getting kicked by an angry mule. He wouldn't be good for much, not without medical treatment.

Still, a quick search turned up a bundle of zip-ties, so I bound him hand and foot. Hernandez and Al'awwal, realizing what I was doing, had gotten in on the action as well, and in under a minute, we had the six guards trussed up all nice and neat—and safely out of reach of any inquisitive hands.

"Ten minutes until the handshake," Hernandez said. "We need to move." The rest of the exfil went butter smooth.

We ghosted through the halls of the prison, with each security door popping open as we neared, monitored by the watchful eyes of Silas and LaSorte. We didn't—quite—walk out the front door. Silas's directions had navigated us around toward one of the loading docks of the prison. A van waited there, a simple, unmarked, white panel van, little more than a box on wheels. It didn't even have a windshield for manual override. But the back door popped open to reveal Silas bent over a bank of screens and LaSorte, grinning through his model-perfect teeth.

"Somebody call for a taxi?" he asked.

"Two minutes," Silas said as the engine revved to life. "I would prefer to be farther away before the scheduled system handshake alerts the world that something has gone wrong here, Detective. I have triggered the locks on the guard towers and shut down all of the lights, but we are not out of the woods yet. If a guard happened to be outside of his tower..." He trailed off, the implications clear.

"Good to see you, too, Silas," I said as I hopped from the loading dock. I reached back to help Tia down—because it was a four-foot drop, not because it felt good to hold her for a moment. Hernandez and Al'awwal managed on their own, and then we were all piling into the van. It started pulling away even before we had the doors shut, responding to Silas's rapidly flicking fingers.

I opened my mouth to say something else, but before I could, Tia, who had pulled off her mask, was pushing me from my half-crouch into a seated position. My first words were smothered by the kiss she planted on me—not that I minded. She was warm and soft and lovely—and, let's be honest, kind of super hot in the battle dress and toting a twelve gauge. It was a quick kiss, but intense, and it took me a second to gather my breath. That was apparently a second too long, because she was already pulling at the crude bandage-job I'd done on my arm.

"What is this? Is that a knife wound?" she demanded. "And what kind of hack wound care is this? Do the prison doctors not know how stitches work?" She glared at me. "You haven't even been keeping it clean."

I couldn't help it. I started to laugh. I'm not sure if it was the absurdity of the situation, the relief at breathing free air, or the crashing adrenaline, but I sat there, curled up against the interior of the van, cackling like a maniac while my friends stared at me in shock. It really *was* good to see them all again.

Chapter 5

The nearly imperceptible motion of Floattown was almost calming. It was hard to believe that three hours before, I'd been locked in a cell. It shouldn't have taken three hours to get from the New Lyons jail out to Floattown, but the route we'd taken hadn't exactly been direct. We'd switched vehicles—twice—in each case the original driving off under whatever programming Silas and LaSorte had installed in it. And we'd driven routes that took us miles out of our way, partly to avoid the cameras, and partly to avoid the riots.

"The shit's really hit the fan, Campbell," Hernandez had said, popping LTL rounds out of her magazines and replacing them with the real deal as the van bounced along the city roads. "Silas and company did exactly what they said they would, and let the cat out of the bag as soon as the deadline was up. The whole fucking world had been holding their breath for it, too. So as soon as the information started showing up, every wannabe black hat hacker looking to spread a little chaos started propagating it all over the place. So did every whacko and crackpot—or maybe I should say former crackpot—who had been screaming that synthetics were human. The best cybersecurity in the world couldn't do shit about that."

"Unless they shut down the entire 'net," Tia added. She'd cleaned the knife wound on my arm, then turned her attentions to the week-old injuries I'd suffered breaking into Walton Biogenics. Her questing fingers hurt as they pushed on the various bruises and cleaned out the long litany of scrapes, but the warm feel of her hands on me far outweighed the pain.

"Right. Taking away their slaves is bad enough, but can you imagine the outrage if they turned off the 'net? All hell would break loose." I said it half-jokingly, but the hell of it was, there was more than a grain of truth there. Enslave an entire people? Yeah, sure, a little outrage. But interrupt peoples' internet access?

"It already has," Hernandez said, and I heard a bit of regret in her voice.

"What?"

She sighed. "Look, Campbell, I'm on board, okay? Shit needs to happen. I get it. But there's a price, and it's a big one. In the week since the files dropped, we've burned... How many, Silas?" she asked.

He didn't even turn his head from the screens he was monitoring. "Fifty-six, Detective. One in every state and a few at the federal level." There was a distinct satisfaction in his voice.

Hernandez grunted. "Fifty-six politicians. Burned them on affairs, bribery, misappropriation of government funds, and damn near all manner of criminal asshat-ery that you can imagine. And it's created the worst kind of feeding frenzy I've ever seen." She shook her head. "We've got people protesting the government, people protesting the treatment of synthetics, counter-protestors out in *support* of the government, or demanding that synthetics be destroyed. We've got roving gangs of thugs out to kill any synthetic they come across, and we've already had a shitload of attack first and ask questions later scenarios that have led to real people being killed."

She waved in the direction of LaSorte and Silas. "Sorry. You know what I mean. Humans killing non-synthetic humans because they thought they were synthetics. Fuck." She shook her head. "And NLPD is stretched beyond the breaking point. We're ground zero here, *hermano*, birthplace of the revolution. You know how it was before you turned yourself in? It's ten times worse, now."

I winced at that. The protests and demonstrations had been in full swing as the deadline for Silas's truth bomb approached, but nothing had quite spilled over into outright violence. It sounded like that ship had finally sailed. Sailed, and maybe sank. "What's the damage so far?"

"A handful of deaths. More people beaten up. That's just locally, of course. Nationwide? Dozens."

"And that does not consider the synthetic deaths," Silas interjected, still not looking up from his screens. "There are not many accurate ways to track that. My sources indicate that in New Lyons that number is already in the hundreds."

"Yeah, well, if my little visit from Woodruff is any indicator, that's going to get a lot worse before it gets better."

* * * *

The accommodations here were, arguably, worse than those I'd been experiencing as a guest of the City of New Lyons Department of Corrections while awaiting trial, but the salt in the air and the subtle movements of the VLFPs, the manmade islands dubbed "very large floating platforms," felt like home to me.

Of course, home had been on top of the platforms, in the prefabbed structures that gave the concrete islands all the charm of a stack of storage containers. Not in the network of spaces commonly—and inaccurately—referred to as the Ballasts. The platforms themselves were massive structures of concrete and steel. I'd had enough science courses in my distant school days to have known, on some level, that the fact that they floated at all meant that there had to be air pockets built into the structures to change the density. Or screw with the water displacement. Or however the hell floating worked. And of course, there were normal needs like plumbing and sewage and electric and all the other lifelines that made modern living possible. All that had to go somewhere.

It turned out the "where" wasn't much different from the mainland. Just beneath the streets, the sewers and infrastructure ran. Beneath that, space had been carved out for a hodgepodge of machinery. Pumps, generators, emergency equipment designed to deploy last-ditch float bags if shit went south.

And below *that* were the Ballasts.

They consisted of…rooms…chambers…cells? Shit. I didn't have a good word for them. Metal boxes thirty feet on a side and ten feet high, stacked side by side and on top of each other, in a very shallow "U" shape. Each cell had watertight hatches leading to its neighbors, and ladders welded into the walls for ease of access, along with low-energy lighting embedded in the ceilings. And not much else beyond that—just empty air for providing the necessary buoyancy. The thought of those hatches all closing at once—there had to be a mechanism to do so to prevent all the cells from flooding in the event of a breach—and trapping me with a limited air supply made my throat feel tight.

The cells weren't empty anymore. They weren't exactly overflowing, either, but every one we'd passed through on our way to whatever metal box Silas had designated as Central Command had a few people in it. Well, a few synthetics, anyway. I knew they were synthetics. They were too… "too" to be human. Too pretty. Too handsome. Too muscular. Too tall or thin or pale or short. Too purpose-built for whatever task they were genetically engineered to perform. For the most part, they fell into parameters that regular humanity might hit, but their "average" was our exceptional. The average Toy made most underwear models look frumpy, and the synthetics built for labor had muscles that I didn't even know existed.

It was disconcerting, moving through those poorly lit chambers, feeling their eyes on me, hearing the whispers that popped up in my wake. Did they see a savior? A champion? Just another human, which, to most of them, meant a monster? Or something else? And what would they see if Woodruff wasn't feeding me a line of bullshit? Would they view me differently if they learned that I helped trigger the event that might bring about their extinction?

I shook the thoughts from my head as I descended another ladder. This chamber was different. The others had a few cots, some bedding, a cooler or two. Bucket-like contraptions that I didn't really want to think about, since sanitation was always a problem where biological beings gathered. Instead, this one was filled with screens. I had no idea how Silas was getting a signal down here, but he clearly was, since almost every available inch of wall space had some kind of screen stuck to it. There was a table in the center of the room, a few more around the edges, and some scattered chairs and what looked like military-issued foot lockers.

A few other people—synthetics all—were already in the room as my rescue party and I entered. I caught a few more glances, but whatever they were doing, it seemed more interesting to them than I was, because they quickly turned back to their screens. It was hard not to be distracted by the screens. Better than half of them looked like they were churning away on some sort of net analysis or crawl, but the rest were tuned to various news streams, live vlogs, or drone shots of the streets, not just of New Lyons, but the rest of the world.

The sound was off, but every single screen was showing some scene of protest, riot, or police response. The scrolls along the bottom presented their own streams of facts—stores vandalized, businesses shut down, number of injured. Number of dead. That was bad enough, but it wasn't the worst of it. Every few seconds, one of the screens would cut away to a different shot. A still image of a middle-aged man, looking haggard and somehow sad.

My mug shot.

The screens were splashed with words like *Breaking* and *Escaped Prisoner* and, my least favorite, *Nationwide Manhunt Underway*.

"That didn't take long." I turned, to see that Tia had made her way down the ladder and stepped up beside me while I was enthralled with the flicking images. She hadn't bothered ditching the guns and gear—none of us had—so she still had the shotgun dangling from a tac-strap. Even with the pistol grip and shortened stock and barrel, the thing seemed almost as big as she was. But she'd put it to use, and, I had to admit, the whole G.I. Jane thing was a good look on her.

"Yeah," I grunted. "Guess we had to expect that, though. You don't spring public enemy number one out of jail and get a light response from the law. They'll be looking even harder now than they were before."

"True," Silas said from somewhere off to my left. "But they also have more to occupy them than just you. They will have to make a show of it, of course, but I do not think they will be looking quite so hard as you might imagine."

I grunted at that and looked at the screens not showing my ugly mug. Protest. Demonstration. Riot. Response. Rinse. Repeat. Yeah, the cops had a few other things on their minds. But I didn't think for a second that Fortier, for one, and the Federal Marshal service, for another, were going to let me walk. I watched a moment later as Hernandez and Al'awwal made their way down the ladder. Whatever else we'd managed to do, between the information the synthetics had released and my own prison break, we'd kicked the shit out of the anthill. And Woodruff was still out there somewhere, sitting on top of whatever plot he was waiting to hatch like a demonic hen.

"We need to talk," I said, turning to face Silas. I glanced around at the synthetics working the screens and wondered if, instead of a safe house, this was the real deal. Silas's secret stash. It would be a hell of a thing, to think that he'd been living beneath my feet in the bowels of Floattown for god alone knew how long. "Maybe somewhere with fewer people."

"This way, Detective," Silas said.

"I'm coming, too," Tia said. Hernandez stepped up beside me, and Al'awaal was already following Silas. Well, they'd earned it.

"Let's go."

Silas led us through one final hatch, this one to the chamber next door to his...shit, I had to call it something, and command center seemed to work. So, next to his command center. This cell was set up like a cross between military quarters and a ready room. I saw a bunk in the far corner, but closer to the door was a makeshift conference table cobbled together from a half dozen folding plastic card tables. A bunch of folding metal chairs sat around it. Wherever Silas was getting his revolution budget, it was clear that the big bucks were being spent on tech and office furniture was pretty far down the list.

I dropped into a chair, taking a deep breath as I did so.

The others followed suit, first divesting themselves of their gear and firearms. In a few short minutes, the table was bristling with ballistic vests, balaclavas, blades, tac-lights, and enough firepower to take down a fortress. Or a prison. Tia dropped into the chair on my left with Hernandez taking the one on my right. Hernandez gave me a big grin and a "Welcome home, *pendejo*," as she sat. Silas and Al'awwal sat across from us. LaSorte had peeled off back in the command center, so it was just the five of us in the room.

Hernandez got right to the point. "Okay, Campbell. We're as secure as anything gets in this fucking city these days. Why the call to bust you out? Spill."

My lips twitched in a smile. "It's not that the tender mercies of the New Lyons detention system were getting too much for me," I said. "Though I'd definitely leave a one-star review." I rubbed my hand lightly over the bandages that Tia had wrapped around my arm. It was a stall. I didn't really know how to begin. The rest waited, some more patiently than others, for me to find the starting point.

Fuck it. Subtle wasn't my strong suit. "I think Walton Biogenics is planning some sort of mass genocide of the synthetics. A final omega protocol to wipe out every one of them. Maybe it's their version of a recall, or maybe it's the only way to cover their assess and try to stop heads from rolling." I paused. "And I think they're going to do it soon."

There was a long, heavy silence at the table. It wasn't the reaction I was expecting. Outrage. Disbelief. Calls for action. But not the quiet.

It was Al'awwal who spoke.

"We know. And we think it's already starting."

Chapter 6

The coughing was the worst.

One of the chambers in the Ballast had been converted to an infirmary of sorts. Cots were laid out in rows, and patients lay on them. There weren't a lot of them—maybe a dozen forms shifting restlessly on their thin beds. It was a sight that, among humans, may not have been all that disconcerting. Everyone got sick at some point, and most of us had seen the inside of a hospital.

But I'd never seen a sick synthetic. Not once, in all my years. And now here were a dozen of them. Their discomfort was bad enough, the constant motion of their pain creating a steady rustle. But the coughing. It created a rhythm all its own, a syncopation of throat clearings and low barks that swelled to a crescendo of deep, wracking hacks that left the synthetics gasping for breath in their wake when the fits finally settled, only to be taken up by a different synthetic. The result was ear-splitting and more than a little maddening.

I had pulled on a surgical mask, as had Silas and Tia. The rest, perhaps wisely, had remained behind.

"We don't know how it spreads," Tia said, jolting me from my reverie as we moved among the sick. Silas, being Silas, was stopping at every bunk. He had a warm touch and soft word for each of his people, and I could see in their eyes, that they truly were *his* people now. "We don't even know what it is. It presents like flu, but…"

"But no synthetic in the history of synthetics has ever had the flu," I guessed.

"Right. We're still going through the haul you guys pulled out of the Walton lab, but according to that, synthetics have immune systems that make ours look like…" She floundered at a loss for words. "Look, you know how when the flu—the everyday, vanilla flu—comes through, it's always the very young and very old who are at the greatest risk?" I nodded, wincing as a particularly harsh cough ripped through a patient Silas was speaking with. I swear I saw little flecks of red spittle forming at the corners of the man's mouth. "Well, if I use that analogy, then compared to the synthetics we aren't even the old or the young. We—humanity I mean—we're like babies born weeks premature, who have to go into a sterile environment to stave off all the little things that can do us harm. That's how much stronger their immune systems are than ours."

"Which makes all this." I waved my hand at the coughing synthetics…

"A fucking nightmare," Tia said. I started at that—I wasn't sure I'd ever heard her curse before. I pulled my eyes away from the miserable forms tossing and turning on their beds to look at her. Most of her face was obscured by the medical mask, but her eyes were filled with a mix of sorrow and honest-to-God rage. Tia may have been an assistant medical examiner, but I didn't think that was her true calling. She cared too much about the living.

"When did it start?" I asked as Silas continued to make his rounds.

"A couple of days ago," she replied. "So far, whatever it is, it doesn't seem to be spreading fast." Looking at the dozen figures, I opened my mouth to object, but her raised hand forestalled me. "I know, I know. A dozen people in a few days sounds like a lot, but trust me, given our conditions, it isn't. We've got hundreds of people, Jason—hundreds—scattered throughout these stupid metal boxes, in close proximity to one another, with no real fresh air circulating. It's a nightmare," she said again. "If these were regular people, half, maybe more, would be sick already."

"Small mercies, I guess," I muttered, but she was shaking her head.

"If this was the flu, maybe. But if you think this is some sort of bio-engineered weapon—and it would almost have to be to get through the natural defenses the synthetics have—then the slow speed makes it worse, not better."

I was no doctor, but that didn't make a lick of sense to me. She must have been able to see the confusion on my face, even through the surgical mask, because she let out a bitter little chuckle. "Incubation periods, Jason. Look, if someone gets really sick, really fast, they know it, right? They stay home from work. They don't travel. But if they don't know that they're sick, or if the symptoms are minor, then they do all those things. See more people."

"Spread the virus," I said, understanding dawning.

"Right." It was her turn to shake her head, this time in frustration. "Honestly, I'm *way* out of my depth here. I'm not a virologist or immunologist. Or even a doctor, yet. I'm barely competent to talk about this with respect to how it would spread among different populations of people. But no one's ever looked at how synthetics interact with each other or even *if* synthetics interact with each other. I have no idea how this spreads or why it spreads or how it progresses or if treatments that help us will help them or…"

I could see the tears forming in her eyes and hear the panic creeping into her voice. I reached out and pulled her into my arms. She hugged me back, hard. "It's okay," I murmured, not really believing it myself. "Whatever it is, we'll figure it out." It wasn't much, but it was all I had to offer.

Maybe it was enough, because after a moment, she pushed away from me. She didn't wipe at her eyes—because poking your fingers into your face when you were in a room full of sick people probably wasn't the best way to stay healthy—but I could tell by the slight rise in her cheeks and the corners of her eyes that she was offering a wan smile. "Thanks. Doctors shouldn't cry in front of their patients. Bad form. Not that I've been able to do much for them. Make them as comfortable as possible, is all, since we don't even know what we're dealing with. We need to figure that out, somehow."

"We do," Silas agreed, approaching us after making his rounds. "But that is not the most important question, Ms. Morita."

"Isn't it?" I asked. "We need to know what we're dealing with if we're going to stop it."

"Yes," he agreed. "But we also need to know what is triggering it. You may not know much about the habits of synthetics, but I do. A normal virus spreads through human,"—his eyes narrowed on the word—"contact. People gather together. They exchange touches, breathe the same air as strangers. Any number of things to expose themselves to contagion. But synthetics? For the most part, we reside in relatively small, relatively isolated groups that do not see many other synthetics from the outside." His massive shoulder rose and fell in a ponderous shrug. "The gathering here is an exception. We have many synthetics who filled different roles before escaping their tormentors. But most synthetics encounter only a small subset of other synthetics or normal humans throughout the course of their day. They do not often find themselves in contact with unfamiliar synthetics."

"Which makes it difficult for the virus to spread through their population," Tia suggested, nodding.

"Which makes it a pretty fucking terrible weapon," I added.

"Agreed," Silas replied. "And while I would certainly call Walton Biogenics terrible, the minds behind them are a long way from stupid."

"Which means we're missing something," I grunted.

"Something that we need to uncover as soon as possible, Detective. Or the solution to the 'synthetic problem' may be a rather final one."

* * * *

We were back in what I couldn't help but think of as the briefing room, just off of the command center, gathered around the plastic tables. It was the usual suspects—me, Silas, Hernandez, Tia, Al'awwal, and LaSorte. There was another synthetic I hadn't met, a stunning woman named Danielle who, according to Silas, was the closest thing to a doctor among the gathered synthetics. I got the impression that her knowledge was academic, rather than practical, but she was also one of the people making sense of the packet of information Dr. Kaphiri had left for us. Which meant she was a hell of a lot smarter than I was, and that was good enough for me.

"What, exactly, did this Woodruff tell you, Campbell?" Hernandez asked, her voice slipping into the rhythms of interrogation. I smiled at that. I wasn't sure if Hernandez was still on the job or not. It hadn't been long since I'd turned myself in to her, but it seemed like the whole world had fallen apart while I was in the detention center, and we hadn't exactly had the chance to talk. Still, I smiled at the familiar tones.

"Not a lot. He hinted that some eager overachiever within Walton was behind the attempt on my life, and that killing me so soon would be getting off too easy. Then he said that Walton Biogenics would never have released the synthetics into the wild without some sort of kill switch or omega protocol. He didn't go into details, but I got the impression that it was a way to kill them all. I'm not sure I understand why, exactly, though."

"Because if every synthetic were to drop dead en masse, do you really think anyone would continue to pursue justice for them? The dead file very few complaints, Jason," Silas said with a humorless smile.

I considered that. If Silas and all the other synthetics expired, what would I do? Could I really walk away from it all? Just accept the extermination of millions with a shrug and an "at least I tried?" The thought made me more than a little uneasy. And yet, at the same time, what would I accomplish if I did keep pursuing it? What did that leave?

Revenge.

And making sure nothing like it ever happened again.

"You might be surprised," I muttered.

The pale synthetic waved one hand in dismissal. "Perhaps. But it is neither here nor there. Your god willing, it is something we will avoid, but not if we keep allowing ourselves to be sidetracked."

"We have no real evidence that the sickness we're seeing here is actually some sort of biological weapon," Tia chimed in. There was more than one skeptical grunt at that thought, mine among them, but she didn't back down. "Well, we don't. I'm not saying it isn't the most likely thing. But we have zero equipment here to do the kind of tests and analysis that we need to do in order to even identify what we're looking *for*, much less what we're looking *at*."

"She's right." The soft voice belonged to Danielle, and I turned my attention to the woman. She was, like most Toys, almost painfully beautiful, her skin a light brown, a shade or two too dark to be called olive. Her hair fell in loose curls, framing a narrow, almost elfin face with deep brown eyes that seemed impossibly large. "There are too many unknowns and too many assumptions being made. Yes, the timing is suspicious, but I would wager that this is also the first time so many synthetics were gathered in such tight quarters. While it is unlikely, this could be a natural outbreak. After all, that is the assumption we were working on before Mr. Campbell returned to us."

"But the urgency has definitely been stepped up," LaSorte chimed in. "If it's Walton trying to end us…"

This wasn't my kind of fight, but it was the fight before us, so it was time to get work. We needed more information, and we needed it fast. "So, what do we need? And how do we get it?" I looked from Tia to Danielle and back again.

Tia shrugged. "We need to run tests. See if we can isolate anything unusual in the blood and tissue of the sick. Take some samples from some who aren't sick as well, and see what we can see there. If we can identify it, maybe we can fight it." She shook her head. "But, Jason, you have to understand…there's entire *professions* dedicated to this kind of thing. You don't just get a random group of people together and have them discover a brand new virus or whatever. We can do some comparative analysis, but…"

She trailed off. I felt the pall fall over the table at her words. Not that it was her fault—she was only telling us what we already knew and didn't want to admit.

"We have to start somewhere," I said at last. "So where do we start? Blood tests? Where can we run them? I assume we can't just buy the equipment and bring it here." It struck me again that I had no idea how Silas was funding his revolution.

"Most hospitals would have the equipment. Private labs. And…" Tia hesitated, but forged ahead. "And the morgue. We have a fair amount of equipment for forensic analysis there." She looked uncomfortable mentioning it, and I knew why. She'd broken the law on multiple occasions now to help the cause, and I couldn't fault her dedication. But it had always been "offsite." She'd never taken things into her own backyard, and if she got caught running off-the-books analyses, it could ruin her career.

"I can dummy up a case file," Hernandez cut in. "Or just attach the samples to something open. We've gotta have a few bangers laid out in the morgue that Guns and Gangs are looking at. If anyone notices, it won't be for weeks." She shrugged. "One way or another, I'm guessing weeks is too long to matter." That answered the question of whether or not Hernandez was still employed by the NLPD. I was glad to see that she still had a steady paycheck, as much for her own sake as for her daughter's. Of course, if she got caught fabricating files, that job would dry up and blow away. I tried not to think about that—Hernandez was smart. She knew exactly what she was risking being here, and it was her choice to make.

"Then we have a plan," I said. "Hernandez creates a request for some bloodwork, and Tia tests the synthetic blood in its place."

"To the limits of my knowledge and the equipment available at the lab," Tia added.

"What do the rest of us do in the meantime?" LaSorte asked.

"The hardest thing—we wait."

Chapter 7

Waiting sucks.

It's bad enough when you're waiting for something that *you* have to do. It's worse when you're waiting on others to do something. And when those others are your friends, and they've gone into danger, it's pretty much unbearable.

I spent the next two days trying to keep myself occupied. Silas had gotten me a new screen, and I'd wasted a few hours setting up my personal filters. Once I'd finished that, I'd flipped it on to get my first real glimpse of the outside world since Silas had launched his campaign.

It wasn't pretty.

The news anchors looked just as put together and impeccable as ever as I started to play back the stories my queries delivered. But the content… "Riots continue to rage throughout the city," the male anchor said, the screen cutting to a video of a mob of people—most with their faces covered in makeshift balaclavas or tee shirts tied around their noses and mouths—running through the streets, throwing bottles and rocks at store fronts, jumping on cars, and generally making a mess of things. "The riots are in response to a massive release of evidence lending more credence to the notion that synthetics are, in fact, thinking beings capable of the same thoughts and emotions as people. Other files, released at the same time, implicated politicians across all fifty-three states in crimes ranging from simple corruption to—in one case—murder. Those investigations are ongoing and have added fuel to the fires spawning the protests. The information was released by the group fronted by former New Lyons Police Department Detective Jason Campbell." The screen cut to an image of me. I winced a bit. Did they have to use the mugshot? No one looked good in a mug shot, and I had enough problems in that department already. And when had I become the "front man" for Silas's organization? I guess when I had opened my big fat mouth on New Year's Eve. But still...

The screen cut back to the female anchor. "We're joined now with Roberto Stringer, attorney for the group SynthFirst. Mr. Stringer, what's your take on all of this?"

The screen focused on a middle-aged man of Hispanic descent. "What we're seeing now is the inevitable conclusion of decades of oppression," Stringer said, his tone serious despite the million-dollar smile he flashed at the camera. "At SynthFirst, we've been saying for years that so-called synthetics are, in fact, people, and people who should have all the same rights as the rest of us. The people of this great country have been lied to by corporations and politicians, and they're tired of it."

The screen split to show Mr. Stringer on one side and the anchors on the other. The male anchor spoke, "But what about the violence, Mr. Stringer? Surely, those of you at SynthFirst don't condone the violence that we're seeing in the streets."

"Of course we don't," Stringer replied. "But the information released shows us that we can't trust the government in this matter, and illustrates the corruption that we have collectively ignored for generations. I ask you, what are the people to do? If they feel they can't find redress for these wrongs among the corrupt politicians, and they can't turn to the corporations that have pulled the wool over their eyes for decades in pursuit of profit, what avenues are left to them? Civil disobedience is a long-standing tradition in this country, and one of the few ways the populace at large has ever managed to create direct change. That goes all the way back to Boston Harbor."

I swiped to a different channel. I didn't need a history lesson, and I wasn't sure the analogy really fit in this case anyway. I kept swiping across my screen, not really paying attention, until the image flashed into the greasy, piggish face of Francois Fortier.

I stopped swiping and the sound kicked in. "Jason Campbell is a criminal, pure and simple," Fortier was saying. The camera panned, showing that the man was conducting another press conference on the steps of police headquarters. The same place he'd taken me into custody. "Look around you people. He's the one responsible for the chaos in the streets."

"But what about his escape?" a reporter shouted over the general tumult.

"It's pretty clear he had help. Probably an inside job. Look, we've got the city locked down. He can't stay hidden forever. And when we find him, we'll throw his ass right back in jail where it belongs." The camera seemed to linger on the beads of sweat forming on Fortier's brow and upper lip.

That brought a nasty smile to my lips. I was making him sweat. And if they were trying to find out who had helped me from inside the prison, they were on the wrong path. That would buy a little time.

I flipped the screen off. I was restless, and watching the city I loved fall apart on live video wasn't going to help. Neither was trying to keep tabs on the manhunt. It wasn't like they were going to tell the press anything that could help me. And if I had to watch Francois-fucking-Fortier for one more minute, I would probably punch something. I needed to burn off some energy.

There wasn't a gym in the Ballasts, of course. But there were a lot of ladders. Climbing up and down a few dozen stories sounded like as good a plan as any. And if that didn't work, I could always find Al. Not that getting my ass kicked seemed like the best of ideas, but it *would* tire me out. I looked down at my wardrobe—Silas and company had a scavenged collection of castoffs from God alone knew where. The good news was, I'd been able to get rid of the orange prison jumpsuit. The only things that had come close to fitting were a pair of ratty khakis and a bright pink tee shirt. Not the ideal workout clothes, but beggars couldn't be choosers.

Time to get to work.

* * * *

I leaned both hands against the wall of the makeshift shower, head down, letting the thin stream of water wash away the sweat of the latest match with Al'awwal. There were, for whatever reason, a couple of working actual bathrooms in the Ballasts, but they didn't have showers. They were probably for maintenance workers or whoever else had need to come down here to work. Thank God we hadn't seen anyone yet, but it did make me nervous. Bathrooms meant there was at least the potential of people, and whatever else they offered, the Ballasts weren't a place we could clear out of quickly.

The enterprising synthetics had managed to tap in to a couple of exposed water pipes and install showerheads in one of the unused chambers. The setup reminded me of boot—just bare showerheads sticking out of the wall without any kind of dividers for privacy. I supposed that synthetics lost anything resembling body modesty, or anything resembling an expectation of privacy for that matter, at a young age. It did make me wonder what Tia had done those nights she'd stayed here and not returned to her own apartment. She didn't strike me as the type to casually shower in a room full of other people. Though the thought of walking in on her...

That really wasn't a good path to go down, not standing naked in a room that any of the synthetics could walk into at any moment. At least the water trickling down onto my head was cold, putting a dampener on any amorous thoughts I might be having. I forced my mind back to the shower itself. While the ingenuity of the synthetics had allowed for a place to shower, the Ballasts weren't built to provide drainage. That was why the water was barely a trickle, and why I had no intention of standing here very long. The water had to be cleaned up and disposed of. There were mops and buckets and squeegees waiting for me when the shower was done.

I was contemplating the irony of that—take a shower to get cleaned up after sweating only to have to clean up the aftermath of the shower which would involve, wait for it...sweating...when the door swung open. A synthetic I didn't recognize—young, female, beautiful—stuck her head in the door. "Silas wanted you to know that Ms. Morita and Ms. Hernandez are back," she said. She regarded me with a frank look, making no attempt to conceal her appraisal. I, in turn, tried not to jump and squeal and cover my important bits like I was in a bad 'net prank vid.

"Thanks," I managed. "I'll be along in just a moment. Just need to finish, and clean up the mess."

For a moment, she looked like she might offer to do the cleanup for me, but then something—a hardness, an edge—flashed across her face. She nodded instead, and left, pulling the door shut behind her. I wondered about that look as I finished up, all thoughts of Tia or the discomfort of the appraising stare lost in that one, hard-edged flash of emotion. I got the impression that, had I been a synthetic, she would have gladly assisted. But since I was a human, a nominal oppressor even if I had shown myself to be on the side of the angels, there was no way she was going to spend her sweat to help me. I couldn't exactly blame her, and yet...

And yet, I was left to wonder, once again, what kind of world would emerge if we managed to achieve all our goals. As I toweled off, dressed, and started to push the mop around the metal floor, I realized that my commitment hadn't waned. The synthetics deserved to be free. There was no question that they had been mistreated and misused to the detriment not just of them, but also to the very soul of humanity. But I couldn't help the slight quaver of... I don't think it was fear. Uncertainty? Cognitive dissonance? Whatever it was, that hard look, that hatred that I sensed burning just beneath the skin of so many of the synthetics, worried me.

As much as I wanted our little war to be won, the possibilities of victory scared me almost as much as the possibilities of defeat.

I cleaned up the floor, a simple task that, for many humans, had been relegated to synthetics long since, and wondered what the future held.

* * * *

My mood brightened immediately when I walked into our makeshift conference room and saw Tia Morita standing there. I surprised us both by striding over and giving her a quick hug. "I'm glad you made it back," I whispered, then stepped away.

Hernandez, also in the room, arched an eyebrow at me and her lips quirked in a smile, but I ignored her. I then realized that the rest of the usual suspects had gathered as well; Silas, Al'awwal, LaSorte, and Danielle all sat at their places around the table.

"Glad you could join us, *hermano*," Hernandez said as I took my seat.

"Sorry," I muttered. "Had to clean up the shower." I didn't want to get into the unexpected mental complexities that task had given birth to, so I continued. "What did we find?"

All eyes went to Tia.

She drew a steadying breath, and, despite a slight flush suffusing her cheeks, spoke firmly. "I ran the bloodwork, from the sick and the healthy. And I ran my own, too, just in case."

"Smart," Danielle muttered.

"Why?" Hernandez asked. "If it's something that Walton did, you don't think they'd have made it catching to humans, too? Not if it was their lethal omega protocol or whatever." Her voice was part cop-worry, concern for the safety of the citizens, but a much deeper mom-worry, with concern for her daughter. The tough-as-nails, all-business face she presented to the world made it easy to forget she had a burgeoning teenager at home.

"No," Tia said. "But you can be a carrier for something and not subject to its effects. We know that it's not super common for different circles of synthetics to interact with one another, not closely enough to facilitate the exchanges needed to transfer a virus, anyway. But they interact with *us* all the time."

"So they make us the carrier, and Walton gets to have humanity fuck over the synthetics one last time," Hernandez grunted. "Sick fuckers, aren't they?"

"Are they?" I asked, looking at Tia. "I mean, did they? Shit. What did you find, Tia?"

"Something," she said. Her lips tightened a bit and her eyebrows drew down in a frown of frustration. "I honestly don't know *what* I found, except that there was definitely *something*. My guess would be that it was viral in nature, but it's not something I can identify."

"No," Silas interjected. "Of course not. If it is something that Walton has done, then it would be new. Even if you had the appropriate training and knowledge, you still would likely not be able to identify it, Ms. Morita."

"I have the samples," she said, pulling a data cube from her pocket. "And the test results. All of it. But we're going to need someone with a lot more specialized knowledge…and maybe equipment, too." She hesitated, and I could tell that whatever was coming next wasn't going to be pleasant.

"And…and it's in my blood," she said, voice falling to barely a whisper. "Whatever this thing is, it was in the blood I tested of the sick synthetics, not present in the healthy ones, and…and present in me." She drew a breath, let it out as a shallow sigh. "I thought about not coming back… I think I'm a carrier. But…"

"But if you are," I said, "then so am I. So is Hernandez. And God alone knows how many other people."

"And how many other synthetics," Danielle interjected. "The healthy synthetic blood Tia tested showed negative, but she didn't test everyone. We've all been around the sick, and while we've taken some small measure of precautions, we certainly haven't exercised any real quarantine procedures."

The table was quiet as that fact settled in.

"So we have no idea who might be sick, no idea what we're up against, and no idea what to do about it," I said. "That about sum it up?"

There were a few desultory nods around the table.

"Well, too fucking bad," I growled. "We didn't come this far to give up. I didn't get thrown into, and then break out of, jail just to watch this whole thing fall apart. So, what can we fucking do about it?"

"Tell the people," Silas said at once. "They are starting to believe, to truly believe, that we are what we say. I do not think they will stand for genocide."

I wasn't so certain. A lot of people might wring their hands and weep, but if the synthetics went away, then so, too, did the problem. I'd been a soldier and a cop far too long to have the kind of faith in my fellow man to think they wouldn't be happier just sweeping problems under the nearest available rug.

I shrugged. "That might get us some sympathy, and might get other eyes looking at the problem. Hell, if we get lucky, maybe that even gets someone with the medical and scientific know-how and equipment on the job. But what if it doesn't? What else can we do?"

Danielle spoke, her voice heavy with an emotion that I don't think I'd ever heard in a synthetic, though I'd glimpsed it, ever so briefly, on Annabelle's face. It held sadness, yes, but also the edge of shame. "We have to monitor the sick. Track the progress of the disease. We don't know that it's lethal yet." Hernandez choked off an incredulous snort at that, and I couldn't help but agree. No one had died from it, not so far, but it would be the kind of miracle to restore humanity's declining faith in all things divine for this not to end in death. Danielle, to her credit, ignored our cynicism. "But we must be meticulous, gather every data point that we can, even if we can't yet analyze it properly. We must be ready to give over as much information as possible. We can't…we can't afford to waste any time."

At first, I didn't understand her shame. Her words made perfect sense. Anything we could learn could only help. It dawned on me, though, that synthetics, while used to watching humans inflicting pain on them, and maybe even on other humans, had no capacity to do the same. They underwent intense conditioning against harming humans and, presumably, each other, or I'm sure we would have seen synthetic fights to the death as prime entertainment long since, and coldly recording the pain and probable deaths of their fellows must have been a concept foreign to them. It had been standard procedure in humanity's medical system—while trying to administer compassionate care, of course—for so long, that I didn't bat an eye at it, but from the outside, how must it seem? That we measured and weighed and calculated every aspect of encroaching death so effectively and efficiently?

I shook that thought from my head. "Right. We monitor the progress. Danielle, I assume you and Tia can take care of that?" Danielle nodded, but Tia gave me a frown.

"I don't think that's a good idea, Jason. We *know* I'm carrying whatever this is. I think I need to go to the hospital. I can fake the symptoms we've seen among the synthetics. If I can get them to do bloodwork, maybe they'll be able to do something. Identify it or get some sort of treatment plan. It's a long shot, but if something as simple as robust antibiotics can help, we should try. They'll probably only give me a few weeks' worth for my use, but we can spread that around a few test patients and see if there's any improvement in the short term."

That sparked an entirely new larcenous chain of thought. "What are you giving the synthetics now?"

It was Danielle who answered. "Just the basics, really. Fever reducers. Cough suppressants. Without UniCare cards, we don't really have access to antibiotics." That sadness and shame filled her eyes again. "If things progress to the point where there is significant pain, we can acquire some of the harder recreational drugs."

That was true enough, and easy enough. The war on drugs had ended long ago, in a rousing defeat. Opiates would be the easiest and most effective to procure. Easier than getting antibiotics. It had something to do with not overusing the drugs and breeding super-viruses immune to anything we could throw at them. Which, under the circumstances, seemed pretty fucking laughable. Why worry about viruses evolving, when your friendly local biogenics company was cooking them up in the lab?

Still it prompted a larcenous thought. "Would antibiotics help?" I asked.

My question was met with general shrugs. "We don't know enough to know," Tia replied. "If it's truly viral, then no. If it's bacterial, maybe. But at this point, they probably can't hurt."

"So, why don't we get some?"

Hernandez cut in, "Are you suggesting we...what...go rob a pharmacy?"

A chuckle escaped me. "You broke me out of a fucking prison, Mel. Are you going to balk at liberating a few antibiotics?"

"*Dios mio.* What have you gotten me into?" There was no heat in the words, just a sort of bemused resignation.

"There is one other thing we might want to consider," Silas interjected.

"Yeah?" I asked, mind already skipping ahead to planning how to knock over a pharmacy.

"Do you recall the raid we executed to retrieve the information Dr. Kaphiri had gathered?" Of course I remembered. It had only been a couple of weeks ago. Oh, and it had ended up with me in prison.

"Yeah. It kinda sticks out," I replied.

"I am certain it does," Silas conceded. "But do you recall how we escaped?"

"Walked out the front door," Al'awwal said, chiming in for the first time. I swear to God, the grin he gave me was one of pure fucking delight. Right before walking out the front door, we'd gone through a half-dozen cops like a pair of blenders. I think Al—the only synthetic I knew of to *not* have the conditioning that prevented his fellows from harming humans— had enjoyed getting back a little of his own. I had another flash, or maybe premonition was the right word, of ambivalence at the thought of what we might be unleashing.

"We did. But in order to facilitate that egress, I triggered a certain alarm," Silas said.

Everything had been happening so fast—and I'd been suffering from a few hard blows to the head—that I hadn't really been paying too much attention to the details of what Silas had done during our escape. But something started to come back to me. "You said something about a biological hazard, or bio labs or something."

"Correct, Jason," the big albino said with a slight smile. "When we were in their systems, I found a node governing alarms for labs with bio-safety levels. Not unusual for a bio-genetics company, I will grant you. But one of those labs was designated as BSL-4. That is a level of quarantine procedure reserved for the deadliest contaminants and biological agents. Why would a company like Walton Biogenics need such a secure laboratory?"

It was Tia who answered. "To develop biological weapons."

"Shit," Hernandez muttered, and it summed up my feeling exactly. "Are you telling me these assholes are building doomsday devices in the heart of fucking New Lyons?"

"A suspicion, only, Detective Hernandez," Silas said. "We have no proof. But I thought it odd at the time that such labs would be present, given the stated scope of Walton Biogenics' work."

I drew a deep breath as all that sank in. "Okay. We've got a lot to do, people. And maybe not a lot of time to do it. Tia—you're right. You should go to the hospital. Let them run tests. But watch your ass, okay? If anything feels off or wrong, even a little… Listen to your instincts. Walton's smart. I'm sure they're going to be monitoring their little superbug and listening for where it shows up. And we know they don't mind doing a little wetwork to keep the populace quiet. You can't bring a gun into your doctor's office or the hospital or whatever, but you ran that shotgun well. Keep it in your car. And keep it loaded." She didn't look particularly comfortable with that thought, but she seemed to understand the need, and reluctantly nodded.

"Good. What about the rest of us?"

"I think I can handle acquiring antibiotics," Al'awwal offered. "We may not need to resort to strongarm robbery on that front. I've got a few doctor friends. If I spread a little cash around, I might be able to get a supply big enough for those here." He hesitated.

"What?" I asked.

"If this spreads… Well, we're never going to be able to get a big enough supply. Not without tapping government resources."

"I know," I admitted, "which is why we need another approach."

"We need," Silas interjected, "to acquire some additional intelligence from someone who works at Walton Biogenics. Preferably, someone who works at the specific lab Dr. Kaphiri once called home. I suppose LaSorte and I could try to find someone who fits the profile."

I thought about that. The pair of them—the best of the best among the tech-savvy synthetics—would be better off getting the word out about the potential dangers. Silas, in particular, still had a network to run and I'm sure he had channels by which he could communicate with other synthetics. We'd never discussed it, never dragged his methods out into the light of day, but the entire revolution would have been swept under the rug in a matter of weeks if he didn't have some kind of organization in place. That single point of failure bothered me—but at the same time, I couldn't begrudge him the lack of trust he must feel toward... Well, everybody.

Fortunately, as I thought of our last little trip to Walton, I realized that we really didn't need to turn Silas and LaSorte loose on tracking down lab employees. We already knew one.

"Don't bother," I said. "We already know the name of at least one person on the payroll there, and a doctor to boot. I'm not sure what type of doctor, medical or philosophical, but in the end, it probably doesn't matter. She has access, and that's what we're going to need right now."

"Larkin?" Al asked, an incredulous note in his voice.

"Larkin," I agreed.

"And this Larkin is going to what... Help us out of the goodness of her heart?" Hernandez asked.

"Not bloody likely," Al replied. "Last time we talked, we sort of tied her up, robbed her office, and threatened to kill her. A little."

Tia gave me a bit of a glare at that. "You threatened to kill her? And how do you just do that 'a little?'"

I opened my mouth to launch into an explanation. But I was cut short when Silas coughed.

Silas.

Coughed.

Chapter 8

Silence reigned in the room.

We all just sort of sat there, staring at the big synthetic, watching, waiting for him to say that he was just clearing his throat. But he wasn't. That was clear from the look on his face. Part confusion, part discomfort, and, most terrifying of all, just a little hint of fear. In all my interactions with Silas, I'd never seen him afraid. Not until now.

Tia moved first, pushing back her chair and walking, without particular haste or undue concern, to Silas's side. "Hold still for a moment," she said, pressing one hand against his forehead. She then took his pulse, and asked him to stick out his tongue. I'd seen caricatures of the procedures all my life, though modern medicine had rendered them subservient to a variety of far more precise machines. They must have still taught the basics in med school, though, because Tia was assessing Silas's health with a calm, professional certainty.

While she worked, she asked questions.

"How are you feeling? Any discomfort in your throat? Your head? Any pressure, here?" Silas fed her answers, but I didn't really hear him. The network, the rebellion, the revolution was built upon Silas. The NLPD could arrest me, a Walton hit squad could take out Al'awwal, Tia could get hit by a friggin' bus, God forbid, and the revolution would go on. But what happened if Silas got sick?

"We're going to have to isolate you," Tia said. She raised her hands at the look of protest that flashed across his face. "I know, I know. You have work to do. Fine. We'll isolate you in here, or even in your room, somewhere you can have access to all the screens in the world, but you're not going to do anyone any good if you're around those who might not have contracted this thing yet. For that matter, we should almost certainly put Jacinda and Evelyn somewhere away from everyone. Full quarantine procedure for them. That little girl is probably at more risk than any of us."

"*Dios mio*," Hernandez whispered.

"Amen," I muttered. I hadn't even *considered* that the child would be at more risk. The thought of her getting sick, and possibly dying... I'd spent so long thinking of the synthetics as adults—and hale and hearty adults at that—that the normal warnings about the very young and very old with respect to illness hadn't sunk in to my mind yet.

"As you wish, Ms. Morita," Silas was saying, jolting me from my reverie. "But let us acknowledge that it is probably already too late for any of these actions to matter, as far as those of us here in the Ballasts are concerned. We will take every precaution, but we have been down here for weeks. The damage is very likely done. We are better served trying to find a way to combat it than limit its spread. We should not waste time worrying about my health."

"Uh-huh," Tia said, ignoring his words as she continued to give him a once over. "And we'll all do just that. Once you're taken care of."

"This is quite ridiculous. It was just a cough," Silas grumbled.

I stared in amazement as Tia deflected every protest the synthetic voiced and ushered him from the command center. It was amazing to watch the tiny woman bully the much larger man into submission with nothing more than a calming tone and a professional demeanor. She was back before we knew it, a smile that I couldn't quite read on her face. The whole thing filled me with a weird combination of pride and the edge of something I could only call lust. Watching her work was kinda hot.

"Danielle," she said as she returned. "Can you make sure he stays isolated, and also see to getting Jacinda and Evelyn situated somewhere?"

"Of course, Tia," the synthetic woman replied.

"Well," I said, "that leaves the rest of us. LaSorte, can you work with Silas on getting the word out? Without needing to be in the same room with him I mean?"

He shrugged and looked at me through hooded eyes. "Most of the time I've worked with him it's been remotely. But... Campbell... If Silas gets sick...." He trailed off, but I could see more than just worry for the revolution on his face. I could see real fear over the potential loss of a friend.

"I know," I said. "But we can only do what we can do. Right now, that means trying to solve this thing before anyone starts dying. And that means Tia goes to the doctor, Al'awwal tries to secure some antibiotics, you and Silas get the word out, and Danielle tries to contain the spread of this thing as much as possible."

"Shit," Hernandez muttered.

I arched an eyebrow at her.

"I guess that means I'm the one who has to help you kidnap a Walton Biogenics employee."

I grinned. "Something like that."

* * * *

Hernandez still had access to department resources. That made things a little easier.

"Are we really going to kidnap this Larkin, Campbell?" she asked as we made our way through the steel corridors and up an endless series of rusting metal ladders to the street level.

"I hope not. I hope that she'll listen to reason, tell us what we need to know. But if Walton Biogenics really has released some kind of pathogen or whatever, I need to get answers." I paused for a moment, and gave Hernandez a long, level look. "I *need* to get answers, Mel. By any means necessary."

"You think you could do that, Campbell?" she asked. "You think you could...what? Beat it out of her? You'd go that far?"

I hadn't really considered what I meant by 'any means necessary.' But it certainly implied some sort of force. My training as a cop and as a soldier told me that those kinds of tactics rarely worked. But *rarely* wasn't the same as *never*. But could *I* do it?

The thought made my stomach turn. But so, too, did the thought of the synthetic population being wiped off the face of the Earth as the result of a bio-engineered plague. One woman's pain, against the fate of millions.

"Fuck," I growled. "I don't know, Hernandez. I really don't. You know what's at stake here."

"Better than you, *hermano*. Better than you. But you'll see soon enough." That comment struck me as odd, but then, I'd been locked up for a week, with little access to the outside world. Hernandez had been out in the shit.

As we'd talked, we'd been navigating our way through the Ballasts, climbing ladders, traversing walkways, and generally moving from the bowels of Floattown up toward the surface of the man-made island. We'd reached the last hatch.

"Me first," Hernandez ordered, shouldering me aside.

I nodded and gestured toward the ladder. Having her stick her head up into wherever we were emerging would be odd if anyone bothered to notice, but it was better than me sticking my ugly mug through the hatch and risking that someone—or worse, some unseeing electronic eye—would make note of it and alert the authorities.

"Keep your eyes off my ass, *pendejo*," she said as she placed her first foot on the ladder rung.

I choked back something that was half-chuckle, half-sputter. Before I could either defend myself or get myself in trouble by insisting that I didn't think of Hernandez that way, she was already moving up the ladder. Probably for the best. Getting caught checking out a woman was just as bad as her thinking you didn't *want* to check her out.

I still looked though. I'm only human, after all.

It only took Hernandez a few seconds to shimmy up the ladder. She paused at the top, grunting with effort as she levered the manhole cover out of the way. Then she peeked out, taking her time. With a final shove, she pushed the cover completely to the side and climbed out of the darkness. I took that as my cue, and climbed up after her.

I'd borrowed one of Silas's raincoats, which managed to be both comically large through the shoulders *and* barely fall to mid-thigh on me, but at least it covered the ridiculous tee shirt. It also had a pair of nice, deep pockets. One of them held a shitty little ganger gun—an inexpensive, damn-near disposable, firearm popular with criminals because it was cheap enough to throw away. I'd be lucky if the damn thing put a bullet within a foot of where I intended it to go, but beggars and choosers. Hernandez had scavenged the piece from somewhere. Apart from Al's and Hernandez's personal firearms—and you couldn't just ask someone to give up those— the only other guns our revolution had managed to put together were the nine-millimeter in my pocket, the twelve gauge that was on the way to the hospital with Tia, and about a half-dozen relics that may or may not go bang when the need arose.

Which is why the *other* pocket held a collapsible baton, probably older than I was, but it was hard to screw up a telescoping steel bar. The neoprene grip had long since worn off and been replaced first with duct tape, and then with what looked to me like the cloth tape hospitals used to bandage wounds. Whatever it was, it provided a nice, secure grip. It also helped balance out the pistol in the other pocket.

My ensemble was completed by a floppy rain hat with a broad, malformed brim that reminded me of an oversized boonie cap, also from Silas's personal collection. Between the ill-fitting clothes and the ridiculous hat I must have looked like a drunk homeless person. Which, come to think of it, was probably a much better disguise than anything I could have planned.

We emerged into a narrow alleyway between two of the prefabbed cubes that gave Floattown its questionable charm. A quick glance showed that no one was around, so I took a moment to bask in the sea breeze and taste the tang of salt on the air. After the caring ministrations of the New Lyons Corrections Department and the dank darkness of the Ballasts, it felt good to be outside.

"You done?" Hernandez asked. "We have things to do."

I smiled, keeping my head ducked so my face would be obscured from any prying electronic eyes. "Lead the way, oh great purveyor of inferior firearms and ill-fitting clothing. Where you lead, I am sure to follow."

She snorted. "I should lead your big *gringo* ass right back to jail." She pulled out her screen and started swiping. "I've got a car coming to this location. And I've pulled the last known address on your Dr. Larkin. Records indicate she should still live there. It's a gated community, though."

"And what do you want to bet that it just happens to be one hundred percent Walton Biogenics employees that live there?" I asked.

"No bet. Pretty much guaranteed. How do you want to play it?"

"We can't just drive in, not through the security I assume they'll have in place at whatever 'gate' leads in to the subdivision." I hefted my coat, shifting the weight of the pistol. "And I don't really feel like fighting our way past whatever rent-a-goons Walton hired. Only leaves one real option."

"Through the wire," Hernandez said.

"And over the hills," I agreed.

"To *casa de la abuela* we go."

* * * *

The drive proved...enlightening.

When the car pulled up a compact two-seater that barely had enough room to fit the both of us—Hernandez punched in the destination. But as soon as the little vehicle started to move, the set of her shoulders changed. I could read the tension in them, and in the way that her head went immediately on a swivel, continuously scanning for danger.

"That bad?" I asked, forced to keep my head ducked down and obscured by the hat so as to avoid any prying electronic eyes.

"You've no fucking idea, Campbell," she replied. Even her voice had tightened. "The car's computer should try to take us around the worst of it. Just thank your lucky stars that we don't have to go downtown."

Floattown looked normal to me. That wasn't surprising. It was one of those areas where, while money was tight, almost everyone had a job to supplement the basic living stipend. In the evening, the gangers would come out to play, and the tenor of the neighborhood would shift, but even they had day jobs to earn enough money to keep on keeping on. It wasn't the kind of place where protests and riots happened. Everyone was too close to the brink, too reliant on their jobs to maintain their standard of living. It was the kind of place where, simply put, no one could *afford* to protest.

I wasn't really sure if that was a good thing or a bad thing. It made the first part of our journey much easier. But the idea that free citizens were de facto financially excluded from some of the rights I'd bled over filled me with uneasiness.

Once we crossed the bridge things started to change. The first thing that struck me was the lack of people. The streets of New Lyons weren't exactly Ney York City or London, but there were always *some* people around. Not today. A few cars moved through the streets, but the sidewalks were empty. I kept my head down— you never knew where a camera might be pointing—but at least the odds of being recognized by another person were looking slim. Still didn't explain the tension Hernandez was oozing, though.

"Where is everyone?" I asked.

"The smart ones are staying inside," she replied. "There's an official recommendation to keep off the streets."

Something about the way she said it—and the continuing tension—told me there weren't a lot of smart ones. "And the rest?"

She shrugged. "We'll see them soon enough, *hermano*. They're doing what people always do when a large enough group gets angry. They've taken to the streets. And the people who disagree with them have done the same. You know the drill."

I did know the drill. Groups of angry protestors were nothing new. They'd been a part of our nation's story since the very beginning. But the line between "angry protestors" and "angry mob" was vanishingly thin. Judging from Hernandez's discomfort, it was a line that had been crossed more than once in the past few days.

"Shit," Hernandez muttered under her breath.

I tilted my head up some, risking exposing my face to the watching eyes to get a look at whatever had drawn out the expletive. The way ahead was clear, but we were about a thousand feet from an intersection. Thick, black smoke was pouring from somewhere down the side road and I could hear a low hum of noise that I couldn't identify.

The distance to the intersection closed, and the noise rose, moving from a hum to a roar. I could see the intersection now, see the living sea of people rushing seemingly at random, expanding to smash against the nearby buildings, contracting and coming together in a flurry of fists and feet. Signs were being waved, but they were too far away to get a good read on them. There were cops and soldiers in the mix—men and women in blue or green, trying to form a thin line against the destruction. Gas cannisters flew out, opening holes in the crowd as people stumbled, coughing and gagging away from the smoke. It was useless, and the cops knew it. Short of live fire, nothing was going to disperse a crowd that size.

I watched as the cops—did the smart thing. They opened up ranks, clustered into tight, defensive knots bristling with weapons that even the angriest protestor would think twice about confronting, and let the crowd go.

Which sent a stream of people into the intersection, and rapidly closing on our path.

"Mother fucker!" Hernandez exclaimed. The car was slowing, detecting the potential issues of a large crowd of people entering the street. Great safety feature...right up until the people in the street had blood in their eyes and murder in their hearts.

"No you *fucking* don't!" Hernandez growled, rapidly tapping at the car's built-in screen. She was still on the job, still had a valid badge number, so she still had the authority to override the self-driving features of the vehicle. In response, a steering wheel pushed its way out of the dash. I couldn't see the pedals, but I knew they had emerged from the floor as well. I braced myself as Hernandez stomped on the accelerator and laid the wheel over.

The tires squealed as the car simultaneously surged forward and angled hard to the right, avoiding the oncoming riot. Bottles, rocks, and other small objects rang against the metal and plastic frame of the vehicle as the protestors, angered that anyone or anything might try to defy them, unleashed a barrage of missiles against us. Something heavy crashed into the rear-window, causing a spiderweb of cracks to burst into existence all along the safety glass. But then we were past them, and the frustrated crowd, visible now only in the mirrors, took out their angst on buildings, vending machines, parked vehicles, and anything else that drew the uncaring eye of their ire.

"*Jesu Christo*, that was close," Hernandez muttered. She didn't return the car to auto-drive. One close call was more than enough to make her want to keep control of things. Not that I blamed her.

"Did you see who they were?" I asked.

She laughed, a short, bitter laugh. "Yeah. That was our side, Campbell. You know how it is. At a certain point, it doesn't even matter which group is on the side of the angels. Unless you're in it, every violent mob is pretty much the same."

"Fuck," I muttered. There really wasn't much else I *could* say to how close we'd just come to being beaten and quite possibly killed by the people who *agreed* with us.

"Pretty much. But as much as I hate to admit it, we need them. Everything we're doing—Silas's group of rebels, I mean—depends on the people getting pissed and taking action. Otherwise, we're just glorified agitators."

I nodded glumly. Silas's revolution—okay, maybe it was time to start calling it *our* revolution, given how deep I was in the shit—was really an information control campaign. Our only weapon of any note was the intelligence Silas had spent a lifetime gathering and curating from his fellow synthetics. The old saying was true; knowledge absolutely *was* power, but only if you could do something with it. Silas could take all the raw data in the world and turn it into actionable intelligence, but someone still had to act on it. I didn't think for a minute that anyone in power would do that out of a sense of the greater good. Politicians were creatures that acted best when they were acting for their own survival. Which meant the voters had to not just be pissed, but they had to be *seen* to be pissed. They had to be protesting in the streets. The knowledge that they'd been lied to by the people they elected, and the constant stream of corruption Silas's campaign continued to reveal were fuel for the fire. Flareups in the form of violent outbursts were inevitable.

"Sucks, though," I grunted.

"Sucks hard," Hernandez agreed. "But if it's the price we gotta pay, then we pay it."

I've said it before, but Hernandez was good people.

Chapter 9

Crossing the wire was almost too easy. It wasn't really wire, not in the barbed-wire barricade sense of the word. It was, however, a concrete barrier like the noise reducers found alongside highways, standing a good eight feet tall. There was no good place to leave the car—the Walton-owned subdivision was, apparently, self-contained, so there were no gas stations, convenience stores, or groceries nearby. So, we found the most remote side road near the subdivision and bailed on the vehicle. Hernandez re-engaged the auto-drive, and sent the car off the nearest inconspicuous place…which was far enough away that a quick egress wasn't going to be on the menu. Better than leaving it somewhere it would be noticed and raise questions, though.

"We need to get over fast, Campbell. We're risking too much already, standing by the side of the road."

I nodded. "I'll boost you up. You can vault and drop, make sure it's clear, and then I'll pull myself over."

She raised one eyebrow and tilted her head ever so slightly to the side. "You sure, *hermano*? That prison food must have been high in carbs or something, because you look like you maybe put on a pound or two." But she was moving as she said it.

"Low blow," I replied, setting my back against the wall and bending at the knees. I made a stirrup with my interlaced fingers, and nodded at her. She took a couple of steps back, got a bit of a running start, and stepped up into my hands. I grunted as I took her weight—Hernandez wasn't big, but she was solid muscle—her hands barely seemed to touch the top of the wall, and then she glided over it, like we had done it a thousand times before. I was kind of proud of that. Until I heard the vitriolic cursing coming from the other side.

"You okay?" I hissed. Then I had to say it quite a bit louder. I mean, the wall *was* intended to be a sound barrier, after all.

"Landed in a fucking thorn bush, *pendejo*," came the growl back. "Next time I'm throwing your fat ass over the wall without looking."

"That's just hurtful," I replied as I drew a deep breath and jumped. I really didn't need the jump to reach the top of the wall, but I weighed closer to two-fifty than two hundred and those guys who do a bunch of pullups? Yeah, they're all skinny fuckers. I needed the extra thrust from my legs to help me scramble over the wall. Even then, it wasn't pretty, and I added a few muttered curses of my own as I dropped next to Hernandez.

"Need a hand?" I asked, watching her pluck thorns from her jacket.

"Fuck you," she replied. "Let's find this *puta* and then I need to get some disinfectant."

I chuckled at that as I tried to take in our surroundings. We'd picked a segment of wall that butted up to some trees, but with subdivisions like the one Walton had put up, you never really knew if the screen was a tree or two thick or went on for a hundred yards. This one fell somewhere between. I could make out the houses—pocket mansions, really, probably pushing five thousand square feet—nestled one on top of the other through the branches, but it looked like we had enough cover that no casual glance would reveal our intrusion. The real problem was, as soon as we cleared the treeline, we were guaranteed to be on camera. The heart of New Lyons was bad enough when it came to watching electronic eyes, but the suburbs? And corporate-owned suburbs at that? Every street would be under surveillance.

"How do you want to play this?" I asked Hernandez.

"Oh, darling," she said, voice dripping honey, "we're just another happy couple, strolling through paradise while the world burns down around us." She reached out and grabbed my hand, her fingers interlacing with mine. It felt...weird. I'd been way closer to Hernandez than this—her own preferred methods of fighting were heavy in jiujitsu—but there was a difference between arm bars and hand holding. "Come on dear," she cajoled, pulling me toward the edge of the woods. "I'll smile all pretty for the cameras, and you keep your fucking face down, so the 'hospitality patrols' pay us no mind. *Comprendes*?"

Sneaking about would only draw attention, and it wasn't like we were going to make it very far without being seen. "Your lead," I agreed, trying to adopt a natural-seeming slouch that just happened to tip the brim of my hat down and obscure my face from any camera mounted higher than three feet from the ground.

"Oh, baby!" she squealed. Squealed. Hernandez. It took every ounce of control to keep my head down as she pulled me forward. I *really* wanted to see the look on her face. "I'm just so fucking happy to be buying a home in the suburbs."

She towed me out onto the street, emerging from the woods with confidence as if it was an everyday event, making a beeline for the nearest sidewalk and picking a direction. The second we were in the open, I started to feel the cold tingle of fear run up and down my spine. The sun was shining, birds were chirping, and I could literally hear children playing in the streets, but I was still creeped the fuck out. Walking down the open road when you were at the top of not only the government's fugitive list, but probably several corporate hit lists as well was…uncomfortable. It was made all the worse by the fact that my head-down pose afforded me only about ten feet of forward visibility, and beyond those few feet, I had no idea what was coming for me. I felt my muscles tensing as my body started to go into fight or flight mode.

"Will you fucking relax?" Hernandez growled from my side. "I'm going to have a hard time smiling if you break my hand."

I realized that my hand, along with everything else, had been tensing, and I now had a white-knuckled grip on Hernandez. "Sorry," I muttered. I drew a deep breath and tried to force some of the tension from my body as I exhaled. It didn't work, but at least I loosened my death grip on Hernandez.

I focused my attention on what little my limited field of vision offered. The houses were nice, beautiful really. Monsters of brick and siding that, taken individually, wouldn't have looked out of place on some mythical country estate. That effect was killed by the fact that they were close enough together that if you managed to lean far enough out the window, you could probably touch your neighbor's house. It also took only a minute or so of walking to realize that the entire community had been built using three floorplans. There were small variations, of course, little cosmetic changes that gave a brief illusion of individuality, but the bones of the houses were all the same.

"Getting close, now," Hernandez muttered, and the low buzz of stress in her voice brought me back to what we were doing.

I felt like an idiot. Sure, Hernandez was leading, and sure, I was watching our surroundings—to the limits of my vision, anyway—but I'd lost sight of what we were actually *doing* here. This wasn't a stroll through suburbia. I should have been trying to figure out where the hell Dr. Larkin lived.

Hernandez was on the job though. Our arbitrary turn out of the woods seemed to have been in the right direction, and she'd been leading me down turns and cross streets for a few minutes. We'd arrived, I noted, at a cul-de-sac, and the little shiny numbers on the mailboxes were lining up with the street address we had on Larkin.

Hernandez had slowed a bit, not enough to be obvious, but enough to buy us a few more seconds of time before the house was in front of us. "How do you want to play this?" she asked.

We'd done what little homework we could on Larkin. She was twice-divorced. One kid from the first marriage, off at college somewhere out of state. No known live-in love interests. Parents deceased. She seemed to spend most of her time at work, and there was a good chance, early as it was, that that was exactly where she was right now. The house should be empty. If we could get in without raising any alarms and be waiting for Larkin when she returned home... But we couldn't know for certain that the house was empty, and breaking into an occupied home could lead to all sorts of unpleasantness.

On the other hand, Dr. Larkin was unlikely to open her door to a pair of strangers. If she recognized me, that went from unlikely to snowball's chance in hell. Hernandez still had one advantage working for her. If she was willing to use it.

"Knock and talk?" I suggested. "If anyone's home, I mean. If not, we try to bypass whatever security's in place and wait."

I could feel the tension ratchet up a notch as she squeezed my hand almost to the point of pain. "Dammit," she muttered. She didn't say anything after that, but she didn't have to. A "knock and talk" was a common investigative technique where cops would knock on a person of interest's door and request consent for a search. Or, barring that, just try to get some information. It worked more often than you might think.

One thing that a knock and talk absolutely required, though, was identifying yourself as a police officer. If even half the help Hernandez had given us to date was revealed, she'd be stripped of her badge faster than you could say the words, and, at this point, probably put in a cell to boot. But despite that she still thought of herself as a cop, and using the knock and talk as a prelude to a push-in assault had to stick in her craw. Hell, *any* push-in assault had to stick in her craw, but we had a job to do.

She sighed. "Okay. If we have to, we have to. But we go on my lead. If she is home, and we can talk ourselves in, we do it that way. And we talk *first*, *hermano*."

I nodded, though, gun to my head, I wasn't holding my breath that this would end without violence. The woman I remembered from the Walton Biogenics lab didn't seem the type to roll over from a stern talking to. "Understood," I said. "But... Hernandez... If it looks like she's going to bolt or scream or trigger some kind of alarm, we have to take her down hard. We've only got one shot, here."

She nodded, and picked up the pace, pulling me once more toward Larkin's house.

It was a monster. Three stories of red brick and beige composite siding crouched on the end of a cul-de-sac like some sort of fat suburban gargoyle. There wasn't much to the ultra-modern style of it that I found alluring—it seemed all hard lines and right angles. Even the four-hipped roof, bereft of gable ends or any real architectural flair, seemed cold and functional. Maybe I was seeing the owner—or Walton Biogenics—in the house itself, but the whole thing felt empty and soulless to me.

As we reached the door, I kept my head low. *Every* house had security cameras. Hell, the neighbors probably had cameras pointed at the houses all around them, just to make sure they could see the latest bit of hullabaloo.

Hernandez released my hand as we climbed the stairs. I flexed my fingers, then shifted my weight, feeling the uncomfortable heft of the pistol moving in one pocket and the baton in the other. I *really* needed to get a proper holster and belt.

Hernandez took up a position in front of the door, in full view of the security camera nestled at about eye-level. I moved as my training dictated, stacking up to the right side of the frame, where there was a little more space and cover. The tactical flexibility was hindered by the fact that I was still having to keep my head low, but if the fecal matter hit the rotary air impeller, I'd at least be in place to support Hernandez. She gave me a glance with a lifted eyebrow, and I nodded in return. She raised her hand and knocked, three quick, hard bangs.

After those raps, we immediately stilled, ears straining, listening for any hint of what might be headed our way. No dog started barking—always a good sign. You never knew how a dog would react to a stranger, but if things went sideways, I wasn't sure I could drop the hammer on a mutt. People, yes. Dogs? Not so much. After maybe fifteen seconds, we heard the sound of footsteps.

I pressed myself tighter against the wall, and tucked my chin deeper into my chest. It limited my field of vision further, but I didn't want to risk any chance of Larkin seeing me. If she did, I suspected our knock and talk would become a kick and scream.

The door swung open. From my vantage, I could only see the bottom third of it, which presented me with a view of jean-clad legs that could have belonged to damn near anyone. But I recognized the voice at once. "Yes? Can I help you?" It was that same calm, controlled voice that had managed to hold it together at gunpoint.

Hernandez flashed her badge. "New Lyons Police Department, ma'am," she said, voice brisk. I thought of it as "business cop" voice. Most of us had three: nice cop for talking to victims and kids; business cop for witnesses; and authoritative cop for when you needed the bad guy to do what you said. "We need to ask you a few questions related to a recent break-in at Walton Biogenics."

A long silence followed. I would have given a lot for a glimpse of Larkin's face, the set of her shoulders, anything other than the tennis shoes on her feet. You couldn't read much in a person's reactions from the knees down. Neither Hernandez nor I tried to breach the silence—sometimes it was best to let the interviewee stew. "But," Larkin said at last, "I thought I'd already given you people everything you needed. The other detective... Fortier...? said the matter was closed."

I ground my teeth at the mention of Francois Fortier and his smug piggy face. If there was any karma in the universe, before this was all over, I'd get a chance to have a conversation with him. By hand, preferably.

"Of course, ma'am," Hernandez was saying. "But there have been a few developments, as I'm sure you know."

"Campbell escaped," Larkin said. I was expecting—and dreading— the fear in her tone. But it wasn't there. She sounded just as calm, just as conversational as she had when she'd opened the door. "I suppose you can come in." The door swung the rest of the way inward, and the pair of legs moved back into the hallway.

"Thank you, Dr. Larkin," Hernandez said as she stepped forward first. I realized that we hadn't planned out what happened next. I hadn't expected Larkin to be home at all, not late in the afternoon on a workday.

As we entered the house, I reached across and grabbed the door, swinging it shut behind me. The click of the latch seemed to echo in the foyer.

"You may as well take off that ridiculous hat, Mr. Campbell," Larkin said as I turned back toward her and Hernandez.

Chapter 10

My hand dropped to my pocket, digging into it with an awkward shove that had me cursing the lack of a proper holster. Even as I was scrambling for my weapon, I was moving to the left, only stopping when my shoulder bumped the wall of the entryway. Hernandez had moved right, clearing my line of fire, and her weapon was already in hand. I tore the rain hat from my head as I struggled to clear my own firearm.

Dr. Larkin stood before us, hands upraised. She looked a little less calm as Hernandez leveled her weapon at the woman and I finally managed to bring my pistol to bear. She also seemed different, somehow, from when I'd last seen her. The power suit had been replaced with a pair of blue jeans and a Tulane University sweatshirt, and her hair was pulled back into a tight ponytail. There was a puffiness about her eyes, and lines on her face that I hadn't noticed. She looked sadder, older. She looked more human, somehow. That would only make things harder.

"Keep your hands where I can see them," Hernandez barked, slipping into authoritative cop mode.

"This isn't necessary," Larkin replied, though she did, I noted, keep her hands where they were and stay very still. "I don't know why you're here, but I have no intention of resisting. I wouldn't have let you in if I did." The hint of a smile flicked across her face, nothing more than a momentary upturn of the corners of her mouth. "Mr. Campbell's disguise might fool the cameras, but I knew at a glance who he was. You don't forget someone who sticks a gun in your face."

I winced. This was the *second* time I was sticking a gun in her face, and while she may be complicit on some level with the goings-on at Walton Biogenics, I had no proof of her personal involvement in any of it. Proof didn't have to matter, I supposed—I wasn't a cop, and I wasn't headed to court. But it still did matter. At least to me.

Hernandez, whatever her stance on proof, was putting safety first, and while I had a more difficult time being hard-hearted to women, my partner didn't. "Shut up," she said. "And back up." Through the hallway, the house opened into a great room, where a large, overstuffed sectional sat. "Back toward the couch. Is there anyone else in the house? Any alarms that you triggered? I swear to god, *chica*, you'd better tell me the truth, or things are going to go very badly for you." Larkin's calm slipped a bit at that, and I couldn't blame her. Hernandez's tone was so cold that the temperature in the room dropped a few degrees.

"No. No one's here. No alarms." The words were clipped and a little breathy. I could see a wildness starting to rise in Larkin's eyes, kind of like the look a deer got when it realized it was actually in danger and it was trying to decide on fight or flight. It was interesting that *I* hadn't been able to get that reaction out of her, even when Al'awwal and I were holding her at gunpoint, but Hernandez had managed it with a few words and a harsh tone.

"If you cooperate, you'll be fine," I added, hoping to calm her down. I didn't say that she wouldn't be hurt. That would only spook her more. Besides, I didn't want to make any promises that I wasn't sure I could keep.

We had arrived in the living room, and Hernandez kept Larkin covered as the doctor edged around the couch and, at a flick of the pistol from Hernandez, dropped into a seat. Hernandez settled into a chair, easing her service weapon into her lap, but not, I noted, holstering up. I dropped the borrowed nine-millimeter back into my pocket—after making sure the hammer was down and the weapon was safed. I took my own seat at the other end of the sectional, so I was looking at Larkin across the coffee table.

"You haven't freaked out yet," I said. "Why not?"

She was still eyeing Hernandez askance, not focused on the gun, but rather on my partner's cold-eyed stare. At my words she glanced away, dropping her gaze to the plush carpet beneath our feet. "I…" She hesitated. Her hands came into her lap, one gripping the other, wringing and twisting. "I…may have been wrong. About Walton Biogenics."

Hernandez snorted. "You think?"

The sudden exclamation reminded Larkin of the woman with the gun, and her eyes snapped back to watching and monitoring what she perceived as the real threat. "Why the change of heart?" I asked.

She shrugged. "I got copies of the information you released. And… I watched you turn yourself in. It made me think that if nothing else, *you* had to believe what you were saying, if you were willing to go to prison just to get it in front of everyone's eyes." She met my gaze, but only for a moment, then her stare went back to Hernandez. And her gun. "So I started reading through Dr. Kaphiri's research." She fell silent. I could tell she wanted to keep going, that she was struggling with something. Her breathing had become a little ragged and the set of her shoulders had tightened.

Do enough interrogations, and you get a feel for when a suspect is about to talk. Sometimes, they need a little push to get the words out. Other times, that push will have the exact opposite effect, and set back the entire process. Larkin wanted to talk, *needed* to talk. And I could tell that she would get there on her own, that pushing her would only slow things down. I shot a quick look at Hernandez, who gave me the barest of nods. She saw it, too.

The silence stretched on for a few more moments, and then Dr. Larkin's hands stilled. Her breathing slowed. Decision reached, she opened her mouth to talk.

And the reflection of a red dot fluoresced against the wallscreen.

Chapter 11

I reacted on instinct, hurling myself bodily across the coffee table while simultaneously shouting, "Down!" toward Hernandez. She didn't even hesitate, rolling out of the chair to the floor even as her weapon came up and to the ready. I hit Larkin—hard—and the two of us went over the back of the couch. I landed on top of her, but the *whoosh* of the breath leaving her as my weight crushed down was drowned out by the muffled *crack* of gunfire and the tinkling of shattering glass.

"Fuck!" Hernandez snapped. I'd ended up behind the couch so I couldn't see her, but I heard her shuffling along the floor, presumably moving into a position with more cover. "You hit?" she asked.

"Negative," I replied.

"Larkin?"

I wasn't sure. I looked down at the woman who, I realized, I was still lying on top of. Her eyes were wide in shock but I couldn't see any blood. I rolled off her, doing my damnedest to stay below the line of the sectional. "You okay?" I asked.

She was gasping a bit, like a landed fish. "Wind. Knocked. Out of. Me," she gasped. But even as she struggled to find breath, she was running her hands over her body, looking for holes. Satisfied that there weren't any, she went back to concentrating on breathing.

"We're okay," I shouted back to Hernandez. "Situation?" As I asked the question, I struggled again with the nine-millimeter in my pocket, finally getting a good grip on it and yanking it out. I heard a tearing as the stitching gave way. Good. Stupid pocket, anyway.

"No fucking idea," was Hernandez's reply.

No more shots had come our way. I ran the scenarios in my head. If the shooter was using a laser, they were close. Too close. Probably within a house or two. Too many obstructed sightlines for anything else. They could be waiting, hoping for someone to pop a head up to present a nice, juicy target. Or they could be on their way in right now, alone or with a group of friends. Either way, this had just turned from an interrogation into a rescue mission.

"Gotta be Walton," I said.

"Yup," was Hernandez's succinct reply. "You need to find a better spot, Campbell," she said. "Looks like the shooter is somewhere west of us, but if there's more than one, or if they move, you've got too damn many windows."

I glanced around. Behind me, the great room opened into a kitchen, where cabinets that I assumed were full of bullet-deflecting pots and pans offered the tantalizing promise of safety. The couch was in front of me, beyond which was a wall with a pair of large windows. To my left, another exterior wall of the house, this one opening to the back yard and boasting a broad sliding glass door that, at the moment, had a wonderful view of both me and Dr. Larkin. And probably Hernandez, too. To my right, the hallway we entered through extended, traveling in a nice straight line to the front door. I hadn't gotten hit in the first spray of bullets, but any bad guys inbound would have a good time of it. Couldn't have that.

I turned back to Larkin, who was now breathing more naturally. Her eyes still had that deer-in-headlights look to them, but at least she wasn't screaming. Not that I'd blame her. "We've got to move to the kitchen, okay?" I said, trying to keep my voice as calm and certain as possible.

She just nodded. Maybe she was in shock, but I didn't have time to worry about that. Getting somewhere with a fighting chance was priority one. Getting the fuck out of here before the cops showed up was priority two. Larkin's mental well-being was a distant third. "Good. Now, we're going to move as fast as we can, but we're going to try to stay as low as possible. A running crouch, okay?" She nodded again. "Good. Ready?"

"Yes," she whispered. It wasn't much, but at least she was talking.

"Go!" I shouted. "Go, go, go!" I put action to my words, grabbing her arm and propelling us both forward. Since I couldn't see the shooter, I figured speed was better than stealth—not that there was much hope of stealth in the brightly lit living room anyway. We moved fast and low and, sure enough, as soon as we cleared the couch the gunfire started again. Fortunately for us, real life wasn't like the vids, and it was a hell of a lot harder to hit a moving target than most would-be shooters realized. We only had a few feet to cover, and it looked like we were going to make it.

Right up until the point where Larkin lurched, cried out, and fell into a heap on the floor.

"Fuck!" I shouted. "Larkin's hit." I didn't, however, stop moving. I grabbed her by the collar of her sweatshirt as I passed, twisting my fist harshly in the fabric. It was tight enough that I was probably choking the woman, but that didn't matter. You could live for a much longer time without air than you could getting riddled with bullets, and while moving targets were a tough nut to crack, a body lying motionless on the floor was pretty much the definition of a sitting duck.

Larkin was a slim woman. In normal circumstances, I could have thrown her around with just a little bit of effort. With the adrenaline of a life-or-death situation pumping hard through my system, I didn't even feel the weight as I dragged then flung her bodily behind the counter, diving in behind her once more.

"*Jesu Christo,* Campbell. I can't see the shooter. Can't even return fire," Hernandez called from her position by the wall. Randomly dropping the hammer in a residential neighborhood when you had no idea of the location of the bad guy went far beyond a bad idea and into the realm of the terminally stupid. "How's Larkin?"

"Wait one," was my succinct reply as I turned my attention to the woman we had come to maybe torture and whose life we were now trying desperately to save. She was looking back at me with a glassy-eyed stare, but at least she was conscious and breathing. There was a spreading stain high on her right thigh though, close to the hip. "You're going to be fine," I told her, not sure if I really believed it. "Probably just a flesh wound." I glanced around the nicely appointed kitchen, then snagged a tea towel that was hanging from the oven. I pressed it against the wound. "This is going to hurt," I said and, before she had a change to react, I pressed down. Hard.

Larkin's eyes went so wide I could see the whites all the way around and a little gasp of pain escaped her lips. But that was it. Tough lady. "Good," I said. "Hold it there. I need to turn you over. Check for an exit wound. Okay?"

Her hands moved mechanically to the towel—already darkening—and clamped it in place. "It hurts," she whispered.

"I bet," I agreed. "But we can't focus on that. Not right now. We've gotta get all of us out of here alive, okay?"

"It's Walton isn't it? They've come for me."

"Probably." As I said it, I placed one hand on her right hip and lifted and turned, rolling her over onto her side. "Damn," I muttered. There was an exit wound, sure enough, just below her right buttock. A bigger, nastier wound than the entry. Either the bullet had tumbled, or the shooter had forgone jacketed rounds for something that would mushroom out more on impact. It was bleeding, but it wasn't spurting or gushing, which meant that, with a little luck, the bullet had missed the femoral artery. Who was I kidding? If it had clipped it, she'd already be dead.

"Do you have tape, string, anything like that here in the kitchen?" I asked, watching the blood seep out.

She shook her head.

"Great." I glanced around, looking for inspiration. Larkin must have liked to cook, judging from the quality of the appliances and accoutrements that I could see. "What about plastic wrap?"

"By the stove," she said. "Cabinet." Her words were getting softer, weaker. I snatched another tea towel and pressed it against the wound on the back of her leg, moving one of her hands to cover it as well.

I duck-walked back to the stove and, sure enough, there was a small cabinet beside it. Within I found the standard array of aluminum and plastic. I grabbed the Saran Wrap and returned.

"Shit!" Hernandez suddenly growled, and I heard her diving to the deck at the same time another volley of gunfire sounded. "They're on the move, Campbell. You need to get the fucking lead out. We're going to have company in a minute."

I dropped down beside Larkin, who was starting to look glassy-eyed. The kind of look people got before passing out from little things like shock and blood loss. Not good. I tore the roll of plastic wrap from the box. "Move your hands," I said to the injured woman.

She did it with a slow, mechanical motion that said she was right on the brink. I didn't hesitate, just started to tightly wrap the wound in the plastic wrap, pressing the makeshift bandages provided by the tea towels tight against the entry and exit points. "What's the plan here, Hernandez?" I called as I worked.

"Larkin mobile?" was the terse reply.

"Negative. I can carry her, but it's going to make my aim shit."

"Shittier," she replied, and I grinned even as I tied off the makeshift wound. We might be about to die, murdered by some corporate wetwork squad, but not even that would stop Hernandez from taking the easy jab at me. "From the glimpse I caught, we got a few seconds, and that's it."

"Entry?"

"Back yard, side yard. Didn't see anyone out front."

Which didn't mean they weren't there. "Okay. Larkin's as squared away as she's gonna get." I glanced around, noting a door set in the kitchen wall. Ten would get you twenty that it led to a garage. But would Larkin own her own car? Even for suburbanites, cars had fallen off the "must have" list with the introduction of driverless ride-sharing services. I thought about the neighborhood, the meticulous, Stepford nature of it. The high-powered corporate town. Keeping up with the Joneses. Yeah. She'd have a car.

"Can you make it to me?" I asked.

"You better cover my ass, *hermano*."

"That's the one thing these dinky little nines you insist on carrying are good for," I shot back. "At least I've got a lot of bullets to lay down some covering fire." I drew a breath, and, in a more serious tone, said, "Ready?"

"Ready."

I picked up the pistol from Larkin's side, where I'd laid it when attending to her leg. I risked a quick glance at the woman. Her eyes were half-lidded, and her breathing was ragged, but at least she *was* breathing. I settled the weapon into my hands, trying to find the balance of the hunk of metal and composite, then I moved into a half-crouched position. I drew a deep breath of my own, then released it in a shouted, "Go!"

As I spoke, I popped up, not moving fully to standing, but just enough to clear my head and shoulders over the counter top. I extended both arms before me and settled the butt of the pistol on the countertop—no need to waste a perfectly good bench rest—while I took in the first full view of the room I'd had since diving over the couch.

The windows that had been facing the part of the sectional where Larkin had sat were now a shattered mess of glass. There must have been more shots than I'd first realized, and from more angles, because the sliding door, too, was now riddled with bullet holes. That glass must have been made of stronger stuff, because instead of shattering, it had just spiderwebbed around the holes punched through it by the rounds. Hernandez was in motion, pushing herself to her feet against the far wall and starting a mad dash in my direction.

I caught a flash of movement through the obstructed glass remaining in the sliding glass door. My mind had barely registered the threat before my body swiveled, almost like a tank turret, and the posts of the pistol dropped onto the shape. I pulled the trigger once, twice, a third time, three quick, but controlled, motions that took less than a second to execute. The shape on the other side of the door got much closer, and then the crash of a body falling through the stressed glass added its own crescendo to the ringing echo of gunfire. I tracked right, muzzle dipping automatically as it traversed past Hernandez, now halfway to the "strongpoint"—if it could be called that—in the kitchen.

I caught movement outside the window, but it was gone too fast to hit. So, instead, I moved the muzzle an inch or two to the right, and put a few rounds into the window frame. The nine-millimeter could probably punch through the two by four framing, but I was firing at a downward angle, so the risk of the rounds finding a target in some unsuspecting passer-by were slim to none. It did have the desired effect of causing splinters of wood to fly out in all directions and even made some more glass fall out of the frame. Not exactly a direct hit, but hopefully enough that whoever was on the other side would keep their head down for a second more.

That second was all I needed as Hernandez came sliding bodily across the countertop and dropped down beside me. She rolled to her knees, popped up to where she could clear the counter, and took a couple of shots of her own. The slide on her pistol locked back on an empty magazine, and she dropped back down, hand moving automatically to the mag holder at her left hip. Her reload was smooth and effortless, the result of countless hours of practice and practical experience. The weapon was back in battery in the blink of an eye.

"Now what?" she gasped, head sweeping back and forth, trying to take in all the possible entry points.

"Any idea how many bad guys we got?"

She grunted. "At least three more, I think."

"Fuck," was my succinct reply.

"Yup."

I glanced down at Larkin. The woman had finally succumbed to either blood loss or shock, and had slipped into unconsciousness. Not great. Time was as much our enemy as the bad guys with the guns.

"We're going to have to try for the garage and hope that Larkin owns a car," I said.

Hernandez threw a quick look around the kitchen, eyes locking on to the door that I had already seen, the door that I hoped led to at least a chance at salvation. "No way to confirm?" she asked. I wasn't sure if she was looking for confirmation that the door led to the garage, or that there was a vehicle in there we could use. I couldn't offer much hope for either.

"Larkin's out," I replied. "Don't see any other options."

"Fast or slow?"

"Fast," I replied. "And hard."

"Ooooh, *papi*," Hernandez said, voice dripping sarcasm.

I snorted out a laugh. "Shut up, Hernandez. You want me to carry Larkin, or you got her?"

It wasn't an easy question, and I gave Hernandez a couple of precious seconds to ponder it. Larkin was a petite woman, but so was Hernandez. She'd feel the weight a lot more than I would, and be slowed by it more. But you couldn't exactly fight while carrying a hundred-plus pounds of unconscious person, either, and if we ran into trouble, we might be better off if I was hands-free.

"I got her," she said. She put action to her words and shimmied over beside Larkin. I popped up once more and put another round into the frame of every entry point I could see. That left me with four rounds left in the nine. Unlike Hernandez, I didn't have any reloads. It was hard enough carrying a pistol in your pocket without trying to cart around extra magazines. The entries still looked clear, which was both a relief and frustrating. What the fuck were they waiting for?

I dropped back down to see Hernandez on one knee, pulling Larkin over her shoulder into a fireman's carry. "We ready to do this?" she asked. I gave her a short nod. "Good. Spot me on the way up." She shoved off the ground, lifting Larkin bodily and settling her across her shoulders as I added what lift and stability I could. If the bad guys had chosen that fraction of a moment to make their assault, we probably would have been dead.

We didn't waste time on more talk, moving for the door I was praying opened on to a garage. Hernandez had managed to manipulate the carry so that she had one arm free, and had redrawn her pistol. Mine was still in hand as I grabbed the door knob and yanked it open.

And found myself staring full into the face of a synthetic.

With a gun.

Chapter 12

I knew the man was a synthetic. I'd spent so long in their company over the past months that I had no doubts. It was something about the face, somewhat shrouded by a black cap, but otherwise visible. It was far too perfect to be human.

My brain did a mental hiccup as it tried to resolve the synthetic in front of me with the tactical gear and sub-gun he was carrying. He seemed to be in mid-breach, as one leg was lifted and ready to plant into the lockplate, with the weapon held at the low ready. His own eyes had widened in surprise at my sudden appearance, and for a fraction of a second, we simply stared at one another. My mind couldn't process whatever was happening here, but my instincts didn't fail me.

I stepped forward, turning my shoulder and body checking the synthetic. The press of my torso prevented him from bringing his weapon up, and the sudden impact, with him balanced on a single leg, sent him reeling. I had time to register that we were, in fact, in a garage, and that there were two steps down to the floor of it and then I heard the report of Hernandez's pistol. I didn't see any rounds impact on the synthetic who had just crashed to the floor, so I had to assume that she was firing back into the house. Looked like the bad guy I had just knocked down wasn't the only one coming to the party.

There was no time to screw around, to play nice, or to demand answers. The synthetic landed hard on a concrete floor and, for just a moment, appeared stunned. I put a round into his head as I rushed down the stairs. But then I stopped, as something tickled the back of my mind. Hernandez's gun barked again, and she shouted, "Come on, Campbell! Move your ass! This *puta* isn't getting any lighter."

I needed to move, but my brain was still churning. Shit. What *was* it? The synthetic—the soldier?—lying on the ground was wearing fairly standard gear that would be recognized by soldiers of almost any nation. Including, on one shoulder, the IFAK—individual first aid kit. Something clicked. "Two seconds, Hernandez," I shouted, as I dropped to a quick knee. Some part of my brain registered that Larkin did, in fact, have a car—thank God—and that, in addition to the garage door, there was an open man-sized door through which the synthetic must have entered, but I was already tearing into the IFAK. I tossed most of the supplies away until I found a tiny squirt bottle of saline solution, used for cleaning wounds. I emptied the contents and, doing my best to ignore the disgust slowly churning in my gut, shoved the applicator tip into the edge of the head wound. I used the suction of the bottle to fill it with a couple of ounces of blood.

"The *fuck* you *doing*?" Hernandez demanded, sending three more rounds down the hallway. "I'm almost dry, and reloading carrying this *chica* ain't happening."

I shoved the bottle into a pocket, looked longingly at the sub-gun strapped to the corpse, and darted to the car. It was a small two-seater with a sort of half-seat, half-cargo space behind the seats. The locks were biometric, which weren't a problem. I covered the door—me and my four bullets—while Hernandez pressed Larkin's thumb against the appropriate screen. I heard the beep of the screen accepting Larkin's thumbprint at the same time I saw a flash of movement down the hallway. I popped off two rounds. No real target, but I was hoping to at least keep heads down and the door clear.

"I've got it, Campbell," Hernandez said.

I didn't bother taking the time to look and confirm. I took her at her word and rushed to the door on my side of the vehicle. In my peripheral vision, I saw Hernandez leaning a bit out the window of the car, pistol extended and held rock-steady on the doorway. Then I was in the vehicle. Hernandez had already used Larkin's unconscious hand to activate the vehicle, and the manual drive feature was on. The Walton employee was wedged unceremoniously into the tiny cargo space. I felt bad about that, particularly with the woman being injured, maybe dying, but we didn't have a hell of a lot of choice.

"You think they've made it to the front of the garage yet?" Hernandez asked.

"No way to know," I replied, flipping through a screen menu to try to find the garage door control. "I got one outside, and the one in here. Saw someone just a second ago, so there's at least one still in the house. Found it," I grunted. "Hold on...and try to stay low."

Hernandez managed to contort herself so that most of her body was lower than the windshield while simultaneously managing to keep her firearm trained on the door. I saw another flash of movement. Hernandez must have seen it too, as she sent a rapid-salvo of rounds down the hallway. Her slide locked back, and in less time than it took to say it, she had the weapon reloaded. "Last one," she grunted.

I flicked the screen, and the garage door immediately started to open. The motor was electric, smooth, and damn near silent. It also moved faster than I'd anticipated. I hadn't been planning on waiting for the door to rise fully in any case. It took only a second or two for it to clear the bumper, and when it did, I stomped on the accelerator. The tires squealed for a moment on the smooth garage floor, but then caught and the car lurched backward. The vehicle had low clearance, but even so, there was a long, tortured screech as the roof clipped the ascending door. Then we were free, out into the darkening evening.

And then more bullets started flying.

Three neat little holes appeared in the windshield as I laid the wheel hard over, spinning the car off the driveway and jouncing the rear end into the well-manicured lawn. Hernandez was twisting with the motion of the car, trying to find an angle on the shooter and answering back with some fire of her own. At least that meant that she wasn't hit. I hadn't felt any impacts, either, though I knew the adrenaline might be deadening any pain. I floored the accelerator, and with a spray of mud and grass we were off.

Hernandez slumped back down in her seat. "You hit?" she demanded.

"Don't think so. You?"

"Negative." She through a glance over her shoulder at Larkin. "She's still breathing, at least."

"We need to get her to Tia."

Hernandez snorted. "We need to get our own asses out of here, first."

I'd studied maps of the area, so I had a fair idea of where I was headed. I nodded to the screen on the dash. "See if you can find the main gate controls on there. And pray that Walton security doesn't have it locked down already."

Hernandez started swiping through menus. "What was that with the body back there, *hermano*?" she asked.

I took a turn, too sharp, and got yelled at by a man out trimming his hedges. In February. The suburbs. "I'm pretty sure he was a synthetic, Mel," I said, taking another corner as I tried to escape the maze of streets.

"Not possible. They were shooting at us."

"Yeah," I agreed. "We all know they can't do violence. But then, there's AI. Who sure as shit can not only *do* violence, but is friggin' *good* at it.

And Silas, who overcame his conditioning, at least a little." I shook my head. "His *conditioning*, Hernandez."

"Shit," she muttered. "And it's Walton that does the conditioning. Or doesn't."

"Or does some other kind of programming," I agreed. "Like, maybe creating their own little super soldiers. Ones they haven't needed to date, but now that we're tearing down their whole world, the gloves are coming off."

"Fair enough," Hernandez said. "But that doesn't really explain why you were shoving a bottle into that corpse's brainpan."

We were coming up on the gate. I couldn't see any vehicles or obvious signs that the bad guys or the cops or anyone else was inbound. "You got the gate?" I asked. In response, Hernandez hit a button on the screen and the iron and steel monstrosity started to slide open. I adjusted my speed so that we wouldn't have to come to a complete stop and wait. So far, the rearview was still clear, but I wasn't feeling great about that. Outrunning a car wasn't too bad; outrunning a radio was pretty fucking impossible.

I turned my attention back to Hernandez's question. "I just got to thinking…if I had an army of genetic super soldiers, and I *also* had a plague that I was releasing to kill off the synthetics, I'd probably make sure my soldiers had some sort of resistance to it. Maybe Tia or the others can figure something out from it."

Hernandez was silent for a long moment. We bounced over the gate tracks and I turned out onto the main road. We needed to come up with a spot to switch out Larkin's car—which could almost certainly be tracked—with the vehicle Hernandez and I had arrived in, but I needed a little more distance between us and the shooters first. "Pretty smart, Campbell," Hernandez said at last. I had to smile at that. At least, until she added, "Must be Tia's influence."

"Shut up, Hernandez."

* * * *

We managed to slip our pursuers. Hernandez linked with our escape vehicle and arranged for it to meet us. I let Larkin's auto-drive take over while I turned around and did my best to check on the woman. She hadn't regained consciousness, but her breathing seemed easier. I ran my hand over the makeshift bandages wrapped around her leg. The plastic wrap was non-permeable, so I wasn't expecting much in the way of blood, but there also wasn't much in the way of…squishiness. Blood didn't seem to be pooling behind the bandage, and none was leaking from the top or bottom of the wrap.

"She okay?" Hernandez asked.

"Best I can tell," was my reply. "She needs better care than I can give her, though."

"Working on it."

We made the switch in a little-used park whose parking area benefited from the cover of several mature oaks. We had to be careful on the timing, since with Larkin still unconscious, we weren't the least conspicuous trio ever to cross through the area. But we managed to get her from her car and into the incognito one without attracting any attention. From there, it was another long, circuitous route back to Floattown. I had some doubts about bringing Larkin into the revolution's sanctum sanctorum, but we didn't have a hell of a lot of choice. As the general tenor of New Lyons continued to darken, it was getting harder and harder to find safe places to keep out of the sight of the NLPD and the rest of the alphabet soup.

Getting Larkin into the Ballasts was another thing entirely. It's damn hard to carry a hundred- plus pounds up and down a ladder when the weight is properly secured and distributed. It's a hell of a lot harder when it's a friggin' body. The human body just is not easy to cart around, particularly in the vertical. Larkin was like a hundred pounds of cooked spaghetti, and between us, it took everything Hernandez and I had to get her down the first few ladders without dropping her.

"This sucks, *hermano*," Hernandez said after a particularly arduous ladder. We'd stopped at the bottom to catch our breath. I checked on Larkin again—still out cold.

"Almost there," I grunted. "One more ladder and…"

I was interrupted as several flashlight beams cut across the darkness, transfixing us. My hand moved reflexively for the pocket where the nine -millimeter—and the pair of rounds left in it—was stashed, but I let the hand fall. I couldn't make out who was behind the glare, but we were deep in the Ballasts. If the bad guys had made it this far, we were pretty much fucked no matter what, and I was too damn tired to fight. Then the lights were moving out of our eyes, splashing off the walls around us and providing more illumination.

As my eyes adjusted I saw the big form of Al'awwal. He had his Israeli-made bullpup on him—smart since he and Tia were probably the only ones in the compound capable of pulling a trigger—but the weapon was dangling from its tac-strap. "Sorry about that," he said with a dazzling smile. "Wasn't expecting you to be sitting down on the job. Thought I'd be avoiding your eyes by keeping the lights aimed low."

I grunted, ignoring the jab at sitting down on the job, still trying to make out the shapes behind him. There were a couple more people—synthetics—with the squat build of tunnel rats. I pushed myself to my feet and offered a hand to Hernandez, who took it. With some effort, I pulled the compact woman up. "Please tell me you're here to help transport Ms. Larkin here," I said, waving one hand at the doctor, laid out as comfortably as we could manage on the cold steel floor. "She needs to see Tia, ASAP."

Al nodded and the two tunnel rats moved forward. Their expressions were unreadable. They didn't know who Larkin was, but she was obviously a human, and they probably *did* know that our mission had been to retrieve some information from Walton Biogenics. They were smart enough to put two and two together and come out in the ballpark of four. If they had been human, I might have given some warning about making sure she got there in one piece, but with their conditioning, it wasn't necessary. On the other hand, they didn't have to hurt her directly. At this point, a little creative work slowdown might be enough to finish the woman. Maybe a warning *was* warranted.

"She has information vital to figuring out this whole thing," I noted. They gave me those blank stares as they knelt, one hooking his arms under her armpits, the other grabbing her legs behind the knees. "Which she offered to us willingly," I added, hoping for some kind of reaction.

I got a slight, begrudging nod in return, and then the pair was off, moving more quickly and surely through the Ballasts than I ever could. "What's the sitrep?" I asked Al, as we started to make our own way into the depths.

"Ms. Morita returned from the doctor. Not a lot of traction there. The hospital is running bloodwork, but it will take a bit for the labs to get back. In the meantime, they've sent her home with some antibiotics. She's distributed them to some of the sick, but…" He shrugged.

"Not too likely that simple antibiotics are going to stop whatever Walton has unleashed," Hernandez agreed.

"Which is why we went after Larkin in the first place," I added.

"Which will be great, *hermano*, assuming she survives."

* * * *

The plastic chair groaned alarmingly beneath me as I shifted my weight. It had probably started life as a piece of cheap, throwaway patio furniture marketed to BLS-ers. How it had made its way down into revolution central, I had no idea. Now it had been pressed into duty as part of a makeshift waiting room outside the chamber Tia was using to perform meatball surgery on Larkin. She had a pair of synthetics assisting her, which left me and the others with not a lot to do but wait and hope.

Hernandez had gone off to find a post-mission shower. I'd done a quick and cursory job of cleanup, but my clothing was still stained with blood. Most of it was Larkin's but some belonged to the synthetic... Shit. The synthetic. I stood up from my chair in one explosive motion, causing the plastic to crack and buckle. Al, who had been drifting off to sleep in his own poorly constructed seat, started awake, hand dropping for a sidearm that wasn't there.

"What is it, Campbell?" he asked, a note of irritation in his voice that still surprised me coming from a synthetic.

"I need to talk to Silas," I grunted. "It's important."

"Then let's go."

I eyed him a moment. Silas had been quarantined in his own chambers until we could figure out anything at all about the sickness making its presence known among the synthetics. Whatever else he was, Al'awwal fell firmly into the synthetic category. Volunteering to go into a sickroom...

He must have read my mind, because he chuckled. "This whole quarantine is a farce, Campbell. Pointless. We know humans are carriers, and you, Morita, and Hernandez have been roaming about freely." He waved a hand, dismissing the implied guilt of the statement. "Not that you could do anything else. Besides, do you really think that something Walton Biogenics engineered to silence the synthetic population is going to be stopped by...what? A closed door?"

His logic was as irrefutable as it was sobering, and I couldn't think why I hadn't figured it out before. No. That wasn't true. I knew *exactly* why I hadn't thought of it. I didn't want to believe it. What Al'awwal was really saying was that there was no way to control the spread of the sickness, not just among our little band of outlaws, but anywhere.

What he was saying was that if we didn't find a cure, and fast, Walton Biogenics had already won. I felt the crushing weight of that knowledge pressing down on me. By going along with Silas and pressing forward with his plans, we had inadvertently triggered what might be total genocide for the synthetic population.

But no pressure.

"Shit. Come on," I said. "This can't wait for Tia to finish. I need to talk to Silas now." I thought about it for a minute. "And we'd better get Hernandez, too."

Hernandez, as it turned out, had finished her shower, and ran into us on the way. She had traded her business wear for a more practical pair of sweatpants and a hoodie which proudly displayed NLPD in bright blue letters across the chest. "Larkin?" was the first word out of her mouth as she neared us.

"Nothing yet. But we need to talk to Silas. Figured you'd want to be there," I said.

Hernandez nodded in response, and fell into line with us as we navigated the maze of metal boxes that was the Ballasts. In short order, we found ourselves before the door to the chamber serving as Silas's personal quarters...and quarantine. I raised my fist and knocked, eliciting a hollow, booming thud.

"Enter," came the response from within. I levered the door open and stepped into the dimly lit room, Hernandez on my heels. Al'awwal, earlier declarations aside, held back a bit.

Silas looked terrible.

His skin was pale, as always, but a feverish flush suffused his cheeks. On someone else, it might have been mistaken for the blush of health, but against the pallid backdrop of the albino's skin, it shouted sickness. Despite that, he seemed unfazed. We hadn't even fully entered his room when he was on his feet. "Is Larkin talking?"

"Not yet," I replied. "Tia's still working on her. But we've got other problems."

"We always seem to," Al drawled from where he leaned against the doorway.

"What is it?" Silas demanded. He cleared his throat, not quite a cough, but I sensed every person in the room tensing at the sound.

I reached into a pocket and pulled out the little bottle of blood. In the rush to get Larkin to safety, I'd forgotten about it, at least until Al had reminded me. I set it on a nearby table.

"I don't understand," Silas said, looking at the vial.

"You know we were attacked at Larkin's," I said by way of preamble. Silas nodded, cleared his throat again. "We assume they were sent by Walton. But at least one of them..." I paused, trying to think of some way to ease them into it. Came up empty. "Shit. One of them was a synthetic. With a gun."

Silas's eyes went immediately to Al'awwal, who answered the unasked question with a shrug. "So far as I know, I am unique. The only synthetic to be grown outside of the control of Walton's indoctrination programs."

"I suppose it was inevitable," Silas said. "In fact, I am surprised we have not seen it sooner."

Hernandez frowned. "If they'll send a bunch of corporate hitmen to kill one of their employees, I suppose they wouldn't hesitate to try to breed an army of synthetic soldiers."

"Exactly," Silas agreed. "Public opinion continues to sway in our favor. We already know from Jason's encounter with Mr. Woodruff that we have pushed them to a point of desperation. It is not such a far cry to think that, in such a time, they would have more than one contingency plan. A group of specially conditioned synthetics—their own private army whose loyalty is above question—would serve them well."

"They'd certainly be more reliable than psychopaths like Fowler," I grunted. "And, at the same time, probably a lot less squeamish than whatever run-of-the-mill human mercenaries Walton is employing. Even the rent-a-cops in the sewers balked a bit at trying to put me and Hernandez into the ground."

"Still tried, though," Hernandez said. "The idiots." Something in her voice made me glance at her, and I saw real pain there, if only for a moment. Hernandez was probably the single toughest human being I'd ever known, and that included a parade of spec ops guys from my service days. But she was a cop at heart, not a soldier. The mission, at least for her, wasn't killing bad guys. It was putting them away. What we'd had to do in the sewers weighed on her. I could live with the fact that we'd had to put down the Walton rent-a-thugs to lead us to Al'awwal and, ultimately, Kaphiri's cache. But Hernandez wasn't built for that kind of killing. Which probably made her a much better person than me.

"Fuck," I muttered, forcing my mind back on track. "None of this is the point. Yeah, they probably have some kind of army of super soldiers. A bunch of Captains America, or maybe Captains Corporate or whatever. Maybe it's their own fucking A-Team. Doesn't matter. What matters is that Walton has a group of synthetics they're sending out into the world to kill people. Sending into the world *now*," I stressed, looking at the blank and staring faces around me.

"So?" Al'awwal asked.

"So…" A new and welcoming voice sounded from behind him, and a smile sprung unbidden to my face. "So," Tia repeated, her voice tired as she slipped past Al into the room, "there happens to be some kind of killer disease targeting synthetics floating around at the moment. Would you send out your crack team of trained killers if you knew they were susceptible to it?"

All eyes went to the young doctor-in-training, who, if truth be told, also looked like shit. She was wearing a pair of scrubs, maybe the same pair that I'd got for her when I'd first brought her into this mess, but it was hard to tell, given the amount of blood speckling them. Her arms were flecked with blood as well, though her hands were meticulously clean. Her hair had been tied back into a rough ponytail, and she wore an expression of exhaustion. She spared me a slight smile though, which, all things considered, felt pretty damn good.

"Larkin?" I asked.

"Should survive," Tia replied. "If she doesn't catch some kind of infection. We're doing our best, but these aren't exactly sterile conditions." She shrugged. "She lost a lot of blood. But I managed to do some rough-and-tumble repair work. She may limp for the rest of her life, but she should live."

"Is she awake?" Silas asked. "Able to talk?"

I was glad he jumped on that grenade. Doctors tended to be protective of their patients. On the NLPD, I'd had to work my way around them more than once to talk to a victim or witness who had been hospitalized, and they were never happy about it. But it needed to be done.

Rather than getting angry, Tia just offered another shrug. "She was out during the surgery, thank God. We don't exactly have much in the way of anesthetic. If she doesn't wake up on her own soon, we're going to have to try to wake her up. Without the right drugs..." She trailed off. "Well, let's just say there's not a lot we can do beyond yelling her name and shaking her. We're pretty much in the Dark Ages here."

"Can we get back to the army of super soldiers immune to the plague?" Hernandez asked. "That sort of seems more important."

"The solution—or at least the broad steps we need to take to find a solution—are now made clear," Silas said. I grimaced at his typically eccentric way of phrasing, then felt guilty as he ruined it by unleashing a sudden, hacking, racking cough. It went on for some time, maybe ten, fifteen seconds, long enough that I could see Tia's hands twitching to try to help. The humans in the room had all experienced something similar at some point in their lives. We knew the lung-wrenching feeling of not being able to draw breath and were familiar with the shaking and gasping aftermath. For Silas, for Al, it was something new. I could see the faintest glimpse of fear in Silas's eyes when the fit finally subsided and Al'awwal had edged a bit farther back from the door.

"Excuse me," Silas said, not letting the coughing—or his fear—slow him down. "Our course of action is made clear. We must find wherever these soldiers are being grown and infiltrate that location. Somewhere within, we will find our cure."

I was about to follow that up with a quip about, sure, sounded easy enough, but was interrupted by the sound of heavy and quick footsteps closing in on us. Hernandez and Al must have heard it too, because almost on instinct, all three of us spread out, taking up positions within the chamber Silas used as his room and turning toward the long avenue of interconnecting boxes that served as a conduit between Silas and the rest of the facility.

It wasn't an NLPD assault force breeching the Ballasts. Instead, it was a lone synthetic, young, but then, most of them looked to be in their early twenties, and with the long-limbed grace and beauty—and in the case of the males, lean musculature—of the Toys. I didn't know his name. The synthetics had continued to trickle in to revolution central and we'd passed the point where I could keep track of everyone. Not so, with Silas, apparently.

"What is it, Thomas?" he asked, holding up a hand to stop the synthetic from entering the room. Not much of a safety measure against contagion, but it was the best we had.

"We need Ms. Morita, quick," he blurted. "Sanjay's dying."

Chapter 13

I went with Tia.

The others stayed behind, since there was no point taking Al'awwal into yet another sickroom, and carting Silas through the halls was likewise contraindicated. Hernandez and Al were going to talk tactics, try to figure out what resources we had available to infiltrate what, we could only assume, would be the most holy of holies for Walton Biogenics. But damned if I was going to let Tia go into whatever we were headed for alone. Sure, there was a chance that I was clean, clear of whatever carrier agent the psychopaths at Walton had engineered to turn regular humans into an attack vector for the synthetics, but the odds were against it. I'd spent too much time in too tight of a space with too many synthetics to be in the clear. So fuck it. Might as well lend some support to a friend.

I reconsidered almost immediately as we entered the infirmary.

It wasn't the frequent coughing. It wasn't the few synthetics stretched out on their beds who were writhing in apparent pain. It wasn't the pall of physical misery that hung over everything. I'd seen more than my share of that. It wasn't that it didn't faze me, but if you've seen enough human misery—synthetic misery, whatever—it just doesn't surprise you anymore.

It was the fear.

The room stank of it.

I'd seen a hospital bed or two in my time, including one in a MASH unit in the middle of the desert. People shot, torn to bits by explosives, bitten by venomous creepy crawlies, or just laid low by the rank and file infections and viruses that had been a part of human history for so long that we barely noticed. Sure, people in those places always had a little bit of fear in them. But there was hope, too. Hope, and whatever ingrained human stubbornness that made a terminal cancer patient look their doctor in the eye and say, "I'm gonna beat this thing."

Resolve.

The infirmary had all of the fear, but none of the resolve.

And why should it? Synthetics didn't get sick. They didn't grow up experiencing the thousand little indignities that the frailty of the human frame inflicted on us. No migraines or nausea. Not even a common cold. The thought was enough to make me feel a little surge of…jealousy? Anger? Whatever it was, it was squashed by walking into that room.

I couldn't imagine what they were going through. Sure, they'd never suffered the indignities of illness—countless other indignities, but never those—but that also meant they had no idea how to deal with them or what was going on in their own bodies when, for the first time in the history of their species, they were laid low from within. And knowing that it was a targeted, genocidal attack, whose ultimate goal could only be death… That just made it all the worse.

The pall that hung over the infirmary had little to do with physical discomfort, and more to do with soul-crushing despair. Which was only heightened by the low, keening moan coming from the back of the room.

Tia, either inoculated against the despair by her medical training or just made of sterner stuff than I, was moving confidently among the beds. It was her job to run toward the sounds of pain just like it was mine to head toward the gunfire. Most people probably thought I had the harder gig, but there was no way in hell I could have done what she did, day after day. I had to lengthen my stride considerably to catch up, but we made it to the bedside of Sanjay at the same time.

The man was in bad shape—no—he was dying. I supposed you could argue that everyone in the room was dying, but Sanjay seemed a lot more serious about it. Without looking, Tia thrust a surgical mask back at me. It seemed pointless, but I pulled the loops over my ears and settled the wire-and-cloth around my nose and mouth. I didn't really understand why she bothered, given she was already a carrier, and it would be a miracle if it turned out I wasn't.

The reason became a lot clearer when the next cough from Sanjay included a fine mist of brownish-red blood.

There were none of the machines that I associated with modern medicine anywhere to be found in the infirmary, but Tia had produced her screen and a variety of other small devices from somewhere within her still blood-splattered scrubs. It took me a moment to realize that they were sensor pads. Tia expertly applied them to various points on the synthetic's body, and then stared intently at her screen. Another wave of deep wariness seemed to wash over her face, and she rested one hand lightly on the man.

He grabbed her hand, clutching at it like a drowning man. "I can maybe do something for the pain," Tia said. "Would that help?"

Sanjay, coughing enough that he couldn't really speak, nodded.

From within another pocket, Tia withdrew a syringe. I didn't know what was in it, but she gave the man's hand a squeeze and said, "Try to stay still, just for a moment." The synthetic nodded, drew as deep a breath as he could, and stilled. With deft hands, Tia injected the man. Almost immediately, he had another coughing fit, but then his pain eased. He smiled up at the coroner's assistant turned revolution doctor, and then he slipped away into unconsciousness.

"I doubt he'll wake up again," Tia said, her voice barely above a whisper. "His blood oxygen levels are way too low. And I don't have the equipment to intubate him and put him on a respirator." She shook her head, and I saw the first tears spill out from the corners of her eyes. "There's nothing I can do to help him. I wish we could take him to a hospital, but…"

But it was illegal for hospitals to treat synthetics, even in the case of accidents. Walton had seen to that. They had their own facilities for dealing with injured synthetics, and Sanjay would just be shipped off to one of those. It would be worse than a death sentence. I took her into my arms, offering what comfort I could. I was aware that we were in a room full of sick—dying—people. I had a sense that their doctor's despair was probably not the best thing for them to be seeing at the moment. But she was in pain, so I offered what help I could. I doubt I could have done anything else and still called myself human.

We stood like that for a long moment, her silently sobbing, me just holding her. We were a quiet island of sorrow in a broader sea of misery, the stillness broken only by the coughing synthetics and the shudders that passed through Tia as I held her. It was not a good moment. But it was a very *human* moment, and part of me reveled in it. I suspected we might not have many of them left.

The moment was broken by the arrival of another synthetic, one of those who had been assisting Tia in her doctoring. "Ms. Morita," the man said, "the Walton woman is awake."

At the mention of Walton, a low murmur, almost a growl, coursed through the room. I didn't miss the fact that in this company, Dr. Larkin wasn't *Dr. Larkin* or *Larkin* or even *the patient*. She was *the Walton woman*. The body of their oppressor made flesh. And we saved her life. When we couldn't save their lives.

"Too tight," Tia gasped.

"Shit." I let her go, realizing that the comforting hug I'd been given her had tightened with my surging anger. "Sorry."

She waved off my apology as she wiped the tears from her eyes. "It's fine." To the synthetic still waiting in the door, she said, "Can you stay with Sanjay? I think... I think it will be soon."

The...nurse? Tech? Shit, I'd have to figure out what I was going to call Tia's helpers, at least in my own mind. The assistant nodded, and we traded places, edging past one another in the tight confines. "This way," Tia said as we left the infirmary. "We set up a recovery room over here." She gave me a frown. "I was afraid I was going to need surgery and recovery for you or Hernandez, going off to kidnap a corporate executive. I didn't expect to be patching holes in that executive."

I raised my hands in mock defense. "Hey, I didn't put them there."

She snorted. "Yeah, well, it's a good thing that none of the synthetics can pull a trigger, or we'd have to post a guard on Larkin's door. I don't think they like her very much."

"No," I agreed. "I think it's safe to say they don't like her much at all."

* * * *

Larkin looked like shit. It seemed to be going around.

Unlike the synthetics in the infirmary, she'd been given the privilege of a private room—a sectioned off bit of container that wasn't being used for anything else. Not because she warranted it, but because putting her in with the synthetics would have been cruel. To the synthetics, not Larkin.

It was difficult to feel sympathy for the woman, given that she was part of a vast global conspiracy guilty of more crimes than I could possibly name. But genocide summed up Walton Biogenics' most recent transgressions rather nicely. Attempted genocide, hopefully. Some part of me understood that Larkin was just one cog in an immense machine, and, though I hated to admit it, one who had truly believed the lies upper management told. That didn't change the contributions she'd undoubtedly made to the misery of synthetics across the globe. But if I could forgive the people who had used synthetics, whether they accepted their true nature or not, could I be less forgiving with Larkin?

I realized that forgiveness had to happen, at some point. Without a fresh start, some honest attempt at reconciliation on all sides, the anger and resentment would never disappear. It would just go underground, slip beneath the surface to rise up and rear its ugly head at the most inopportune moments. So maybe, just maybe, I could make a start of it by, if not forgiving Larkin, giving her the benefit of the doubt. She had just had her former employers try to shut her up with a bullet, after all.

"How are you feeling?" Tia was asking, moving to her patient's side. She either felt no animosity to the Walton employee or was a hell of a lot better at hiding it.

"Weak," Larkin muttered. "Water?"

Tia poured a glass from a pitcher near the tattered cot serving as a bed. There was no real way to prop Larkin up—it wasn't like we had access to fancy hospital beds. Tia resorted to main strength, levering one arm behind Larkin's shoulders and leaning her forward while simultaneously bringing the glass to her lips. "A little at a time," she said.

Larkin took a few struggling sips. Even that seemed to exhaust her. "Can you grab a couple of those pillows and help prop her up?" Tia asked, still holding Larkin in a more-or-less seated position.

I followed her nod to a pile of... Well, some of them were actually pillows. Others looked like cast-off couch cushions. And one was just a torn-out piece of foam that looked like it might have been ripped off a mattress. I grabbed an armful and dumped them by the cot. I selected as best I could, opting for cleanliness over what I thought would provide the maximum comfort. The end result didn't really look all that comfortable, but Tia was able to free her arm and settle the woman into an upright position against the supports.

Some of Larkin's strength seemed to be coming back. She reached out and took the glass from Tia, waving a hand to indicate that she wanted to try on her own. She only dribbled a little as she sipped from the glass. But by the time she lowered it, her hands were shaking enough that Tia had to retrieve the cup before she dropped it.

"Why am I so weak?" Larkin asked, voice a little slurred.

"Mostly, that's the blood loss," Tia answered. "And a little bit of the drugs. We gave you some pain killers. We don't have much." Her words were clipped, professional. But something in them made me revise my estimate of the animosity she felt. She was exercising a doctorly bedside manner, but it was too textbook, with none of the warmth I'd come to expect from the beautiful young woman.

"Thank you," Larkin said. First to Tia, then she looked at me. "And thank you, Mr. Campbell. I know you and your partner saved my life."

I wasn't in the mood to pussyfoot around. "From a corporate hit squad. Of synthetics."

"What?" She tried to sit up straighter. Hell, maybe she tried to jump out of the bed. Whatever she tried, it was aborted as she gasped in pain and reached for her leg. Tia was quick to intercept her hands.

"Keep your hands away from the dressings," she said. "We've got a hard enough time keeping things sterile without you poking at them. And try not to move too much. You've been shot, remember." She eased her back against the cushions, but by the ashen-faced, glassy stare, Larkin wasn't planning on trying to move any time soon.

"Not possible," she gasped. "Programming."

"For fuck's sake," Tia sighed. I stared at her in shock, partly because she'd taken the words right out of my mouth, and partly because she swore so rarely that I almost couldn't believe the words had come from her mouth. She looked mildly embarrassed at her own language—which I found adorable—but plowed on. "*Doctor,*" She invested the title with more than a hint of sarcasm. "Programming. Indoctrination. Brain washing. Call it whatever you want. But if you can program synthetics against violence, what in the world makes you think that you couldn't program them *for* violence as well?" Her voice had risen, and while she wasn't shouting at the end of it, she was close. Her face was red, eyes pinched with anger. She'd taken even more of a liking to the synthetics than I'd realized.

"But the laws..." Larkin started, but trailed off as she realized the idiocy of that sentiment.

"Yeah," I said, placing one hand on Tia's shoulder and giving a gentle squeeze to calm her. She'd hate herself if she caused actual harm to one of her patients, and at the moment, it felt like a real possibility. "Turns out, laws don't stop a lot of people from doing whatever the fuck they want, any more than they stop bullets." I nodded at her injury. "Never have. Never will. It's why we have cops in the first place. Well," I amended, "when the higher-ups haven't been co-opted by assholes like the Walton execs."

It took Larkin a moment to process that. Her face set in a stubborn line, but then relaxed into a more resigned expression. "Yeah," she muttered. "Yeah, that makes sense. And I suppose if the company wanted to, there's no reason they couldn't program the synthetics to be killers." A shudder coursed through her body, whether from the thought of vengeful synthetics with the capacity to cause harm, or the more primal fear endemic in humanity that our creations would one day turn against us.

"Great," I grunted. "Now that we all agree your bosses—or former bosses, since I think being the target of a hit squad can be considered your termination notice—are evil fuckers, we can get to the real question at hand."

Larkin gave me a confused look. "Which is?"

"Which is where the fuck are they making them?" I growled. She winced and I shot a guilty look at Tia, fearing condemnation, but she just stared poker-faced at Larkin. She *really* must have been pissed at Walton. Still I couldn't be that big of an asshole. "Look," I continued, "we've got a plague your loving and caring corporate offices have released into the world. I don't know where or how they did it, or even when, except that it must have been recently. But they've made us—regular humans—carriers of an illness that can wipe out the synthetic population."

"To say nothing," Tia interjected, "of what could happen if the virus mutates. I'm sure your geneticists and virologists are top of their fields, but no one can control for all the possible variables and mutations. A few dozen generations of viral evolution and we might find ourselves with something that could wipe every primate off the face of the planet." *That* was certainly a sobering thought that hadn't occurred to me. Could the plague make the leap from synthetic to human? And why not, when we'd been saying all along that there really weren't any differences between the two?

"And we figure," I said, playing off Tia as naturally as if we'd been interrogating perps together for years, "that there's no way Walton Biogenics lets their killer synths walk around susceptible to this plague they've released. Which means that, somewhere, there's a facility where these soldiers are being created, and that facility may well have the cure…or at least some sort of vaccine."

Larkin was looking more than a little shell shocked, and who could blame her? She'd barely come to terms with the fact that she'd been working for the gold standard of evil for god alone knew how long. Throwing killer synthetic assassins and potentially world-ending plagues on top of that had sent her into full landed fish mode. She lay there, mouth opening and closing as if trying to talk, but no words came out. This went on for a full thirty seconds. If she hadn't been laid up with a bullet wound, I may have smacked her, just to bring her back to her senses. But, again, I couldn't be *that big* of an asshole, and besides, I doubted that slapping was a doctor-approved method of dealing with shock.

Tia leaned in and said, "Ms. Larkin. You need to answer our questions. I understand you've had a lot of new and painful information dumped on you, but we don't have time for you to adjust to it. Countless lives are at stake. If you know anything that can help us, anything at all, then you need to pull it together and start talking." She kept her voice calm, professional. There wasn't a whole lot of emotion in it, though I could hear the faintest hint of anger beneath her words. It seemed to do the trick, because Larkin's mouth snapped closed and stayed that way. Then she drew a long breath.

"The lab where I worked, the one you broke into, that's where Walton Biogenics does a lot of biological research. If there is a virus…" Tia started shaking her head, and I felt my teeth grinding at that partial denial, but Larkin plowed on. "If there is a virus, it was probably developed there. But there's no way that they're growing synthetics there. And even if they were, there's no way you're getting back in. Security has been tripled, and at least a third of it is dedicated to just looking out for you, specifically, Mr. Campbell, since your escape."

Tia looked at me and I shrugged. "We weren't planning on trying to break in there," I said. "There may be something that we could use to help, maybe even good data on the virus, but trying to infiltrate the same site twice…it's problematic. We'll do it if we have to, but it will be a hell of a lot harder." Then I turned my attention back to Larkin. "Where are the synthetics grown?" I asked.

She threw up her hands helplessly, then winced as the motion tugged at something in her leg. "Dammit," she muttered. "That hurt. To answer your question, they're grown…everywhere. I mean, all over the world. There are facilities in the United States, in Mexico, Brazil, several European countries, China… There's dozens of them."

"Shit," Tia whispered, and I saw the hope draining from her.

"It wouldn't be a regular site," I pressed. "They're not going to be growing and training their super soldiers at the same place they're growing Toys and Domestics. No chance in hell. And it's not something that's going to be well known. It's going to be a rumor. A myth. The Area 51 or Bermuda Triangle of Walton Biogenics. And no matter how tightly held the secret, it's going to have spread. The only thing that travels faster than light is gossip through a government or corporation. You know *something*, even if you don't know that you know it."

I was reaching, grasping at straws, but I couldn't let Larkin, or Tia, know that. The logic tracked. Even when it was better to do your business out in the open, and mask it as part of your legitimate operations, people seemed to have an almost pathological need to hide their secrets. Hernandez could wax eloquent on all the gang operations they never would have busted if the bad guys had just made a little *less* effort to hide what they were doing. And the only force I'd found more powerful than the need to hide secrets was the need to *tell* them. If there *was* a black site, Larkin had heard of it. If she could only remember…

Larkin, for her part, appeared to be trying. Her face had gone slack, her eyes half-lidded. She was drawing deep, slow breaths, almost as if in meditation. Her hands were more active. She kept reaching toward her leg, as if wanting to massage the wound, then snatching her hand away. She settled on clasping them, then wringing them. Worrying at them as she thought. Tia held her silence, and she kept that calm, bedside manner expression glued to her face. For my part, it took every ounce of interrogation-room-built poker face and willpower not to let my frustration show.

If Larkin couldn't come up with a lead worth following, we'd have to break into her old job. There was a chance at that, before Walton Biogenics sent a hit squad to remove her. If we could have used her credentials, or even got her to act as an inside man, we may have been able to get what we needed from the virus development site. But it looked like Walton was too smart for that. They must have been watching Larkin like a hawk, and sent teams the minute we'd made contact. Now, they'd probably added her name to whatever short list their security had to actively watch for. Watch for, and shoot on sight.

"The Potato Farm."

The non sequitur broke me from my reverie. "Come again?" I asked.

Larkin was staring at me, brown eyes wide, as if she'd just come to some realization. "The Potato Farm," she said again. "It's a synthetic growth facility located in the middle of nowhere in Idaho. It's a normal site, for the most part, focusing on the growth of Laborers."

"For the most part?" Tia asked.

"It's like Mr. Campbell said. There's always been rumors about it. It's part of why it got its nickname. I mean, we joke..." She paused, and winced as if in pain. "We *joked*," she corrected, "about how all of the synthetic growth sites were vegetable farms. Because as soon as the synthetics reached the proper age, they are...harvested. And sent off to the conditioning centers."

"Harvested," Tia said. There was a tone in her voice that I could only call loathing. I looked at her and the mask of professionalism was gone and she was staring at Larkin with a seething anger. I think, in that moment and for the first time in her journey to become a doctor, Tia was regretting saving someone.

Larkin, for her part, refused to meet Tia's eyes. "Yes," she said softly. "Harvested." She looked down at her leg once more, maybe feeling the same thing from Tia that I had and wondering how near a thing her survival had been. "And taken off for programming."

"Indoctrination," Tia snapped. "Brainwashing."

"As you say," Larkin agreed.

"The Potato Farm?" I asked, trying to get the conversation back on track.

"Right," Larkin said with a sigh. "It's called that because there have been rumors for a long time that there's more going on at the facility than the norm. That the real work is being done underground, both figuratively and literally. It's one of those things that started as a joke, but became so common that I've heard senior executives referring to the site as the Potato Farm. Most think it's some sort of underground lab. I always kind of laughed at that, since we did that kind of work right here in the city proper. But the rumors persisted."

"Idaho," I sighed. It had to be somewhere thousands of miles away. And somewhere where the conditions on the ground in the middle of February would probably be best described as *arctic*. "Do you know where?"

"Yes," Larkin said. "The main site has never been hidden from anyone. I've even worked on projects with some of the staff there. I'm sure I have the address in my contacts."

Which may or may not have been purged by Walton. But hopefully they missed that little detail. My mind had already flipped into planning mode, categorizing what we would need. Getting out of the city would be a problem, but Silas or one of the synthetics who worked the sewers could probably find a path around the checkpoints. It would require switching vehicles a lot and spending a considerable amount of time walking through the sewers, but that was manageable. The team we put together would have to include me, Al'awwal. Hernandez if she was willing. Probably Tia, though I hated to risk her. They needed her at the makeshift hospital, but I was afraid we needed her more. She might be able to make the dying more comfortable, but for us to have a chance we needed every person capable of fighting. We just didn't have enough trigger pullers.

A sound reached the recovery room. A sound that had me dropping my hand to the pistol that was no longer in the pocket of the pants I was wearing.

Chapter 14

"What is that?" Tia demanded, as the tinny sound of...screaming? Shouting? Something. Reached our ears. To penetrate the steel-walled ballasts... It had to be nearly every synthetic in our makeshift headquarters.

"Stay here," I said. "We may have been found out. If you hear gunshots... try to get out." I realized we'd never done any sort of evacuation drill, maybe the first oversight in Silas's master plan. Or, maybe, we'd been driven to his last refuge and there was nowhere else to go. Either way, we were on an island, so unless the albino had boats waiting, we were probably fucked.

I rushed out of the room, cursing under my breath for ditching the pistol. It was a dumb call made on comfort, and now I was paying the price. No time to try to get to my room to retrieve it. I'd have to hope that if Al or Hernandez were putting up a fight, they had a spare piece.

As I tore up a ladder, moving toward higher levels of the Ballast, working my way ever closer to the noise, it started to become clearer. I'd been on a raid or two, and they were normally prefaced with explosions—flashbangs in the NLPD, more serious ordinance in the Army. I hadn't heard any explosions, or gun shots for that matter. The sound of a terrified crowd was to be expected, at least when you were hitting a large group. But while I definitely heard the sounds of a crowd, what I was hearing lacked the panicked note of terror. In fact, it sounded like...celebration.

I entered another cell of the honeycomb of chambers that made up the Ballasts and stopped dead. Or was stopped. There was simply no way to move through the press of bodies before me. The room might be called a lounge, or recreation room, if one was very generous with either term. It was little more than a few large screens, salvaged from god alone knew where, and mounted on the walls. A scattering of tables and chairs—always at a premium in revolution central—normally filled the space.

Normally, because through the press of bodies, I couldn't tell what had been done with the tables or chairs. There must have been fifty synthetics crammed into a space that could accommodate half that number. The proximity of so many bodies only minutes after watching the first synthetic succumb to the effects of the Walton plague made me itch. Still, as shocking as seeing that many synthetics gathered despite the warnings we'd circulated, it was more shocking to see them so excited.

And they *were* excited. Like, yelling and screaming and jumping up and down excited. It was more emotion than I had witnessed from synthetics... ever. Even the birth of Evelyn's child paled in comparison.

"What the hell is going on?" I demanded, grabbing the nearest synthetic.

She was beautiful, dark skinned and slimly athletic. Almost certainly a Toy before escaping. Her teeth gleamed perfectly white as she shouted something in return, but her words were lost beneath the general tumult. I couldn't miss her outthrust hand, pointing toward the screens.

The mass of synthetics had thrown me for a big enough loop that I hadn't really registered what was happening on the screens. Now, though, it was clear that the synthetics—those who weren't jumping and shouting and carrying on—were all fixed in the direction of the nearest screen. All the screens showed the same thing: a nondescript female politician standing before a podium somewhere sunny and warm looking. The info-banners on the screens differed from one another, telling me that, whoever the politico was, she was being broadcast simultaneously across multiple sites.

I didn't recognize her. If she was a major player, I would have. At least at our state or the national level, anyway. I tried to tune out the screaming and yelling and focus in on the info-crawl, trying to read what I couldn't hear. The woman was, apparently, Abigail Clark, Assistant Director of Homeland Security. Except, last I knew, which wasn't all that long ago, the AD of Homeland was a guy. Maybe Silas had dirt on him, and maybe his campaign of kicking skeletons out of closets had already reached into the stratosphere of Homeland Security's muckety-mucks. Oh, how quickly things change, in the mist of revolution. I kept reading. Understood the cause for celebration.

The info-crawl was terse. Clipped. "Newly appointed Assistant Director, Homeland Security addresses press. Status of synthetics called into review. General order to all manufacturers to cease and desist operations. Owners of synthetics to be warned that, during this inquiry, temporary rights are conferred to synthetics. Criminal charges against those violating these rights might be possible."

Holy shit.

There was a lot of equivocation in those words. A lot of "temporary" and "might" and "possible." Nothing that conveyed the iron-clad resolve of a people in agreement that a terrible wrong needed righting. But fuck me if it wasn't a start. I just stared at the screen, reading the words again and again as they continued their stately march. The assistant director appeared to be taking questions, now, with screens cutting to reporters and back to the AD. I still couldn't hear what was being asked, not over the roars of the synthetics. I could imagine the questions, though. They had to boil down to just a few things. When had this been decided and when would full implementation begin? Who had made the call? Why? And, most importantly, how was it going to be enforced?

Some of the screens started to change, keeping a window open with the assistant director and her press conference. Other windows opened showing reaction shots—scenes of streets across the United States, across the globe. Times Square in New York, filled with either a riot or a celebration. Hard enough to tell that on a normal day, but the giant, building-wide screens were all showing the news and the crowds were certainly responding. The Mall in D.C. Easier, and sadder, to know what was going on there. Violence being played out on the grassy divide between the Lincoln and Washington memorials. Bodies in the reflecting pool, and riot cops and National Guard already starting to move in. Full-blown chaos in the streets in downtown L.A. Even worse than D.C. I'd been in wars that looked less violent than the drone shots of the streets. New Lyons. Where it had started. Where Walton Biogenics had their headquarters. Two mobs facing off across an asphalt divide, a thin blue line of law enforcement standing between them. If those crowds lost it, the officers were toast. They knew it. They did the job, anyway, trying to keep protestors and counter-protestors, celebrants and assholes from killing each other for the pure, savage joy of it.

More shots. Paris. London. I couldn't tell if their governments were acting in accord with the U.S., or if their citizens were reacting to the efforts of our government. I felt a bitter little surge of spite at the thought of the oh-so-refined Europeans, always quick to point out the barbaric ways of their less-cultured colonial cousins, waking up to discover that we were suddenly ahead on the social curve.

The synthetics were swirling around me, a churning stream of eddies and currents. I couldn't tell if everyone was here, but I *could* tell that the celebration was spreading. That the general din was leaking through the

Ballasts, bubbling upwards and dripping downward, flowing out in all directions. Someone, I realized, should tell Silas. But no. He'd know already. Probably knew before anyone else in the room, and let them discover it for themselves. Let them find the joy of it. That was Silas.

Then LaSorte was in front of me. His face was lit up like Christmas, and tears poured openly from his eyes. Without a word, he grabbed me by the back of the head and kissed me full on the lips. I blinked in surprise as he laughed at my poleaxed expression. LaSorte was a handsome man by any reckoning, but my proclivities lay in other directions. Still, I couldn't deny the happiness on his face, and my laughter joined his as the surging crowds swept him away. Somewhere, someone had started playing the drums. It was an urgent, rapid beat, and, though I never was one for dancing, I felt my feet starting to tap along.

The synthetics were less restrained, throwing themselves into the music with abandon. The chaotic maelstrom of bodies became something else, something that pulsed in time to the music. Tia was swept into my view, being spun by a burly synthetic who probably started life as a laborer. Her hair streamed behind her like a banner, and her face glowed with exertion and emotion. The laborer nodded to me as he spun by, somehow twirling Tia so that she ended up collapsing in my arms, gasping and giggling.

I held her for a moment, reveling in the feel of her, the warmth of her body against mine. Then, as if by some arcane female power, I found myself dancing. Thoroughly against my will. But I was powerless against the combined might of the feel of her in my arms and the terrible weight of her smile. "Isn't it amazing," she shouted. Had to shout, to be heard over the tumult. Someone had found…a violin? A fiddle? Something stringed that was adding a little melody to the driving beat of the drums.

"Amazing," I echoed. It truly was. No promises, no concrete gains. But acknowledgement. Acknowledgement on the international level that what we were doing was not for naught. But most of my amazement at that moment was that I was holding a beautiful woman in my arms and sharing a dance. Something that, after Annabelle, I didn't think would exist for me.

Annabelle. I could think of her name now and not cringe. Not feel the stabbing spike of pain that had shattered my life for a couple of decades. Why was that? Was it Silas and his revolution? The fact that, after so many years of complacency, I had started to *do something* about the problem? Or was it Tia? Was it finding a woman who had, against all my better judgement and irrespective of the years between us, managed to find fertile soil in my heart, a place I'd long thought barren and salted so that nothing could grow? Or was it even simpler than that? Was it finding friends, a family? Hernandez and I had been friends, sure. But not tight. Not like we were since things started unfolding. Hernandez. Tia. Al. Silas. Even LaSorte. It was the largest friend group I'd had...certainly since the Army. Maybe ever.

Silas. Shit.

With that, reality came crashing back down. We could dance and laugh and cavort and carry on. But so what? It didn't matter if the synthetics were freed if Walton Biogenics managed to wipe them off the face of the planet with their super bug. And if that bug mutated? Then we were all equally fucked. How's that for fairness? With all our advances, death still manages a one hundred percent success rate.

"What's wrong?" Tia asked. "You're stiffening. It's like trying to dance with an iron bar."

The twelve-year-old boy part of my brain, still focused on being close to a pretty girl, came up with plenty of rejoinders to that. But not even the strength of juvenile humor was enough to overcome my sudden worry. "This is stupid," I muttered. Well...shout-muttered. I couldn't exactly whisper, not and be heard, but I tried to direct my words just to Tia. "Why are we celebrating? If we don't do something about the virus, none of this matters."

Tia frowned, and then started tugging at my arm, pulling me from the crowd. We slipped from the chamber, and the next one, and the one after that, where the celebration had spilled over. We kept going, until Tia managed to pull me into a quiet little corner of nowhere. "Now," she said. "What are you talking about?"

I sighed, and felt a hopelessness that I hadn't realized I'd been feeling, even in the midst of the impromptu party. "Why are we celebrating?" I asked, again. "What good are maybe-possibly-but-not-guaranteed rights to anybody if they're too dead to exercise them? What's the fucking point?" I growled.

"The point, Jason Campbell," Tia said, annunciating each syllable of my name in a way that reminded me of my mother when I was in some sort of trouble, "is that they have hope. Real hope. How many of them do you think came into Silas's plan with any thought that it might actually succeed?"

"Not a lot," I muttered. Hell, I hadn't believed it myself. I'd just wanted to find out who was killing girls. Not be the voice of a fucking revolution. "Not a lot."

"More like none," she sniffed. "It was a way out that was almost certainly going to end in death, but even so, the one in a million, one in a billion chance that it could actually work was enough. That one little spark of hope against the unending darkness of their lives."

I understood what Tia was saying. And yet... "Dammit, Tia. I get it. But, it's not enough. One little spark in the darkness. One bit of hope that maybe change will happen. When it's weighed against what's coming, what we have to do. Every person down here, with the exception of... who? You. Me. Hernandez. Three of us that might be spared the virus if we fail." I snorted, feeling a bitterness welling up inside me. "Except, that if we fail, we'll already be dead anyway, since we're the ones who are going to have to break into yet another Walton Biogenics stronghold and try to ninja out some antivirus. And because you're one of our only trigger pullers, that means I have to put a half-trained damn near kid who makes me feel things I haven't felt in years in the line of fire." I stumbled to a stop realizing what I had just let slip and hoping, somehow, that Tia hadn't heard it.

She had.

The expression on her face was unreadable in the poor light of the empty Ballast chamber, and her dark eyes seemed even darker. "That's exactly why they're celebrating, Jason," she said, her voice near a whisper now. I had to lean in a little to hear her better, until our faces were scant inches apart. "They know they may die. You were a cop. I was training to be a coroner. We both saw more death than anyone should have to. We both know how fleeting life is. Do you think the synthetics don't know that, too?"

"Yeah," I muttered, only sort of following the conversation, now. Tia was so close to me. If I leaned forward just a little bit...

"So, they're doing the eat, drink, and be merry thing," she said. "For tomorrow we may die." She seemed to think about that for a moment, her eyes staring into mine. A small smile curled up the edges of her lips. "Tomorrow." She leaned forward, and I was suddenly very glad she had pulled me into a secluded spot of the Ballasts to talk.

Her lips met mine and there was an urgency there that I hadn't felt from her before. She pressed hard against me, hands grabbing the back of my head, pulling me down to her. My hands went first around her waist, then lower, exploring her curves. She let out a soft moan as I stroked and squeezed. Then, she pulled harder, and we were on the floor, me on top of her. Her hands were roaming now as well and somehow my shirt was pulled over my head and tossed aside. Didn't much like that shirt, anyway.

She gave me a hard shove and I rolled with it, and then she was on top of me, straddling me. Her shirt joined mine. Then she shimmied out of her bra with that inhuman arms-behind-the-back elbows-at-an-impossible-angle twist that seemed encoded in the female DNA. After that... Well, after that, things got a little hazy.

* * * *

"I'm cold," Tia whispered.

It was some time later, and we were stretched out on the floor. We'd managed to maneuver our clothing beneath us, creating a thin cloth barrier between our bare skin and the cool metal floor. And providing some padding for the more...energetic activities in which we'd engaged. "I noticed," I said, letting my eyes roam over her body.

She slapped me—playfully, but hard—on the hip. "Ow!" I said.

"It's what you deserve, taking advantage of a... What did you call me? 'A damn near kid?' And do you really think that description fits?" she asked with an arched eyebrow and naughty smile. She also writhed about as she did, distracting me from the question in all sorts of interesting ways.

"Definitely not," I said, hands starting to roam again.

She batted them away. "No time for that, Detective." she grinned. "As you were so melodramatically reminding me not too long ago, we *do* sort of have to save the world. What is it you always say? Time to get to work?"

I sighed. Tia was right. No matter how much I'd like to stay here—and truth be told, the metal floor was becoming less and less appealing now that the fun parts were over and the post-coital bliss was fading—there really was a lot of work to be done. Tia was already making her way to her feet, somehow making the movement graceful and sensual. Well, okay, the nudity helped with that.

"You're on my clothes," she said, staring down at me.

I smiled, admiring the view. "Sorry?"

She kicked me. Lightly. "Move it."

"Yes, ma'am."

My rise to my feet was, if I don't say so myself, every bit as graceful. You don't spend as many years as I had getting thrown to the mats without learning how to get up with a certain amount of efficiency. Probably a lot less sensual though.

We sorted out our clothing in companionable silence. Tia kept casting secretive looks and small smiles in my direction, and I couldn't help but admire her as she dressed. It had been... Well, a long time. Too long. Since I'd seen an actual, living and breathing woman in that state of undress. Much less done other things.

When we were once again fully clothed and more or less presentable, Tia went up on her tiptoes to give me a quick kiss. Well, that may have been her intent. Things went on a little longer than either of us had intended.

"We have to stop," she said at last, putting both hands on my chest and pushing me away. "Or we're never getting out of here." She winced and rubbed at her backside. "Besides, the floor in here isn't very comfortable, so if you expect a round two, Detective, you're going to have to find better accommodations."

I grinned at that. Not just at the thought of a repeat performance, but at the thought of Tia already thinking about it. Maybe it was shallow—okay, hell, it was *definitely* shallow—but it suddenly felt really good to be wanted again.

"Let's hurry up and save the world, then. So we can get on with that round two."

Chapter 15

It turned out, making any plans that evening was an exercise in futility. The synthetics were split between jubilant celebration and fixedly staring at the screens, watching the riots and protests and, in at least one case, outright carnivals that had broken out across the world. I couldn't watch those for more than a moment or two.

Silas had merely looked at us with weary eyes when I tried to talk to him about what Larkin had revealed. The man had looked paler than usual, if that was possible, and could only go for a minute or two without a cough. Most were still slight, nagging things. But every now and then he would unleash a torrent of hacking that had Tia prescribing a good night's sleep and as much cough suppressant as she thought the synthetic could handle. He had waved us away, telling us to come back in the morning, acknowledging that nothing was going to get done tonight.

Tia, remembering that she had not just one patient in Dr. Larkin, but a whole slew of them in the ill synthetics, had rather guiltily rushed off, with just a quick peck on the cheek for me. At loose ends, I had wandered through the Ballasts, watching, but not really participating in the celebrations. I witnessed more than one "affirmation of life" that had the simultaneous effects of making me wish Tia was around and marvel at the…flexibility… of the synthetics when it came to celebrating. And at their lack of inhibition. And, in some cases, at their literal flexibility. But voyeurism had never been my thing, so when I wandered into a chamber of the Ballast being put to good use, I left them to it. Besides, I got the distinct impression that, even in the larger gatherings, I—in all my humanness—wouldn't be entirely welcome.

At length, I'd sought my bed. Sleep didn't come easy. My mind kept bouncing back and forth between the news of at least a partial victory, the need to stop the plague, and intrusive thoughts of Tia. Most of those were of the carnal nature, and thoroughly enjoyable. But I also couldn't help but think of the future, and wonder what a broken-down former cop could offer someone like her. That doubt kept me awake as much as worrying about infiltrating another Walton Biogenics facility in a long-shot effort at a cure. Which said something about the human spirit. But I was too damn tired to figure out what.

The next morning, we all gathered in the war room. Silas, cognizant of the fact that LaSorte, Al'awwal, and Danielle were, at the very least, asymptomatic, was joining us via screen from his own personal quarantine chamber. Hernandez threw one look at me and Tia, and let out a snort. "Finally," she said. She walked over and gave Tia a quick hug, and whispered something into her ear that I didn't catch. Whatever it was, it made Tia blush, and then honest-to-god giggle. I gave Hernandez a hard look. She gave me the finger. But she did it with a smile.

"If we are quite ready?" Silas asked, from his electronic position at the head of the table.

"Sorry," I said. Hernandez didn't even have the good grace to look embarrassed. I noticed that LaSorte and Al were both looking at me and Tia and that they had shit-eating grins on their faces. Dammit. I mean, it's not like I was ashamed of what Tia and I had done, but I also wasn't expecting to be the entertainment for my friends.

"Perhaps you could tell us what Larkin said," Silas suggested.

That settled everyone down. "Right," I agreed. "There's a place in Idaho, a facility where they grow synthetics. The call it the Potato Farm. I gather it's because most of the real work takes place underground. Also, Idaho. Apparently, there are lots of rumors about the place. Short of round two at the facility we hit... Fuck's sake. Was it only a month ago?"

"Time flies when you're toppling regimes." Al grinned.

"Anyway. The security there—in all of New Lyons, hell, probably all of Walton Biogenics—is on high alert. Specifically looking for me. And now Larkin, too. Larkin says that the virus was probably developed right here, in her former workplace. But getting in there..." I trailed off. Shook my head. "We've only got three trained shooters. Me. Al. Hernandez. We're already going to have to put a gun in Tia's hands and bring her along, which is risky in itself." I gave her leg a quick squeeze under the table, to take some of the sting from the words. "No way we're breaking into that lab again with four shooters and tech support."

"And what is at this Potato Farm?" Silas asked.

"Dunno," I admitted. "But it's Larkin's best guess at where the synthetic hit squads are being grown."

"Fuck," Hernandez said. Everyone looked at her. "If they're being grown there, they've probably got them on guard duty. We took out the ones at Larkin's place, but they were decent. Better than normal rent-a-cops. Gonna be a bitch."

"Four shooters. LaSorte? You in for the screen work?" I asked.

"Yes," he replied.

"As am I," Silas said.

A silence fell over the room. Everyone seemed to be looking at the screen with Silas's calm face plastered on it. And then looking at me.

Fuck.

"Look, Silas," I began.

"No, Jason," he interjected. "You look. I started this, and I *will* be there at the end. I understand that I may not be at my peak physical shape, but I assure you, there is nothing wrong with my mind. I can operate screens every bit as effectively now as before I contracted Walton's final solution."

"That may be," I agreed. "But if you come along, you're going to be putting us at risk." I said the words as gently as possible. "Coughing could give us away, and we don't know how quickly things may progress. We can't carry you along behind us."

"Too bad," he growled. "Understand me, Jason. All of you. I will not be left behind. And while LaSorte is certainly talented with screens, I am better. Significantly better." I threw a quick glance at LaSorte, who was nodding along, apparently in agreement with Silas's assessment. "And if this is a top-secret facility, you will need me. That is all there is to it."

"And the risk of infecting Al'awwal? The risk of infecting LaSorte?" I asked.

"Acceptable," was the reply. "You know as well as I that we are likely all either infected or carriers at this point. Every synthetic in the Ballasts is as good as dead already. And every synthetic in the world will follow soon after. Unless we do something about it. I am the one who brought this plague down upon my people. I *will* be there to fight it."

I looked at the others. Al gave me a sort of half-shrug. LaSorte looked green around the edges, but he was nodding. I hoped his queasiness was from the thought of already being infected, and not, you know, actual queasiness. Whatever Silas said, I doubted he'd be operating at peak efficiency while hacking up a lung. I didn't need my other tech guy down, too. Hernandez looked worried, and I knew why. You didn't bring sick operators on mission. You bumped them and went to the next guy. Wasn't worth compromising things. Of course, in this case, there wasn't a "next guy" that we could bump to.

I looked at Tia. She must have thought the glance was a question, because she said, "I'm not sure how we're getting to Idaho. Driving, I guess? I don't think you would make it through an airport. We can probably rig up some sort of quarantine for Silas, particularly if we get a van or something. Or maybe an RV. We seem to be able to get a lot of cars... Can we get an RV?"

"We need shooters more than we need transport, Campbell," Hernandez said.

"I know," I agreed. "But we don't have them. With the exception of Al, the synthetics can't pull a trigger."

"Well," Al said, "the exception of me and these synthetic security forces Walton has created." He gave a slight, self-mocking frown. "I'm starting to feel less and less special every day."

"Well, why don't we *get* them, *hermano*? I can put out some feelers with the NLPD. Talk to some people we both know. Maybe pick up a couple more people who are willing to help. People who are actually trained for this sort of shit." She glanced over at Tia. "No offense. And even if we have a full team, I'd just as soon have you along. A good combat medic is worth more than a shooter."

Tia gave her a beaming smile while I turned the idea over in my head. "Silas?" I asked.

"Your call, Jason," he answered. "You know the tactical situation better than I do." He shrugged, though I could only tell from the lift of his traps. His shoulders were too wide for the camera angle to include them. "There are risks. You know them. And, I assume, many benefits as well."

That was the problem. The risks were obvious. If the wrong person got wind of Hernandez's recruiting efforts, we were fucked. Period.

But, if we went into the Potato Farm under-gunned and under-supported, our chances of getting out with said cure were pretty fucking anorexic.

"How sure are you that you could find the right people? And how long would you need?" I asked.

"A day or two," Hernandez replied. "And as sure as I can be." It was her turn to shrug, and then sigh. "Shit, *hermano*, you can never really know what people believe, deep down."

"True enough. I assume it will take a day to get everything else ready?" I asked.

"Yes," Silas agreed. "Assuming Ms. Morita is willing to assist and act as our face in the more mundane matters. Purchasing supplies and RVs. That sort of thing."

Tia nodded. "And we'll need to get some things to set up an isolation chamber for Silas." She frowned., and looked at Hernandez. "Can you steal some gas masks from the cops? The NBC types, if you have them."

It took me and Hernandez both a minute to process that question. I'd been okay with my "retirement" from the force, and I was having a hard time swallowing the notion that we'd come far enough that Tia was comfortable asking Hernandez to steal gas masks intended for response to nuclear, biological, or chemical attacks from the armory at work.

"You think the Walton people are going to try to gas us?" Hernandez asked.

"No. But the current run of military and police masks don't have exhale valves," she responded.

I looked at Hernandez, who looked back at me, and I saw my own confusion mirrored in her dark eyes. "Uhm. Tia. I think you're gonna have to back it up a bit for those of us who don't know what the hell you're talking about."

Tia smiled. I got the distinct impression she liked the mystery. And even more, that she like explaining things. To me. That was going to be... interesting...down the line. If there was a down the line. "Gas masks are respirators. They work by filtering out contaminants. Most of them have an exhale valve. Something that lets the wearer's exhaled breath escape the mask without having to be forced through the filters. Makes the filters last longer."

"But doesn't protect anyone else from anything the person wearing the mask might be exhaling. Like, say a virus," Danielle added, clearly following.

I'd spent some time in the NBC masks, both in the big green machine, and in the NLPD. The things sucked. Drawing in air wasn't exactly easy, and exhaling was every bit as hard. Hard enough that when you really got to panting—like say when you were made to do PT wearing the fucking things in the middle of a desert—you started to worry that the seal would pop. I hadn't really thought that was because my breath was being forced out through the same filter the "fresh" air was being drawn through, but it made sense.

"So, it's a sort of self-contained quarantine for Silas?" I asked.

"And anyone else who starts showing symptoms." She paused. Looked at Al and LaSorte. "Sorry guys," she said with a frown. Al waved her off, and LaSorte, looking a little pale around the edges, nodded his understanding.

I looked at the screen, to where Silas was watching us with intent, feverish eyes. "Sucks to be you, buddy," I said. "Those masks are no *bueno*."

"If it eases your concerns about the fact that I *will* be part of this mission, then I can suffer well the indignities," he replied. Then ruined it, by lapsing into another coughing fit.

"If," I added, looking at Hernandez, "you can manage to swipe a few?"

"And some extra filters," Tia added. "We won't have Silas in the mask all the time, but those filters are only good for a few hours."

"You don't ask much, eh, *hermana*? I can get the masks. With all the riot work, the fucking things are lying around the office. And they're passing out filters like Kleenex. You give me today to do some recruiting, and I can get the masks and hopefully a couple of extra shooters here tomorrow morning."

"All right. Today we plan and prep. Tomorrow road trip to a potato farm. Silas, LaSorte. We need you guys running down everything you can on this place. Assuming she's conscious, we can get you wired in to Larkin, so you can pick her brain. Hernandez has to go into work." I looked over at Tia, Danielle, and Al.

"I'll put together a list of what we need to isolate Silas for the trip," Tia said. "I can do that and check in on the sick as well." A darkness passed over her face. "I... I hesitated to mention it, but we lost another one. We're starting to get some idea of how the virus progresses, but... Well, the timing is all over the place. I suspect it has something to do with the specific purposes for which each synthetic was designed. Progress seems slower in those optimized for manual labor and..." She blushed a bit, but carried on. "And sex."

"Can't have your playthings catching some nasty human disease," LaSorte muttered.

"Enough," Silas interjected, cutting through the burgeoning pall in the room. "Callous as it may sound, we do not have time to mourn. If we are successful in our endeavors, we will mourn for all those who have fallen. If we are not, we can pray that someone will be, and that they, in turn, will mourn for us."

"Jesus," Hernandez whispered.

"Well," Al'awwal said, "On that note, I think I'll help Ms. Morita. There are a number of other items we should secure, in addition to an RV and whatever supplies are needed for the quarantine chamber. I've probably got most of it at home, but, even if I haven't seen myself on any wanted posters lately, that might be a bit risky. I'll add it to the list and accompany Ms. Morita on her shopping expedition."

I felt a tightness in my shoulders that I hadn't realized was there ease. Going out into the streets right now wasn't exactly safe. Tia could handle herself well enough, and I'd make damn sure she brought a weapon with her. But Al'awwal was big enough that his size alone would deter a lot of would-be troublemakers. Troublemakers that would flock to an attractive young woman out wandering around a riot by herself. I gave him a brief nod of thanks, and he winked at me.

"And I'll help with the patients, and continue my studies," Danielle added. "Even if we beat this thing, we'll need to understand more about it." She flashed a smile. "There may be an entire new branch of medical science in the very near future."

Yeah, but would any of us be here to see it? I didn't voice the thought, just looked around the table once more at the faces of my friends and brothers- and sisters-in-arms. No one looked exactly eager—we all had too good an idea of the mountain of tasks that were ahead of us. But I saw the firm set of determination in every face. Even now, with the promise of legal status for the synthetics still fresh in the air, Walton Biogenics' trump card, their final solution, might put us down. But if it did, I had no doubt that every person—human or synthetic—in the room would go down fighting.

Sometimes, that was the best you could ask for.

"All right," I said. "We've got a metric shit-ton to do, and not a lot of time to do it. Let's get to work."

* * * *

I spent most of the day at loose ends.

Everyone else had a meaningful task to pursue, but I was bound by the same limitations that had plagued me since I'd been named public enemy number one. Well I *could* go on forays out into the world if absolutely necessary, the risk of being recognized was too great for something as simple as a supply run. So, helping Al and Tia was out.

Likewise, I lacked the expertise to contribute anything meaningful to Silas's and LaSorte's pursuits on the screens. They understood what needed to be done, what information needed to be gathered. They had a direct line to Larkin, and from all indications, she was honest in her desire to help us bring Walton Biogenics down. Which meant that if I poked my nose in there, even with my experience as an interrogator, I'd only slow them down.

Helping Hernandez was out of the question, for obvious reasons. Even if she thought she could find a couple of sympathetic ears in the precinct, there was no way in hell I could go within a mile of a police station without getting my ass arrested.

* * * *

I made my way back to my room, such as it was, and dropped onto the cot that served as my bed. As it creaked under my weight, I had a brief, tantalizing thought of Tia. I didn't think the cot would pass her standards for comfort relative to a round two. Well, just another reason to get to Idaho and rob a potato farm.

I slipped my personal screen from my pocket and flicked my news app. The screen wasn't really *mine*, of course. I hadn't had a screen that was truly mine, in my account, since I'd walked away from the NLPD. I couldn't remember whether this was my third, fourth, or fifth burner, but it didn't matter. I'd stored my filters on an anonymous cloud, and it was a simple matter to drop them into the news app. If I wanted to look at events over the past few weeks that passed the filters' tests, I'd have to wait a bit, but for current news, it took only a minute or so before the screen chirped, letting me know it was ready for review.

I hit the text only option, not really wanting to watch even the innocuous talking heads of the filter app. The first bullet, unsurprisingly, read: *Law enforcement officials still searching for wanted fugitive and former NLPD detective, Jason Campbell*. No surprise there. Even if we won, I'd have to face my day in court. I had some small hope that, given the circumstances, if we were successful, the courts would show some measure of leniency. There were no guarantees, but I didn't want to live my life as a fugitive. If we lived through the next few days, I foresaw turning myself in once again. The thought made my skin crawl, particularly around the various knife wounds that hadn't yet fully healed, but there you had it.

The next headline was of more interest: *World leaders to hold summit discussing synthetic rights*. I briefly scrolled through the linked article. It didn't flow like a human-written work, being constructed programmatically, but it did convey the important information. At least four of the five "w's" of journalism—Who, What, When, and Where—were easy enough for a machine to do the heavy lifting. "Why" was often more nuanced, but in this case, it was simple enough. The only thing I cared about was the when— and it was weeks away. Too damn long. Too damn long by a long shot.

The third headline filled me with a sense of looming dread. "Reports of illness among synthetics amidst push for full rights." I scanned that story as well. There were plenty of words like "isolated" and "scattered reports" which gave me at least a little bit of hope. But from what I could tell, the gist of the story was still being reported as something more along the lines of a consumer report or a "buyer beware" rather than a medical matter. No indication of an investigation into the illness. No commentary from doctors. Might as well have been a report on faulty airbags for all the health information presented. But the fact that there were enough cases that stories were being generated was beyond alarming. Even if we found a cure, or vaccine, or whatever the fuck we were looking for, could we get enough of it? Or manufacture enough of it? Fast enough to matter?

A wave of blackness swept up from somewhere deep in my gut. Had this whole thing been for nothing? Had getting the attention of the people, of world governments been no more than a pyrrhic victory? What use are rights to the dead?

"Fuck!" I half-growled, half-shouted, the word echoing off the walls around me. That was enough news for one day. I stuffed the screen back into my pocket and pushed myself up off the cot. Maybe I couldn't help the others, not at the moment, but there was still a room full of sick synthetics, and those taking care of them could probably use a hand. I'm sure Danielle and the synthetics acting as orderlies wouldn't turn me away.

* * * *

Danielle was more than happy to see me, and I was put immediately to work. As I moved from sickbed to sickbed in our makeshift infirmary, checking vitals and sharing a few words with each patient, I was struck by two things. First, even in the few short days, the number of sick had increased by a noticeable amount, although it hadn't doubled or anything so grand. If it had moved that fast, the world would probably be in a panic, synthetics or no. But Walton had been smarter than that. More insidious. Their little cleanup plague either moved slow or lay dormant long enough to spread the illness out, so that by the time anyone realized what was going on, it would be too late.

As I sat chatting with the sick, doing my best to lift their spirits in the few brief moments I spent with each of them, the weight of that responsibility settled a little more on my shoulders. If we failed, it could mean the end of the synthetic population. They knew it. But not one of the sick that I spoke with seemed to regret the revolution. A young—well, by appearance, anyway—man that I spoke with, who had likely been a Domestic as he lacked the beauty and grace of the Toys and the bulk of the Laborers, put it best: "I lived my whole life as someone's slave," he managed to gasp out between bouts of energetic coughing. "At least if I die, I die free."

Well. Fuck that.

People deserved to *live* free. Free to make wonderful decisions. Free to make terrible ones. But most of all, they deserved to be free from the tyranny of those who held power over them. Didn't matter if the power was wealth, or the long and sometimes oppressive arm of the government, or actual, physical strength. The synthetics had suffered under all three. And they were willing to die to end it. They couldn't fight, not with their conditioning, but they could still resist, even if it meant death in the end.

How could I do any less?

Chapter 16

"We need to meet, *hermano.*"

Hernandez had screened as I was wrapping up a long day of helping Danielle and the others take care of the sick. It had been a torturous process coupling hard, unpleasant labor with an emotional wringer that left me exhausted. I'd found a new respect for the work nurses and CNAs did. All I wanted to do was sleep.

"About what?" I half-snapped. Then I remembered where Hernandez was, and why. "Shit. Sorry, Hernandez. It's been a long day. What's up?"

She let my outburst pass, which worried me. "I've got a couple of candidates. But I want you to meet with them."

Something in her voice set me on edge. "Who are they?" I asked.

"I'll explain when you get here. I'll text you the address." And she hung up. Just like that. My phone chimed a moment later, but I didn't bother looking at the address, instead trying to think my way through the problem.

Back when I'd first gone underground, Hernandez and I had established some screen protocols, to allow us to keep in contact and keep us both safe. We'd abandoned a lot of them when Silas had set her up with her very own secret-squirrel burner phone, but I still remembered the protocols and I was certain she did as well. She hadn't slipped the duress phrase into the conversation. So, she probably hadn't been found out and detained, and then forced to try to set me up. Probably.

Then why the secrecy? I trusted her enough that if she thought some of our brothers in blue were ready to be brought into the fold, then so be it. I glanced at the address on the screen. It wasn't far. Just off Floattown. A distance I could easily walk, and through a place I knew well enough to avoid the prying eyes. Hernandez had visibility into what the cops were doing, which meant it should also be a place without any extra security.

I thought about going to Silas, or Al, or Tia. Letting any of them know what I was about to do. But they'd just want to discuss it, or come with me. If it was somehow a trap, it would catch two as easily as one. And whatever Hernandez was up to, I knew I was going to go. Talking about it wouldn't change that. I owed her a lot more than the trust to go to a meeting with some possible recruits.

I made my way back to my room and geared up as best I could. My wardrobe was still intensely lacking. I was half-convinced that it was the result of some widescale joke the others were playing on me. But I'd managed to scrounge together a pair of half-serviceable jeans and a zip-up hoodie. Not the most stylish, but it would serve, and the hood would help keep my face hidden from watching eyes.

I still had the nine-millimeter and somewhere along the line, Al had managed to find me a couple of spare magazines. I missed my forty-five, but I was starting to warm to the blocky peashooter. It had served well enough at Larkin's house. I still didn't have a holster, so I tucked it into the back of my pants.

I made my way through the Ballasts, moving toward the surface. I passed only a few synthetics along the way, but no one gave me so much as a second glance. I did *not* run into Tia or Al. Those two wouldn't have let me pass so easily, and I was grateful that I'd managed to slip out of the occupied levels without running into either of them. I'd pay for it later, and I felt a slight pang at the thought that the long, narrow Well, not dishonesty, but certainly avoidance…would do some damage to my burgeoning relationship with Tia. I'd rather risk that damage than put her in danger.

Floattown was quiet as I emerged once more into a sheltered alleyway between some of the pre-fabbed buildings. The sun had slipped below the horizon an hour or two ago, and the moon had yet to rise. The winter darkness always added a sense of stillness to the evening. Not quite peace, not in New Lyons. But something more akin to a sense of waiting. What the city was expecting, I didn't know.

I drew a deep breath, tasting the Gulf in the air, and let it out in a steadying sigh. Then slipped into the shadows. My hood was up, head down, hands stuffed deep into the central pocket of the hoodie. Hopefully, I looked like every other BSL-er walking aimlessly around the streets at night. My steps weren't aimless, though, and they took me through the buildings, past the edge of the commercial zone and to one of the narrow bridges that connected Floattown with the mainland.

The area on the landward side of the Floattown bridge was mostly industrial, with a few commercial enterprises scattered about. The standard workday was over, but given the number of warehouses, transport companies, and other ventures that didn't keep regular hours, there were a fair amount of people walking around. No riots or crowds, though, not here.

I moved among the crowds, keeping my eyes downcast and the hood low, avoiding the cameras as I could, and relying on my "disguise" to spoof the ones I couldn't. Hernandez had chosen a meeting spot in a narrow alley that ran between a truck mechanic's shop and a long, narrow brick building that might have been a small-scale factory at some point. It didn't have any signage to indicate what it was now, though there weren't any broken windows and I saw at least one light burning in the interior, so it probably wasn't abandoned.

As I slipped into the alley, Hernandez stepped out from a doorway on the maybe-abandoned mystery building. "This way, Campbell," she said, waving me over.

"Why the mystery, Hernandez?" I asked. I could tell from the set of her shoulders and the slight frown on her face that she was uneasy. It wasn't worry about the location—if so, she'd be looking around more, instead of meeting my eyes.

"Better if you hear it from him. You trust me, right, Campbell?"

There was actual worry in her eyes, but, for some reason, I felt some tension ease. It wasn't the look of impending betrayal that I saw there. At least, not the kind that would end with me in bracelets. "With my life. Let's do this."

We stepped through the door into a large, mostly empty room. There were a few scattered stacks of pallets. A couple of plastic fifty-gallon drums. Piles of what looked like broken-down cardboard boxes. And a giant of a man standing near the pallets. I recognized him at once. And felt a surge of guilt.

"Shit," I muttered. "Thompson." Hernandez didn't say anything, which I thought was strange. But she led me over to the big rookie. Well, maybe not a rookie, anymore. Given the current situation, he'd probably seen more action in his couple of months on the force than I'd seen in my first couple of years. He looked much the same as I remembered—big, chiseled features, recruiting poster haircut. Okay, so maybe his nose was a little off-center—that was probably my fault.

"Campbell," he said, his voice a smooth baritone. "I'd say it was good to see you but…"

"But last time I put a few bullets into you?" I asked.

He rubbed at his chest. "That really hurt, you know."

"Look, kid, I knew you were wearing Kevlar, all right? I wasn't trying to kill you, but you were in my way. If Hernandez brought you here, then you know why."

He surprised me with a grin. "Shit, Campbell. I don't care that you shot me, not really. I care that you cheated. I still owe you for our sparring session. I was *winning*, dammit."

"No such thing as cheating when it's life and death," I replied. "Thought you would have figured that out by now."

That sobered him a bit. "Yeah," he said. "Yeah." Then he grinned again, a grin that had an almost vindictive edge to it. "But it's cool. Because I get to see your face for the next part."

Hernandez had been suspiciously quiet during all of this. And I realized that despite Thompson having been sent against me and Al'awwal as part of a special response team at the Walton Biogenics lab, there was no way Hernandez would have looked as worried as she did over bringing the rookie into the fold. Which meant there was another shoe to drop.

It dropped. Hard.

"Campbell."

I recognized that voice. That smarmy, greasy voice. Francois Fortier, NLPD Detective, head of the fucking team looking for yours truly, and someone who loved to share the details of the depravities he visited on his own personal Toys. The one cop in all New Lyons I'd happily put a bullet into. He stepped out from behind the stack of pallets, all oily hair and sloppy, seam-straining suit, and I damn near pulled my gun. I could sense Hernandez at my shoulder, ready to tackle me if I did, and I could see the slight shift in the set of Thompson's shoulders, also ready to throw himself into the fray.

* * * *

"What the fuck is going on here, Hernandez?" I growled. Fortier opened his mouth to answer, and I shot him a glare that said all the things I wasn't saying out loud. Damn, but that bastard made my fists itch.

"He wanted to help," she began.

"To help, or some help?" I snapped before she could say more. "I didn't think you'd be the one to help him find me." She winced at that, and I felt shitty. Deep down, I really didn't believe that Hernandez had betrayed me, but Fortier brought out something ugly in me.

"Just listen to him, *hermano*," she said.

Fortier hadn't said anything. Five minutes ago, I wouldn't think you could put him in a room with me and have him shut up for that long. Even being wrong about that irritated me. "Fine. Talk."

He shrugged, and I swear to God, somehow managed to look...*bashful.* "Look," he began. "The thing is... Shit." He trailed off. Looked down at his shoes. Back at me. I was vaguely aware of Hernandez giving him a supportive nod—which sent another little stab of betrayal into my guts. "Look, I can admit when I'm wrong. When this shit started, I wanted nothing more than to put you away. God above," he said with a gritted-teeth smile, "I fucking hate the sight of you, Campbell. Always have. Probably always will. Your holier-than-thou, too-good-for-this-fucking-world attitude. Do you have any idea how fantastic it was to watch you fall from your own little mountaintop and have to live in the shit with the rest of us?"

Thompson and Hernandez both looked a little worried now that Fortier was unloading. But this, at least, was a Fortier I could understand. And to think that he hated me every bit as much as I hated him, even if I thought the reasons were bullshit, made me feel a little better.

"And yeah," he continued. "I liked Toys. Liked having beautiful women at my beck and call." He snorted. "Look at me. I wasn't getting them any other way." Some of the anger drained from his voice. "But I hand-to-God thought they were things." He winced as he said it. "Jesus, even saying it now..." He shook his head, and a look of nausea swept across his face. In that moment, I hated him just a little bit less. A little bit.

"So yeah, call me stupid. Call me naïve. Call me whatever the fuck you want. I don't care. I bought into the line I was sold. I tried to ignore the evidence. Wrote off the pregnancy as a fluke. You ever hear of a liger? And having dirt on politicians. Who the fuck doesn't, and who the fuck cares? Politics is an older and dirtier game than prostitution. Everyone knows it. But then you had to turn yourself in, and you had to do it with a shitload of scientific mumbo jumbo tucked in your back pocket." He shook his head, spat on the ground. Drew an angry breath. "At first I was just happy to put your ass behind bars. But then I got to wondering why you did it. We weren't any closer to finding you. So why do it?"

"To make people listen," I said quietly. "And to make sure Walton couldn't suppress the evidence we'd found."

"Make people listen," he snorted. "Well, it fucking worked, damn you. I wanted to ignore it, Campbell. I really fucking did. But I'm a cop. I've never seen a guilty man turn himself in unless he was bucking for a lesser sentence. I waited to hear about you cutting a deal."

"No deals," I said.

"No deals," he agreed. "Just you, in a cell. In general fucking population. And I got to thinking about that, too. About how fucked up that was. I don't like you, Campbell, but cops don't belong in general pop. And I figured, if you're half as smart as you get credit for, you had to know there was a chance you'd end up right where you did. A good chance some scumbag convict would try to shank you."

I unconsciously rubbed at the knife wound on my arm. "So, you reviewed the evidence. The 'scientific mumbo jumbo.'"

"Yeah. Most of it might as well have been written in Sanskrit. But Kaphiri's journal entries, his explanations. Maybe most of all, him documenting the efforts Walton took to keep him quiet. You don't go to that kind of effort to silence someone if you're not doing anything wrong. So yeah, I started believing." He shifted his weight, dropped his gaze once more. "I... I couldn't just turn my Toys...my... Shit. Whatever. I couldn't turn them out. Just, kick them to the street. They're still at my place, Campbell. I haven't touched them. But they're there. Looking at me. Waiting for me to tell them what to do. Watching and waiting."

"That's pretty much all they're allowed to do," I agreed. "That, and suffer."

The words landed harder than I'd expected, and Fortier winced. The color fled his face, and for a moment, I thought he was going to vomit. He got himself under control with a visible effort. "Yeah. So, they're there, at my house. And it got to the point where I was almost afraid to go home. I had to do something. I've been... Well, sabotaging some of the efforts to find you. A little bit. But it's...it's not enough."

His admission of trying to undermine the search efforts shocked the hell out of me. In a thousand years, I never would have expected it. I could buy the guilt, the realization, the understanding. I'd seen it in other faces. I'd seen it in Hernandez. But aiding and abetting was a far cry from assuaging your guilt, and if you'd asked me yesterday if Fortier had the courage to act, I would have laughed in your face. "And then Hernandez showed up," I said.

"Yeah," Fortier agreed. "You may think I'm an asshole, Campbell, but I'm not half as stupid as you think. I've been watching her. And while she was smart enough"—this with an acknowledging nod toward Hernandez—"to avoid anything that I could actively pursue, there was an awful lot of sick days and family emergencies accruing over the past couple of months. Not enough to go to the brass, even if I'd wanted to. But enough to make me suspicious. So, when she started pulling people aside and asking questions..." He trailed off.

"He sought me out, *hermano*," Hernandez said. "Cornered me, really. I didn't want to let him in, but he told me the same thing he just told you. And I believe him. Besides"—she shrugged—"other than Thompson here, no one else was taking the bait. Figured another shooter can only help." She threw Fortier a smile that was half-hate and half-tease. "Maybe he'll catch a bullet for us."

"You're all heart, Detective," Fortier replied, the snide tone creeping back into his voice just a bit. "But I'm not just a target. Me and Thompson, we brought gifts." With that, he reached behind the stack of pallets and began pulling out gear bags. My heart skipped a beat at the thought of having an honest-to-God holster once more.

"Fine, Fortier. You and Thompson are in. Has Hernandez briefed you?"

"Just that it's incredibly dangerous, we'll all probably die, and if we don't do it, the world is doomed," Thompson said. Then he grinned. "Who could say no to that?"

"She didn't even mention Idaho?" I asked. "That's the best part."

Chapter 17

We spent Valentine's Day on the road.

The RV that Al'awwal and Tia managed to secure was an older, used model that had seen a lot of road. But it had the benefits of being big enough to hold us—complete with a makeshift isolation chamber for Silas—and being within the price range that we could pull together on short notice. I still had no idea how Silas funded things, but even his resources weren't without their limits. And you couldn't exactly walk into an RV lot and hand over a briefcase full of cash without raising an eyebrow or two.

It did have all the required autonomous driving and navigation features. Which was a damn good thing, since without them, we wouldn't have been able to get on the interstates. As it was, we were staring down about sixteen hours of driving to get from New Lyons to the Potato Farm, which was located somewhere within a hundred miles of Boise. That same drive would have taken twice as long back before autonomous driving, when speed limits were set statically at levels thought to be best for the mechanical limitations of the vehicles and the physical limitations of the humans behind the wheels.

Now, speed limits simply didn't exist, not on the interstates. The whole thing was computer controlled, relying on a network of global positioning satellites, a bank of super computers, and the continuous data feed from every car on the road. The system adjusted speed based not only on the flow of traffic, but on the system monitoring of the vehicles themselves. Even our clunky, outdated RV averaged a solid one-hundred-forty to one-hundred-fifty miles per hour, while more modern vehicles sped along the interstates at something closer to two hundred. Not even law enforcement could engage manual drive on the interstates…but then again, there was no need. All they had to do was identify the vehicle they wanted stopped, and if it was on the interstate, the system would take care of it. Slow it down, move it to the side of the road, and then lock the vehicle in place.

It made our journey all the more dangerous, and, to be honest, it made my palms itch. Hernandez looked a little twitchy, too, staring out a window, but with one hand near the sidearm she still wore. Our egress from New Lyons had been easier than anticipated. Silas was still tied in to the NLPD's computers, and we had Fortier and Thompson with all the latest intel that hadn't made it into those systems. We'd slipped past roadblocks and monitors like they didn't exist, using surface roads until we were well out of New Lyons, and then accessing the highway. Hell, with Fortier on board, we probably could have driven directly through any one of the checkpoints, so long as I stayed out of sight. But we hadn't gotten as far as we had by taking risks.

The others had taken the two cops in stride, since none of them had the history with Fortier than I did. Silas had even gone so far as to reach out to his network and ensure that Fortier's former Toys would be either brought into the fold or, at the very least, taken to a place of relative safety. I couldn't tell if the relief of Fortier's face was from thinking that they'd be taken care of, or that he wouldn't have to deal with them himself when all this was over.

We had gathered in what passed for the living area of the RV, with the door to the vehicle's single "bedroom" open but sealed off with plastic drop cloths and duct tape. I knew that the plastic also wrapped around the walls, floor, and ceiling, in an effort to isolate Silas, the room's sole occupant, as much as possible. One of the small windows in the back of the RV had been left unwrapped, and had even been cracked open, the proverbial airhole. I'd questioned that at first, but Tia had explained that the point was to protect those of us trapped in the small metal box from whatever plague Walton Biogenics had released, and not to stop any airborne particles from being sucked out the window and sprinkled over the highway. Her words, not mine. The risk, as she'd pointed out, of the virus actually finding a host that way was pretty slim.

The table, such as it was, was only big enough for four people. LaSorte claimed one of the seats of honor, as he had a half-dozen screens spread out before him. Al'awwal had the other, rounding out one side. Fortier and Thompson had squeezed into the other side, their respective—and very different—bulk making for a tight fit. Some bench seating ran along the wall on the opposite side of the table, and Hernandez, Tia, and I shoehorned onto it. I was, maybe, pressed up closer against Tia than was strictly speaking necessary, but I told myself that it was to give Hernandez a little more room. Besides, Tia didn't seem to mind. Silas had pulled a metal folding chair right up to the edge of the plastic. If it wasn't for the barrier, he could have reached out and touched the people at the table.

Fortier and Thompson were taking turns staring back and forth between Al'awwal and Silas. Al, in typical fashion, wasn't fucking about on the preparedness front. While most of us chose to leave the heavy gear in the bags, he'd strapped his Israeli bullpup to a tac-strap and had it close at hand. Fortier was looking at him with an expression that was half-incredulity and half-fear. "You sure he's a synthetic?" Fortier asked, directing the question my way.

"I can speak for myself," Al said. "And yeah, you're damn right I am." He patted the bullpup affectionately. "And yes, I can use this."

"Pretty effectively," I agreed. "And he kicked my ass when we were sparring."

Thompson stopped staring at Silas and his quarantine room, "And worked his way through a squad of the Special Response Team."

"Jesus," Fortier muttered. "And a fucking plague to boot. You didn't mention *that*, Hernandez."

Silas cleared his throat. Or tried to. It turned into more of a half-cough, half-strangle. No one spoke until the fit had passed. Silas twisted the cap off a bottle of water with one hand and took a long sip. "While I am sure," he said at last, "that we all have many things of which to speak, perhaps we should concentrate our efforts on the matter at hand. We will need some kind of plan when we approach the…" He paused, grimaced. "Potato Farm." A wan smile twisted his lips. "And I fear time is something of the essence."

That was an understatement, but it reminded everyone around the table of just how dire our circumstances were. "What have you been able to find?" I asked.

LaSorte took the cue, and started working his magic. "We're too cramped in here. Take a look at your screens."

I pulled out my personal screen, and, sure enough, found information already blossoming onto it. Most of it was basic—images from corporate marketing materials embedded within what looked like county-filed blueprints, satellite shots used for traffic apps, some heat mapping showing the highest periods of activity. I wasn't sure how LaSorte got that, but it conformed with a fairly standard workday, so maybe it was conjecture. Names and addresses of employees. And, the *piece de resistance*, the basic layout of the physical and electronic surveillance.

"Damn," Thompson said with a low whistle. "You guys are better than Cyber. You pulled this together in…what? Two days?"

LaSorte flashed his charming grin at the big rookie. "Something like that. But this,"—he waved one hand that encompassed all our screens,—"is the easy stuff. Some of it was behind pretty impressive firewalls, but, really, nothing to the degree that one might expect at a super-secret facility."

"Are we sure we have the right spot?" Tia asked. Her presence had earned surprised exclamations from both Thompson and Fortier, but she'd just grinned and shrugged and somehow had the pair laughing along with her in under a minute. I had no idea how she did it, and I could admit the tiniest itch of jealousy to see her laughing with Fortier, though I think I'd managed to keep it off my face. "We're kind of going on pure conjecture, here. And I'm not sure we should trust that Larkin woman."

"We did find one thing, Ms. Morita," Silas said from behind his plastic wall. "There are unusual power levels at that facility. With Ms. Larkin's help, we identified several 'standard' Farms and ran some cross analytics. We have a good estimation of how much energy a Walton synthetic facility would use, based on size. The Potato Farm…" He couldn't finish the sentence as another bout of coughing racked his body. He waved one hand toward LaSorte, who jumped into the gap.

"The Potato Farm is drawing about half again as much power as it should be," the former Toy said. "Something is going on there. Something way outside the specs of the other facilities we hacked. But that's all we could find."

I sighed. I'd been around Silas and LaSorte long enough to know that if they couldn't find something on the 'net it meant one of two things: the thing didn't exist, or it wasn't connected to any part of any network. "It's a black box," I said.

Silas and LaSorte nodded while Al'awwal, Tia, and the cops looked at me with confusion. "It's not connected to the 'net," I clarified.

"No way they can do… Well, any fucking thing without computers," Fortier snorted.

"They have computers, asshole," I said. "And networks and servers and the whole shebang. They're just not connected to any outside network. And if they need to use the 'net for something, I'm sure they can take a stroll upstairs, do what they have to do, save it to physical media, and then return to their work."

Thompson actually shuddered, and everyone else looked more than a little uncomfortable. The thought of being disconnected from the omnipresent 'net, even for the course of a workday, was…daunting. It was like a power outage or stepping back in time. And while some might romanticize the notion, or even practice a level of 'net-free living, most people loved the connectivity of modern life.

Silas broke the silence. "They are certain to have electronic and physical security in whatever this lab is. But we cannot access it from offsite. LaSorte and I will have to go with you when you go inside."

"Do we even know where inside *is*?" Hernandez asked. "I get that it's logical for this place to be here, but we can't logic it into existence. And what are we going to do? Wander around the secure Walton Biogenics facility while we try to find a secret door down into a top-secret and, if they are making killer synthetics down there, highly illegal lab?" She snorted. "I knew this might be a one-way trip, but I need to know we've got at least some chance of getting home again. I've got a daughter to think of."

Hernandez was right. I wanted this to work—needed it to. Millions would die if we were wrong. But if there was zero chance, if we were throwing our lives away in a futile gesture that no one would ever know about... Even if I might have been willing, I couldn't throw Hernandez into that grinder. Or Tia. I glanced over at her. She was frowning. Contemplating the problem, or having second thoughts?

"We still have work to do," Silas admitted. "Walton Biogenics may have set up a black box, but I do not think for a moment that they did the construction themselves. Somewhere, someone was hired. Records were kept. Plans filed. We have hours yet before we near our destination. LaSorte and I will find how to access the Potato Farm. And once we're inside, we can deal with any electronic security." He said it with confidence, and I had to believe him. He'd taken over the network at Larkin's workplace with such ease, and that had been without LaSorte riding shotgun. Silas gave us a smile that had nothing to do with happiness. "The rest will be up to the trigger pullers, as Mr. Campbell calls you."

"So, I guess we better figure out how we're going to get in, take down an army of synthetic soldiers, and get back out again," I agreed.

* * * *

We'd been turning the problem over for hours, with not a lot to show for it but short tempers and long odds. "We don't know enough," Thompson said, slapping his massive palm down onto the table to emphasize the point. The table rattled like a mouthful of loose teeth under the weight of the blow. "Sorry," he muttered, a blush blossoming on his cheeks. It made him seem even younger. "But I don't know how we make a plan when we don't even know how to get in the front door. Or if there is one."

"There is!"

It was LaSorte, his voice equal parts triumph and tiredness. All eyes went to the synthetic, who had pulled a folding chair up close to the plastic wall separating the rest of us from Silas so the two could converse. "There fucking is!" he reiterated. That widened more than one eye, since the amicable synthetic rarely swore. "We found it."

I looked over at Silas. "Want to explain? LaSorte seems a little excited."

Silas offered up a rare smile of his own. "With due cause, Detective," he said, slipping back into old habits. "With due cause." He flicked his screen and my own—and those of everyone else in the RV excepting LaSorte—chimed.

Like Pavlovian dogs, we all checked the message. It was a series of blueprints. No, not blueprints, or at least not the computer-designed building layouts that I thought of when I thought of blueprints. These appeared to have been hand drawn, with cursive notations written in. I had to squint and really concentrate—cursive hadn't been taught for a long time and might as well have been kanji for all the sense it made to most people. Growing up with academic parents had all sorts of unexpected benefits.

"What are we looking at?" Tia asked. "And what's the funny writing? Is that Cyrillic?"

Hernandez and Al chuckled, but the others looked equally confused. "No, Ms. Morita," Silas supplied. "The writing is in cursive, a popular technique used before the omnipresence of keypads. Think of it as the precursor to swipe-typing and you will not be far off. As for the documents themselves, they are an architect's plans for a large lab and synthetic growth facility, complete, you will notice, with several biohazard labs." Areas on the map began to receive color-coded overlays.

"Nice," Thompson said.

"How the hell, and where the hell, did you find this?" was Fortier's contribution.

"In the archived documents of an old estate sale, Detective Fortier," Silas said.

I shook my head. "Estate sale?"

"The path was convoluted," Silas admitted. "But we tracked down the architecture firm that Walton Biogenics had used to design several of their *farms*." His mouth twisted with distaste as he said the word.

"There was nothing on their servers," LaSorte interjected. Then he paused. "Well, okay. There was lots of stuff on their servers, but no plans for any secret bases."

"There were not," Silas agreed, throwing LaSorte an exasperated look. "So, we started hunting down the architects themselves."

Hernandez snorted. "And let me guess. You found that several of them had died under mysterious circumstances. Sounds just like our friends at Walton."

"Correct, Detective. Well, except for the 'mysterious' part. They all died of perfectly explainable, natural causes. Like heart attacks. Including the twenty-six-year-old marathoner." He gave another slim smile. "Which is where we eventually found the plans."

"Huh?" Fortier asked, not following. Not that I could blame him. I was only sort of with them.

"The marathoner was one of the architects for the Potato Farm," LaSorte chortled. "He must've kept plans. Was probably proud of the work or whatever. But when Walton offed him, those plans must have been part of his effects."

"Oh-kay," Fortier said, drawing out the word.

Tia let out a tiny laugh, almost a giggle, of her own. "And documents that don't contain any protected personal information get digitized and monetized when people die. It's part of the estate. Which means that Walton just shot themselves in the foot."

Fortier was still looking lost, and Thompson's face was screwed up into a mask of confusion. Well, they were new to the revolution, and until recently hadn't been thinking of Walton as the bad guys. "If Walton hadn't had the architects killed, odds are the plans would have never found their way into a computer," I said. "Meaning that in trying to cover up their little science experiment by killing off the people who designed it, they actually opened the door to us." I shrugged. "Well, metaphorically speaking. We're still going to have to kick down some doors."

"But now we know exactly where those doors are, Detective," Silas said. He did something on his screen, and the view on mine, and presumably the others', shifted and zoomed. "There are three entry points within the confines of the main building."

"No doubt heavily guarded," Thompson said.

The screen moved again. "And one that is significantly *outside* the main building."

The screen showed a spot in the middle, I shit you not, of a literal potato field. Okay, not in the middle of it. It appeared to be at the back entrance to a farmhouse. Silas tapped a few more buttons, and the image wireframed out and several overlays appeared. It was hard to make out, but it looked like there was what one would assume to be an old-style set of external cellar or storm shelter doors that instead led to a long tunnel. The tunnel traveled for almost two miles, before merging with the diagram of the Potato Farm.

"It's a bolt hole," I said.

"Correct, Jason," Silas agreed. "Or so we believe."

"What's a bolt hole?" Tia asked.

"Escape route," Hernandez said. "Probably for the corporate bigwigs to *vamos* if the police came knocking on their door."

"A back door out," I agreed. "Which means it's also a way in."

"It'll still be guarded," Fortier noted. "They're not gonna be dumb enough to leave the back door unlocked."

I nodded while Al said, "I bet the actual farm is a front. Probably a guard house of some sort." He thought about it for a moment. "Probably also means that the Potato Farm moniker started from someone in the know."

"Which means we're almost certainly at the right place," Thompson said.

"Which means we have a chance," Hernandez agreed.

"Yes," Silas said. He started to say something else, but another round of coughing took him. Once again, we were all quiet, with little we could do but watch the pale-skinned man suffer. Finally, he just waved a hand at us as he retreated, still choking and gasping, deeper into the chamber. Tia was on her feet in an instant, moving to the plastic, damn near pressing her face into it as she peered through, making sure that Silas hadn't collapsed. There hadn't been a way to make an airlock or the equivalent, so if she had to go in, it meant that Al and LaSorte were going to have to put on gas masks, and keep them on for the rest of the journey.

We all stared at each other helplessly for a long moment, and I saw Al twitching in the direction of the bag that held the gas masks. But then Tia turned back. "You guys keep talking. It looks like he's recovering. I don't see any sign of blood. It should be okay."

"Relatively speaking," Al'awwal muttered, and the rest of us could only nod.

"So," I said, trying to get things back on track, "we've got a target. We've got a way in. There's going to be physical security." I looked at Fortier and Thompson. Thought about it. Included Hernandez in my gaze. "We're not going to be able to dick around with whoever is there. Up until this point, we've tried to keep things as bloodless as possible, but that's about to change. There's no chances to surrender, no arrests. No warnings. You're not cops anymore. You're soldiers. Soldiers shoot to kill. Got it?"

"Sir, yes, sir," Fortier said with a mocking, half-assed salute.

"I'm fucking serious, Fortier," I growled. "I can't have this going to shit because someone hesitates."

"We're good," Thompson said softly. "Hernandez explained the situation. We knew what we were in for from the start." He offered a boyish grin. "Okay, the synthetic soldiers were a new twist, but still."

"Me, too," Hernandez said. "Not how I want to do it," she admitted. "But I understand the need." She looked uncomfortable. "I'll be okay with security, *hermano*," she said. "Just like the bully boys in the sewers. But if we run into unarmed civilians…" She trailed off and I nodded my understanding.

"Understood," I agreed. "If it comes to that, I'll do the dirty work. God willing, it won't come to that." She nodded.

Silas had returned to the plastic wall, looking wan and shaky. I noticed a few flecks of either spittle or vomit at the corners of his lips and looked closer while trying to hide what I was doing. Definitely not red. Not blood, then. I wasn't sure how far along in the sickness Silas really was, but until he started coughing blood, we at least had a chance.

"Okay," I continued. "Tia, we'll need you for this, too. Have a seat." She complied without comment, her mind clearly still working the problem of the illness. "We're going to have to break up into multiple teams," I began. It was going to be a long planning session, and time was slipping through our fingers. We'd only get one shot, and I was determined we'd make it count.

Chapter 18

"I've got two hostiles on the southeast corner of the building."

The whispered voice, Thompson, came through the earpiece of the tactical headset I wore. Thompson had informed us that one of the reasons he'd made the Special Response Team so quickly after joining the NLPD had been because he was, in his own humble opinion, a world-class marksman. It was a legacy learned hunting deer and wild hog, but he was a qualified sniper. He'd also brought a pair of his preferred long guns with him. They weren't quite the precision, match-grade rifles that were used by the NLPD, but there was a limit to how much equipment Hernandez, Thompson, and Fortier were able to sneak out. Thirty-thousand-dollar rifles were a bit out of their league. Still, we'd all been duly impressed by the bolt action thirty-ought-six with its night-vision and thermographic-enabled scope. He'd brought a spotting scope along as well, which Tia was currently running. She'd protested not being able to go in with the "ninja squad" as she called it, until Thompson had convinced her how important the second man—or woman—was in a sniper team. He wasn't just blowing smoke, either. An untrained spotter was better than no spotter at all.

The fact that it kept her away from the shooting, at least for the opening act, was just a fringe benefit.

We'd split into four teams. Thompson and Tia were hanging back in an overwatch position. It was their job to spot the bad guys and, if the shit hit the fan, provide some precision covering fire. It would have been nice to have Thompson put his skills to use and thin the herd for us, but no matter how much of a tack-driver his thirty-ought-six was, it spoke with authority. If he started popping melons, the bad guys would know we were here with plenty of time to let the *other* bad guys know we were coming. At that point, the entire operation would pretty much be tits up.

The second team was made up of me and Al'awwal. I would have preferred Hernandez, but there was no way in hell I was putting Fortier and a synthetic together. Particularly a synthetic like Al, who I was pretty sure would be willing to put a bullet in Fortier if he slipped into old habits.

So, it was me and Al, low-crawling through the snow. There weren't a lot of things that could make me miss sand and hardpan, but trying to push yourself through a fallow field covered in at least six inches of snow using only your knees and elbows was one of them.

At least I was properly kitted out, for the first time in what felt like forever. Tactical gray digicam utilities gloves, boots, balaclava. Plate carrier and MOLLE webbing with all the trimmings. An honest-to-god forty-five back on my hip and a sweet little German subgun, complete with silencer, in my hands. If it wasn't for the whole fate of the world hanging in the balance thing, I might even have been having fun.

We were sweeping around the left side of the long driveway that led through the fields and up to the farmhouse while the third team, Fortier and Hernandez, made their way up the right side. The final team consisted of LaSorte and Silas. They were hanging back with the sniper element until we cleared out any enemy shooters. LaSorte had an array of equipment with him, and had said something about sniffing for wireless. I trusted him to deal with that. The only advantage of the empty rolling fields was that there wasn't anything vertical on which to mount a camera. Until we got close to the house, surveillance was going to be limited to the standard issue Mark 1 human eyeball.

"One of the hostiles is mobile. Moving down the driveway. Might be the start of a standard patrol."

"Dammit," I whispered. We'd started well away from the driveway, but there was no way to crawl through the snow-covered fields without leaving tracks. The moon was about half full, and its pale luminescence cast enough light across the snow-shrouded fields that it was possible our trail would be spotted. Then I keyed my mic. "If it looks like he notices the tracks, we're going to have to take him down."

"I've got our end," Fortier's voice came back. He and I were kitted out pretty much the same, meaning we were both carrying silenced submachine guns. Hernandez had made sure that the rounds were subsonic. They didn't carry as much muzzle velocity as supersonic rounds, but the silencers were far more effective. Still not like the vids, but quiet enough that the sound of the subgun's action would probably be louder than the sound of the bullet.

"Roger that," I whispered back. "I'm on it from our side."

"Eyes on," Thompson said.

I shrugged out of my pack and moved it around until it was positioned before me. Then I proned myself out in the snow, ignoring the cold that was creeping through the insulated fatigues. I rested the barrel of my subgun on the pack, using it for a shooting rest. Then I flicked on the holographic sight. The green reticule appeared in the glass panel of the sight and I started scanning the driveway. The same moonlight that could betray us gave us good visibility, and I saw a form moving away from the house. We'd begun our approach about fifty yards from the roadway. I was set up for close combat and the scope was zeroed at twenty-five yards. I wasn't sniper qualified, but I was a fair distance shooter and understood the difference between line of sight and ballistic arc. Most people would think the farther out the shot, the higher you needed to aim, accounting for the effect of gravity on the round. They were right, to a point. But bullets were designed to leave the barrel on a slight upward line, meaning that a round actually crossed a weapon's zero twice, following a natural ballistic arc.

I hadn't even had a chance to test fire this weapon, but I'd used similar ones. Assuming the zero was good, I was actually going to need to move my point of aim a little lower. It would be better if I didn't have to take the shot at all. Once we dropped the first guard we started a clock that we couldn't stop. But we couldn't risk being found out, either. One radio call, one yell, and the entire operation was blown.

"Hostile is almost lateral to your position, Team Two," Thompson said. "Something's caught his eye."

I could see it. My optic offered no magnification, but at fifty yards, I didn't need it. I couldn't make out details, couldn't tell you what the guy looked like, but the track of his head was unmistakable.

"Shit. He's seen the trail. Repeat. He's seen the trail. Take the shot."

I'd already started drawing in a steadying breath before Thompson began. As he said "Repeat" I was settling the reticule just below the center point of the target's torso. I released the breath halfway, holding it for a split moment as I squeezed the trigger. One round. The target lurched, staggered a step. Fell as Thompson said, "Shot." I kept the reticule trained on what I hoped was a corpse. If I saw movement, I'd have to shoot again, to make sure no alarm went out.

"Who has eyes on hostile two?" Al'awwal was whispering into the radio.

"Still by the corner of the house," Tia said. "I don't think he noticed."

"Confirm status of one," I snapped.

"Hostile down," Thompson confirmed. "Wait one. Going thermal to scan the house."

While Thompson did that, I shimmied my way back into my pack. "We've got four more in the house," he confirmed a moment later.

"We've got to move," I said. "The one outside is going to be getting antsy soon."

Hernandez's voice came over the radio. "We'll sweep around to the back. Once we're in position, you take down the front door. We'll crash from the back. Thompson, once we knock on the door, take whatever shot you can."

"Roger that, Detective."

We moved forward, a little faster now, staying low to the ground and curving slightly away from the house, trying to stay out of the direct line of sight of the guy on the front door as long as possible. "Talk to me, Tia," I said, a little breathless from the adrenaline and effort. "What's the hostile on the door doing?"

"He's just standing there," she said. "Wait. He's looking down the driveway. This spotting scope's amazing. I can see his expression. He looks... I don't know. Worried, maybe."

"Shit," I muttered. "Guy's starting to get antsy." We'd closed the direct distance to the house to about thirty yards, but had swept far enough to the side that the distance was closer to forty.

"Do you have the shot?" Al asked.

I dropped to both knees, bringing the subgun back to my shoulder and aligning the sights.

"Hold," Thompson barked. "You've got a hostile at the window. Wait one."

"Fuck," I muttered. I was kneeling in damn near zero cover in the middle of a fucking field. All the hostile had to do was glance in my direction and it was over. "What's he doing, Tia?"

"Still looking down the driveway."

"If he so much as glances in my direction or reaches for a radio, tell me. Roger that?" I asked. I could hear the clipped, urgent tone in my own voice. I breathed deep and slow, trying to calm my racing heartrate. Al'awwal had dropped prone at my side, and he had his own rifle pointed in the direction of the house. I could see him actively scanning the visible windows, trying to find the target that Thompson's thermographic scope had picked out.

"Roger that," Tia replied, and though it was the correct response, it struck me as so out of place that I had to smile. I felt my breathing calm and my heart beat slow, just a little bit.

"Window's clear. Take him," Thompson snapped. This time, I didn't even register the mechanics of the shot. One second the target was up, the next he was down and Al'awwal and I were sprinting for the door. I stepped over the body and took up position on the right side of the door as Al'awwal mirrored me on the left.

"We good?" I asked.

"Yeah." Tia's voice was shaking. "The...hostile...is down. I...saw it."

Damn. Hadn't planned on that, but I had told her to watch the guy like a hawk. "House still seems quiet," Thompson said.

"It's alarmed." LaSorte, chiming in on the radio for the first time. "We've isolated the signal. We're working on trapping it."

"Work fast," Hernandez replied. "We're almost in position."

"And we're holding," I whispered into the mic.

The seconds ticked by and I felt a tightness in my shoulders that started to slowly spread to my back and neck. Maybe three minutes had passed since I'd fired the first shot, but it felt like hours. "We're in position at the back door," Hernandez checked in. "Status?"

"Almost there," LaSorte said. "One minute."

Fortier snapped, "Hurry the fuck up. We might not have a minute." I wondered how long it had been since the fat detective had been on a case where he might get shot at.

"One minute," LaSorte said again. I could hear the tapping in the background and, faintly, the sound of Silas coughing. The albino synthetic hadn't said anything over the radio. I had a brief moment of worry that it was because he couldn't.

"Any time now," Hernandez said.

"Got it," LaSorte replied triumphantly. "Alarm's down."

"Thompson?"

"You've got three on the ground floor and one upstairs," the sniper replied.

"Roger that," Hernandez said. "On my go." Time for one more deep breath, and then Hernandez shouted, "Go! Go! Go!"

Like we'd practiced it a thousand times, Al'awwal stepped into the doorway, raised his leg and slammed the flat of his boot into the door. It exploded inward, the dead bolt no match for the synthetic's strength. I heard the rear door smash open even as I swept past Al'awwal, subgun up and at the ready. Then the thunderous report of the thirty-ought-six sounded, almost simultaneous with the shattering of glass somewhere overhead. Thompson taking down the bad guy on the second floor.

A form came darting from somewhere to the right, and Al'awwal opened up, his bullpup barking once, twice, three times. The body dropped. Two down. From deeper in the house came the roar of Hernandez's twelve gauge. Then the house fell into silence.

"One down," Thompson said.

"One here." Al'awwal.

"And two makes four," Hernandez finished.

"Thermal's clear," Thompson said.

Al and I were still moving through the first floor, clearing room by room. Thermal imaging wasn't perfect and there were plenty of natural and man-made features that might mask a heat signature. "Wait one," I replied as we continued our sweep. We met up with Fortier and Hernandez, and they fell into the stack with practiced ease. I might not have liked Fortier, and he might have looked like someone who sat on their ass professionally, but he moved well and did his job.

"Upstairs," I said, and the others nodded.

It took maybe ten minutes to clear the place to everyone's satisfaction. Every closet, every bathroom, every nook or cranny where a person could conceivably stuff themselves needed to be checked. When we were done, I keyed my mic again. "Clear. Come forward."

"Roger. On the move," Thompson replied.

It was warm in the house, warm enough that between the surge of action, the stress, and the thirty pounds of gear, I was starting to sweat pretty good. Fortier looked like he'd taken a swim in a particularly polluted pond, and ever Hernandez's face showed a light sheen. Only Al'awwal appeared impervious to the rigors of the last few minutes. The synthetic had ejected the magazine from his bullpup and was casually topping it off with a few loose rounds from a pocket. Which reminded me we were sharing the farm with a half-dozen corpses.

"Let's check these guys," I said, earning a combination of groans and nods from the others.

A cursory search revealed that the security we'd taken down were human, not synthetic. I wasn't sure if that was a good thing or a bad thing. They were all armed, and they all had radios. "We should probably grab one," Fortier said, gesturing at a radio. "Maybe we can listen in on the others."

I grunted. "Don't bother. Leave it to Silas and LaSorte. They'll be able to rig something up."

"Your vote of confidence is appreciated, Jason," Silas said as he entered the room. Well, staggered into it would be more appropriate. Apart from the one bad fit on the way to the farm, Silas had seemed not fine, but operational. Now, he looked like two hundred pounds of hammered shit. His skin was pallid with a thin sheen of sweat that had nothing to do with exertion. He stood with one arm thrown over LaSorte's shoulder and while the gas mask he wore blocked most of his face, I could tell from the set of his shoulder and the look in his eyes that he was in physical pain. Thompson and Tia had entered the house as well, and Tia's eyes locked onto Silas. The look on her face, part horror, part compassion, showed that she, too, was shocked by his rapid deterioration.

"Fuck's sake, Silas. Are you okay?" I asked. It was a stupid question.

"The gas mask has put an unexpected strain on my breathing," he admitted. Now that the shock of his appearance had worn off, I could hear the strain in his words. I silently cursed myself. Of course he'd have a harder time breathing. The masks forced you to draw air in through a filter. It was about twice as much work as normal breathing.

"Lose the mask," Al'awwal said with a shrug.

"Agreed," LaSorte said.

"I will not expose either of you to…" Silas began, but LaSorte cut him off.

"Oh, screw that, Silas. We've all been exposed already and we know it's just a matter of time. Maybe we couldn't risk it on the drive, but we're at the end, now. And if we don't win here…" He trailed off. Shrugged. Left the obvious unspoken.

"And you feel this way as well, Al'awwal? You who are the First among us?"

"We need you functional, Silas," Al replied. "If LaSorte has to literally carry you everywhere, I'm not sure you qualify. Plus, your hands are shaking. Could you even work a screen right now?"

"No," Silas acknowledged. "But—"

"Enough," I cut in. "We don't have time for this. They're right. Ditch the mask. We need to hurry the fuck up."

While we were talking, Tia had been looking through a messenger bag she had packed herself. She pulled out a syringe and grabbed Silas by the arm. "Hold still," she said, squirting a little bit of the liquid out of the needle. "I'm going to give you something for the pain."

"I'm not sure that's—"

"Shut up. Take the mask off. And hold still. Doctor's orders." Tia softened her words with a smile.

"Of course, doctor," Silas replied, pulling the mask from over his head. His breathing eased a bit as soon as the seal of the mask was broken and a little bit of the color returned to his face.

"Small pinch," Tia said as she jabbed the needle into his arm and depressed the plunger. Silas drew another shuddering breath and actually sighed. "Better?" Tia asked.

"Much better, Ms. Morita," he responded. "Now, I believe, as may have been pointed out, we are in a bit of a hurry." He straightened, standing on his own. He didn't look super steady, but at least he didn't need to rely on LaSorte for balance. "If someone will help me sit, I'll see what I can do about getting up on this radio. While I do that, LaSorte can accompany you to the bolt hole and deal with any electronic security there."

* * * *

The bolt hole doors—which on the surface looked like simple storm doors to an underground cellar—proved to be something else entirely. It had taken Silas and LaSorte a solid fifteen minutes, while the rest of us stood shivering in the cold, to hack their way through them. When they opened, the doors dropped down about six inches and then slid into recesses along either side of what proved to be a stairway leading down. The doors themselves were damn near as thick as the recesses into which they slid and appeared to be made of solid steel.

"Definitely not a root cellar," I quipped, taking point.

"You think?" Hernandez said. She'd given the shotgun to Tia in favor of her nine-millimeter. She had, at some point, secured an under barrel tactical flashlight, which she flicked on. I did the same with my own tac light, and the high-lumen beams sent shafts of light piercing the darkness. Fortier slotted into position behind Hernandez, followed by Thompson, Silas, LaSorte, and Tia. Al took the rear, securing our six.

"We've got about a two-mile hike to get to the facility," I noted. "We're going to move quick." I gave Silas a hard stare. "If we move too quick, say something. We need you on the other end. Understood?"

"Understood, Jason," Silas replied. He still looked like shit, but he was moving under his own power and he'd managed to hack into the enemy radio frequency. It was just dead air, which meant that there was a good chance it was just the team frequency for the guards at the house, but if it did come into use, we'd have a window into the enemy's operations. Always useful.

"Let's move out."

The bolt hole didn't have much to offer. Once we got past the initial stairway and the landing at the bottom, it quickly became clear that the tunnel was little more than a massive culvert, roughly eight feet in diameter. The sloping walls made it difficult to do anything other than walk single file down the middle. A string of lights hung overhead, but they weren't lit, and I took that as a positive sign. At least we didn't seem to be expected.

The whole setup made me itch. We were lined up like ducks in a row in the proverbial shooting gallery. A blind geriatric could take us all down with a little bit of luck and maybe a mag change.

We made the journey in silence, since we couldn't risk sound carrying. Every twenty minutes or so, Tia, who had more of a knack for this than I'd have thought, made us stop while she sprayed some sort of numbing agent down Silas's throat, taking advantage of the fact that he wasn't wearing the mask. From the expression on his face, it tasted terrible and, in general, wasn't the most pleasant of experiences. But it effectively killed his cough. Kind of hard to sneak down a giant concrete tube if someone is busy hacking up a lung.

After the first mile, we killed the lights, switching to the night vision goggles that Hernandez had been able to secure. There weren't enough sets for everyone—again, only so much equipment could walk away from the precinct without someone noticing, but Hernandez, me, Fortier, and Thompson had the gear. We strung a line between us so the others could hold on. It slowed us down, and the snail's pace was another niggling itch against my tactical sensibilities, but it couldn't be helped. Better to move slow than let the enemy know you were coming.

All told, it took us just over an hour to cross the distance. As we neared the end, we could see a single red-tinged light burning above another set of stairs. There didn't seem to be any guards, and I couldn't make out any obvious electronic surveillance devices. Not that I'd be able to see the high-end stuff with the naked eye, but that was why we had LaSorte and Silas. The light was enough to see by, so I slid the night vision goggles off.

Silas had his hands full trying to stay upright, though he didn't seem to mind the tunnel or the darkness in the slightest. I remembered that he was a Tunnel Rat, grown for exactly this kind of environment. But LaSorte had been moving with his screen out, with some sort of odd, cobbled together antenna sticking out of it. As we got closer to the light he stopped, giving the rope a light tug. We all immediately paused. I sank to one knee, bringing the subgun up, and I could feel Hernandez taking a firing position over my shoulder. I hoped to God we didn't have to shoot anyone like this. In a concrete tube, with her so close, the gunfire might well rupture my eardrums.

My eyes were glued to the light ahead, straining for any kind of motion, but I could hear LaSorte tapping away at his screen. There was a long moment and then a very faint beep. "There were motion sensors ahead," he warned in a barely audible whisper. "And cameras. I've deactivated the motion sensors. I can flip the cameras off whenever, but I can't spoof them."

"Damn," I muttered. I doubted that panic would ensue the moment the screens went blank, but someone, somewhere would be sent to check and see why they malfunctioned. Which meant that the clock would start ticking a hell of a lot faster. But there was no helping it.

I stepped to the side and edged back, Hernandez moving up automatically to take point. I turned so that I was facing the wall, but so that I could keep my companions and the entry to the facility in my peripheral vision. "We're going to do this fast," I said. "When LaSorte kills the cameras, we run the rest of the distance. LaSorte, Silas, when we get there, you're going to have to hack the door fast. We can't afford a fifteen-minute wait."

"It should be quicker this time, Campbell," LaSorte said. "Assuming it's set up like the other end, anyway."

"Good. Once the door's open, all bets are off. We know the layout, but we don't necessarily know what's where. Tia's the only one of us who has any real idea what we're looking for. She's priority one. We have to keep her alive."

"Wait, what?" Tia started to ask, but I cut her off.

"Sorry, Tia. No argument on this. The cure is all that matters, and you're the only one with the training to identify and administer it." In the faint red light, her face was a mask of shadows, and I couldn't read her expression, but she quieted. I continued. "We move quick. We keep it quiet as long as we can. We avoid alarms as long as we can. But once we trigger them—and make no mistake, we will—then it's fast and loud. We go from cat burglars to a smash and grab. Everyone clear?"

I could see them nodding. "Good." I slipped back in position, taking point once more. I pulled the NVGs from my head, stuffed them back in my pack. I heard the others doing the same. We'd have them if we needed them, but odds were pretty good there would be lights on the other side of the door. "Kill the cameras."

I heard a rather emphatic tap at the screen. "Done."

"Move, move, move," I snapped. I put action to my words rushing down the hallway. I covered the ground quick and double-timed it up the stairs, aware of Hernandez at my back. The others fanned out in the landing, those with firearms taking up shooting positions to cover the door. LaSorte made his way up the stairs and knelt before the screen embedded in the wall to the side of the door.

"Same tech," he said. "Two minutes."

I waited, rifle at the ready as LaSorte worked the screens. Then he was stepping back, his personal screen in hand. "On your word, Detective."

"Go."

Somewhere in the walls, gears started whirring, and the doors began to open.

Chapter 19

I took a kneeling position on the stairs, clearing Hernandez's fire zone above me and getting closer to the entry. I peered through the rapidly expanding crack between the doors, straining to pick up on any danger.

I could see little of the room beyond. Just a small, empty space, maybe eight feet on a side with an industrial looking fire door facing directly opposite the bolt hole. Light filtered in from a window set high above the door, giving enough illumination to see, but painting the room in shades of gray. No sign of any people, for which I was grateful. We were still firmly in a shooting gallery. I'd be a hell of a lot happier when we could get some cover.

The doors opened enough for me to slip through. I surged forward, crossing the distance to the other door in two strides and posting up beside the doorframe. Hernandez was on the other side in an instant, with the rest moving in and taking up positions along the wall. LaSorte was the only exception, as he panned a flashlight around the room, keeping it at about knee level. The circle of light traced the wall, pausing at each electrical outlet for a moment before moving on.

"Nothing here," he whispered. "We need to get somewhere where I can hardwire to their network." He pulled his screen out, and from the corner of my eye, I could see him flicking and zooming across something. The blueprints, most likely. Then he worked his way past the line of shooters, having enough sense to stick close to the wall in case the door burst open, until he had taken the position right behind me. "I think we need to go here," he said, pointing at the screen.

I took my eyes from the door long enough to study the map. He'd outlined a path from our current position, past a few larger rooms and intersections and down a long hallway. On either side of the hallway were a number of small eight by eight rooms. Nothing was labeled—the files Silas and LaSorte had managed to track down either hadn't ever shown what the space was going to be used for, or that information had been added later. But the purpose seemed clear enough. "Office space?" I asked.

"I think so," LaSorte replied. "If they are, I should be able to wire into the network."

We knew we couldn't wander blindly around a vast underground facility. So the plan was to find a spot where Silas and LaSorte could plug in, and wait while they cracked open the network and spilled out all the secrets contained therein. We'd then use the information to locate the cure, secure it, and get the fuck out of Dodge, hopefully before we were noticed. That last part was a long shot, but we could hope.

"Right," I said. "Looks like it's fairly close, too. We'll make a play for it. You drop back, and send Al forward." LaSorte nodded. A moment later, Al'awwal was by my side. "We're going to boost Hernandez up," I said. "So that she can have a look through that window and see what's what."

"Roger that."

"I get to have all the fun," Hernandez chimed in from her side of the door.

I ignored her as Al and I both set a shoulder against the door, standing facing each other. We held each other firmly at the wrist, right arm to right arm, left to left. In addition to providing us some extra stability for lifting up Hernandez, the position had the added benefit of putting my bulk and Al's as a barrier against opening the door. It had probably been under two minutes since we took out the cameras, maybe not long enough for security to even have noticed, much less send a response team. If they were on the ball, though, a team would be en route. Or there could simply be people out in the corridor, going about their normal business.

We both sank into a squat position, and Hernandez stepped up onto our crossed arms, putting a hand on each of our shoulders to steady herself. She was small, but fit and solid. Still, we managed the weight easily. Hell, Al'awwal could probably have curled her. We straightened our legs slowly, lifting her until her eyes cleared the bottom sill of the window. "Little higher," she muttered. "I need a better angle." We lifted more, until I was standing not-quite stiff-legged. It was a tiring position, and I could feel my quads starting to tremble. She surveilled for a good thirty seconds. Then, "Down," she said.

We reversed the procedure, and she hopped off our arms. "Long corridor to the left. Nothing to the right. Dead ends, just like on the map. No sign of people. No cameras that I make out. A few doors. Everything seems to line up to the blueprints."

That was good news, at least. "We move quick," I said. "If we meet resistance, we try to take them down quiet. But don't be stupid. If we have to go loud, we go loud. They're not expecting us, so hopefully we can maintain an element of surprise even once the shooting starts."

There were nods all around and then we were moving. I visualized the blueprints in my head while wishing for the augmented reality helmets that would have been part of the standard kit for the Special Response Teams. Still, even without the map projected directly into my field of vision, it wasn't hard to remember where we were going. And even if it was, Silas and LaSorte were non-combatants. Both of them moved with their eyes to their screens. If we took a wrong turn, I had no doubt they'd correct it. We moved in good order, me on point, Hernandez behind me, then Fortier. Fortier and I had the only silenced weapons, though "silenced" would be a relative term in the narrow hallways. The rest were strung out behind us in a tight line.

We passed several doors along the way, but didn't deviate from the plan. Any one of them could have provided access to the network. Hell, any one of them could have held the cure. It was just as likely that they held a security team, or that opening one would trigger an alarm somewhere. We had a solid plan, and we were going to stick to it. From my best estimation, we were maybe twenty or thirty feet from the hallway where what we hoped was office space should be. Another few seconds and…

We turned a corner and ran full on into Walton Biogenics Security.

It was a team of three, wearing the same blazers I remembered from the lab. In that first frantic instant, I couldn't tell if they were human or synthetic, but it didn't matter. The response had to be the same in either case. Firing the silenced subgun would sound about like dropping a stack of books. Maybe quiet enough that it wouldn't be noticed. Maybe not. The security team didn't have weapons out, so I surged forward, letting my gun dangle from its strap. I was vaguely aware of the Hernandez and Fortier moving into action as well.

Surprise was on our side, and the fight was short and brutal. I looked into the widening eyes of the first member of the security team as my elbow lifted above my head and sliced down at a forty-five-degree angle, palm turned toward the bad guy. My elbow smashed across the bridge of his nose in an explosion of blood and I heard the louder crack of the zygomatic bone. He dropped to the ground. I turned, ready for the next guard, but it was already over. Fortier had produced a baton from somewhere in his gear, and while my former nemesis may have been hefty, there was obviously strength there as well. He'd laid out a guard with one well-placed blow, and from the amount of blood pooling on the concrete floor, had probably killed the man. He didn't look too upset about it, either.

Hernandez was behind the third guard, a rear naked choke in place. I hadn't seen her attack, but from the inhuman angle of the security guard's knee and the countless hours I'd practiced on the mats with her, I knew what had happened. She had stepped around the security guard, lashing out with a well-placed side kick that impacted just above the knee, separating the femur from the patella and destroying the MCL and LCL. That alone would have been enough to end any fight, but she had slipped behind the man as he was falling, locking in the choke, and using his own weight and momentum to finish it. It was one of her favorite techniques, though she had never executed it fully in training, for obvious reasons.

I briefly considered the bodies. Three large men, all three down. I did a quick check, and sure enough, found the skin tag on all three. Synthetics. All three were also carrying sidearms. "At least we're in the right place," I muttered. I considered whether to try to stash the bodies or leave them where they lay. Fortier's guy was going to be out for a while. I could see the slight rise and fall of his chest, so Fortier hadn't killed him, after all. At least, not yet. But we weren't about to administer first aid. Still, only Hernandez had managed a bloodless takedown, and even if we hid the bodies somewhere, the pool of blood was going to raise eyebrows. And the alarm.

"We leave 'em," I said. "Let's move."

We turned the corner, and found ourselves in the hallway of what I hoped were office doors. No heads were poking out, wondering at the commotion. In fact, from what I could tell, the offices were dark. No light was bleeding out from beneath the doors. There were also no name tags or any other identifiers affixed to the portals, beyond a simple number. The doors, stark white against the darker gray of the unpainted concrete, were somehow unsettling. I wondered if, instead of offices, we were about to open cell doors. The place had that kind of feel to it.

"That's not creepy at all," Hernandez muttered, shifting her grip on her pistol.

"Any one is as good as the rest, I guess," I whispered in return. I chose a door at random. The number centered at eye level was four. Trusting the others to move behind me and keep alert for threats from other vectors, I let my subgun fall back onto its sling and drew my forty-five. I used my left hand to test the knob—it was unlocked. I threw a quick glance at

Hernandez, who gave me a nod. Then I threw the door open and bolted inside, moving left and sweeping the small interior with my pistol.

Empty. The lights flicked on as I stepped in, triggered by a motion sensor. The room was simple, with a desk, chair, screen, and hutch. The walls were unadorned. The desk was clean. No loose papers or personal effects. "Clear," I said.

The other piled in, and with eight of us in the small space things felt real cramped, real quick. We had to jostle and shuffle around to let Silas drop into the chair in front of the scree, LaSorte standing and peering over his shoulder.

"Something doesn't feel right about this," Hernandez muttered.

"This whole place feels off," Thompson agreed.

"It's quiet... Too quiet," Al chimed in, drawing out the phrase and wriggling his eyebrows. It was trite, but that didn't make it less true. I'm not sure what I had been expecting at a top-secret Walton Biogenics facility, but dimly lit hallways, empty offices, and small security teams weren't it.

Silas and LaSorte were busy working their magic, and all the rest of us could do was stand in tense silence, waiting. No matter how quiet things were, we had just butchered a security team, so we knew the place wasn't completely abandoned.

"We are in," Silas said. His voice was quieter than normal, straining against the numbing agent Tia continued to give him from time to time. "It appears this facility is in the process of being decommissioned."

"Decommissioned?" Tia asked. She looked uncomfortable in her tactical gear, the shotgun that seemed almost as long as she was tall cradled in her arms.

"I suppose once you release a plague designed to kill every synthetic on the face of the planet, it doesn't make much sense to keep the factories open," Fortier said.

"Maybe not," I agreed, wincing slightly at *factories*. Even if it was sort of the right term. "But they've still got security on site. Hopefully that means they've still got something worth guarding. And if we're really fucking lucky, maybe it means a lot *less* security and no civilians to get in the way if things go south."

"I think we've got something," LaSorte interrupted, still reading his screen. "Looks like there's a medical facility toward the north end of the compound. Several laboratories listed, as well as testing and research facilities."

"That's our best shot," I said. "Can you send it to us?" Before I even finished asking, our screens beeped. "Good. What about electronic security?"

"Allow us a few more minutes, Detective," Silas said. "There are measures in place, but I believe that we can defeat them. Many seem to have been deactivated as part of the decommissioning process." I supposed that made sense. Not a lot of point paying for high-tech security on an empty vault.

The minutes ticked by and my skin began to itch. The security patrol had to be missed by now. Which meant that another patrol would be heading out. How large of a security force had been left behind at the "decommissioned" facility? A dozen? More? We'd gotten lucky with the first three. Taken them by surprise. But if we had to go up against a well-trained and well-armed force, things wouldn't be so easy.

"We have done it," Silas said, voice triumphant. "We cannot take over their security measures, but we can deactivate them as we go, turning them back on in our wake. And we can make sure that no alarm or electronic lock will stand in our way."

"Good," I said. "Then let's roll."

We moved out, working our way into the corridor and through the twisting nightmare of intersections. If you didn't know what you were doing, the place really *was* a maze. There were no signs indicating where you were or where you might be headed, no convenient color coding to prevent you from getting lost. Nothing. Not even a legally required emergency evacuation plan. If it wasn't for the blueprint, we'd have been wandering around down here for hours, with no fucking clue. I realized once again just how central Silas and, to a lesser extent, LaSorte, were to the entire revolution.

We'd been moving deeper and deeper into the complex until we came to a door that was quite different from the others. Either Silas's electronic magic was working, or we'd gotten extremely lucky, because if security was on to us, they hadn't managed to cross our paths. Unlike the plain wooden doors we'd seen up until now, this one was made of metal, steel from the look of it. There were two doors side by side, with latches rather than knobs. They reminded me vaguely of hospital doors, the kind that were built to take impacts from gurneys and swing out of the way. Only more solid, somehow.

There was a screen to the right of the doors, glowing a soft red. That lasted for about three seconds, as Silas tapped his personal screen. The glow shifted through amber and to green, and the click of a heavy lock disengaging was clearly audible in the hallway. There was no signage present on the door and no windows. We had no idea what we were stepping into.

I went first, and I went fast. When stealth wasn't an option, speed was often the best bet. I hit the door with my shoulder and followed it in at a near sprint, conscious of Hernandez and the others on my heels. That lasted for about three strides, and then my legs caught up with my eyeballs and I came to a skidding halt.

The room was vast, easily the size of a football field. I should have realized, from the maps that we had seen. The roof stretched a good thirty feet above us. The stairs from the surface level hadn't delved that deep. The room must have stretched up into the building built above it. Or maybe the topography of the land was different, and the overt façade of the Potato Farm was built atop a hill. Or maybe the two miles walk to get here from the farmhouse had been on a steady, if hardly noticeable, decline.

I shook my head, forcing the thoughts aside. Forcing my mind back to the actual reason I'd come to a skidding halt. It wasn't the scale of the room, no matter how impressive. No. It was the contents.

I didn't have a word for the machinery that filled the room. Too many science fiction vids and games gave me an approximation: cryo chambers. But, no. That wasn't quite right. More like specimen tubes. If specimen tubes were made big enough to hold a fully grown human.

Or synthetic.

They stretched from floor to ceiling stacked one on top of the other and stretching into neat rows, like the shelves in an old grocery store before delivery services had made that sort of shopping obsolete. I wished to God that they were empty. But they weren't.

The bodies were recognizable, if only just. The ones I could see were men and women who had, at some point, been fit and trim and in the kind of shape that everyone envied but only professional athletes or early twenty-somethings could actually achieve. Unless, of course, you were synthetic. At some point, because those I could see were several days into the process of putrefaction.

The corpses were unclothed and floating in some sort of transparent fluid. Whatever it was, it wasn't alcohol or formaldehyde, or anything else that might deter microbial action. Bodies decaying in liquid were never pretty, and the bloated, discolored flesh that stared out at us from behind the glass was the stuff of nightmares. No. A single body like that was the stuff of nightmares. We had to be looking at hundreds. Maybe thousands.

"Jesus, Joseph, and Mary," Fortier gasped. Thompson was making a retching sound, reminding me that despite all the action he'd seen, in some ways he was still as green as any other rookie. Hernandez was taking it in stride, at least as much as I was, which is to say, not actively vomiting. I turned a worried eye on Tia, fearing the worst, only to find her pressed close up against the nearest cylinder, examining the contents with a professional eye. She'd been acting as a doctor to the living for long enough that I had almost forgotten her original calling was to minister to the dead.

But as surprising as her interest was, the expressions on the faces of Silas, LaSorte, and Al'awwal were worse. All three wore the same expression. There was disgust there, but that only scratched the surface. Fear. Shame. Guilt. And beneath it all, a hatred so pure that it made me shudder to look at it.

"What the fuck is this?" Thompson asked, wiping vomit from his mouth as he straightened back up.

"This is Walton Biogenics at its finest," LaSorte spat.

"This is the ultimate perversion of my father's life work," Al'awwal added. I could see his fingers white-knuckle tight on his rifle.

"This is how synthetics are grown," Silas said. His voice was the calmest of the three, but there was something in that calm that was somehow all the more terrifying. It reminded me of arctic warfare training in Alaska and learning how to cross frozen rivers and streams. Those seemed calm, too. Right up until the point that the ice cracked and you were swept into the torrent of icy darkness that flowed just beneath the surface.

"These are adults," Tia pointed out, still studying the...contents. "Fully grown. It was my understanding that synthetics could only be grown no later than early teenaged years or certain...psychological problems would develop."

"So we've all been told," Al'awwal said. "But who knows? Maybe that's just another Walton lie."

"It is far easier to brainwash someone before said brain is fully developed," Silas added.

"Then why now?" Fortier asked. "Why start growing people to...to... fuck it. To adults?"

No one answered for a moment as we worked over the problem. Then it hit me. "Soldiers," I said. "Child soldiers aren't much use. They probably started growing these a few months ago, when we began our little rebellion. Against a potential future need."

"I thought they attacked you when you went after Larson," Tia said.

"True. I'm not saying that Walton hasn't had these soldiers for years. But maybe there were only small batches. Maybe even grown the traditional way, to children first and then trained." I glanced around the vast chamber, at the hundreds of capsules. "It's obviously more than a pilot program," I admitted. "But if we're lucky, there were only a small amount to begin with."

"A process which was accelerated with our actions," Silas mused. "Perhaps when we took over the airwaves on New Year's Eve, they implemented this new version of the program."

"And when Campbell turned himself in, and they opted for their final solution, they decided to...terminate?" Thompson asked. He still looked a little shaky, but at least he was able to look at the capsules.

"I think the word you're looking for is 'abort,'" Al'awwal said. He rubbed one hand at the stubble on his face. "Most likely to start getting rid of the evidence. Same reason for the decommissioning of this facility, I'd guess. I doubt they would have done either if they didn't have a more than adequate security force in place here, though."

"Lucky for us," Fortier snorted. "If they had all these things active..."

"Things?" LaSorte demanded at the same time Hernadnez said, "I don't like relying on luck. We need to move."

As if on cue, the gunfire started.

The crack of the first round sounded almost simultaneously with the shattering of the capsule by which we were all standing. Body and liquid spilled out onto the floor, more of it splashing on us than I cared to think about. The smell was awful, a mix of effluvia and rot that, under normal circumstances, would have twisted my stomach into a knot that could only be untied with violent emesis.

But these weren't normal circumstances, and I was in motion before I realized it. My first instinct was to give Tia a hard shove, clearing her from the line of fire. Only then did I dive for cover myself, scrambling to get my weapon into action. More gunfire was sounding now, some from the far end of the chamber, some answering fire from my companions. My dive had landed me behind another of the glass tubes. Intact, at least so far.

I finally brought the subgun to my shoulder. I leaned out for a quick glance, taking in the situation. The lighting was bad, just a few LEDs far overhead. The far end of the room was mostly shadow, excepting only the blinding muzzle flashes. I felt a bullet whiz past my head and ducked back behind the glass.

"Anyone got eyes?" someone shouted over the general cacophony. It sounded like Fortier, but I couldn't be sure.

"At least a dozen," Thompson replied, his voice coming over the radio. It wasn't much better than shouting, but it was slightly more audible over the thundering fire. The shakiness in his voice was gone, replaced with the same calm I remembered from the mats. I gave our side of the room a quick scan. Thompson had unlimbered his rifle, and was sighting down the scope, using a seated position with his legs in front of him and the rifle resting on his knees. The kid really did know his way around long gunning. Fortier and Al'awwal were shoulder to shoulder, each firing from opposite sides of shattered pylon, the rotting body of a half-grown synthetic draped over the glass between them. Hernandez was a little farther back, her pistol out, but not active. Given the ranges, she wouldn't have much chance to hit anything from where she was. Tia was opposite me, across the corridor formed by the rows of coffin-like tubes. Her shotgun was trained downrange and while it may have been slightly more useful than a pistol, she was biding her time as well.

"Shit," Thompson said. "Two on the move." Then the thirty-ought-six roared, the boom echoing in the room. "One down." The words—and, presumably, the casualty—were answered with a barrage of fire from the opposition that made all of us hit the deck and grab as much cover as we could. With the echoing chamber, I couldn't pin down the ordinance the enemy was using, but whatever it was, it could put a lot of lead downrange in a short time. Which meant they had plenty of resources for some of their team members to provide suppressing fire while the rest moved forward to flank and kill us. Now that Thompson had made the rifle's presence known, I doubted he'd get to spot or take a carefully aimed shot again. The bad guys had to know that if they gave us that kind of time, we'd eventually whittle them down. No. They'd come for us now.

Unless we went after them first.

I caught Hernandez's eye and using a mix of hand signals learned from the Army and the NLPD indicated that I was going to sweep around to the right and that she should head left. She nodded, gave me a thumbs up. I held up a single finger, indicating that she should wait, then keyed my mic.

"Al, Fortier. Hernandez and I are going to move up the flanks and try to intercept their fire teams. We're going to need some cover of our own. You game?"

"On your go," Al responded at once.

"And get to say that I saved your ass?" Fortier replied. "You bet."

"In three," I said, holding up three fingers for Hernandez as well. She was on the channel, and could hear me, but verbal communication could be dicey in the middle of a gunfight, even over the radio. "Two." I dropped a finger. "One." Just my pointer raised. "Go. Go. Go."

Hernandez swept left and I moved to the right, even as Al'awwal and Fortier popped out from cover. Neither had selective fire weapons, but they both had good trigger control and speed, and they managed to send enough of a barrage of firepower back into the face of the enemy that their fire slackened. We took advantage of the momentary reprieve, hopscotching forward from cover to cover.

Thompson's big rifle barked again, followed by the bellow of Tia's shotgun. Given the circumstances, neither was likely to hit anything, but it gave us a little more covering fire, and even trained soldiers balked when they heard the roar of a sniper rifle. I slammed into one of the glass cylinders, breathing hard. I'd covered maybe half the distance when the enemy responded in kind. A hail of bullets tore through the air. More glass shattered. More bodies spilled forth.

I heard a curse over the radio, male, but in the chaos, I couldn't recognize the voice. At least if they were cursing, they weren't dead. Then I saw a blur of movement, not at the end of the chamber. Closer. No more than fifteen feet away. The security team had the same idea, and had moved outward to flank us. Two hostiles. They'd taken the time to go wider, and were almost on my position. But they hadn't seen me yet.

I brought the silenced subgun up to my shoulder, and set the holographic sights on the first, squeezing the trigger twice before traversing to the next target. He was whirling in my direction, bringing his own weapon to bear when I squeezed off two more shots. I ducked back down as the target fell, not wasting time to make sure they were dead. "Watch your nine, Hernandez," I hissed into the mic. "They're flanking wide."

There was no answer, and no way I'd hear the pop of her nine-millimeter over the general cacophony. Nothing to do but keep going forward. "Two down," I added.

The thirty-ought-six thundered again. "One down," Thompson said on the heels of my declaration.

"Three more here," Hernandez added. Her breath came in short ragged gasps. "I'm hit, though."

"Fortier's hit, too," Tia said.

"I'm fine," Fortier growled over the radio. "Or I would be if your girlfriend would leave me the hell alone, Campbell."

"Still operational here," Hernandez said.

I could hear the pain in her voice, and in Fortier's. No matter what they said, and no matter what the vids would have you believe, there really wasn't such a thing as getting shot just a little bit. Adrenaline might carry both of them through for a few minutes, but at a price, and it was a price that would have to be paid soon. We needed to finish this, and quick.

"Moving," I said into the mic.

I put action to the words and made my way forward. If they'd sent two my way and three after Hernandez, that meant we'd taken down five. Thompson had put paid to another two with his rifle. No telling if Al'awwal or Fortier had managed to hit anything with their suppressing fire, but at least seven of the bad guys were down. That still left a half-dozen to deal with. We'd better than evened the odds, but we couldn't afford any more injuries.

Our suppressing fire had vanished, reduced to sporadic shots that I recognized as coming from Al'awwal's bullpup. But the other side's volume of fire had dropped as well. They were either hunkering down and waiting for reinforcements, or preparing for their own charge to try to finish us. My money was on the second.

I stalked forward, body lowered into a half-crouch as I moved, stock secure against my shoulder. The stance looked awkward from the outside, but it ensured as stable a firing platform as possible when on the move. I was closing distance, scanning as far ahead as the shadows allowed, looking for any telltale motion to betray the position of the enemy.

But this time, they were careful. And they were good.

Damn good.

I came within a half-inch of death. I saw the motion—the reflection of a barrel oddly distorted by the liquid-filled curved glass of one of the synthetic capsules—at the last possible second. There wasn't time to do anything other than hurl myself forward. I saw the muzzle flash. I heard the whizz of the bullet as it streaked past my head, and then I was on the ground, rolling forward. I crashed into the metal footer of the container at the same time I saw a pair of boots step out into the open.

I lashed out with my legs, scissoring them and catching the pair of boots, and the security officer to whom they were attached, in the sweep. He crashed down on top of me, something hard and rigid striking me just below the solar plexus. I felt the air driven from my lungs as I started gasping like a landed fish.

Another pair of boots rounded the corner, and I knew I was done. Two on one wasn't necessarily insurmountable. Unless, of course, the bad guys had guns, and you lying on the floor in front of them struggling to draw a normal breath. All I could do as I watched the second gun barrel come up was try to maneuver the security guard atop me into the line of fire. I heard a rapid *pop-pop-pop* but didn't feel the impacts. Had the guy managed to miss from less than six feet away? No. The shooter was falling, and the guy on top of me, who had been content to keep me locked up so his buddy could end it, started to put his heart into the fight. There was another, closer, pop and the guy on top of me shuddered, then went still.

Al'awwal appeared, moving in the same half-crouch that I had been, stubby bullpup shouldered. The shots had been from him—he'd dropped the shooter then put one round into the guy on top of me for good measure. That had been risky—the round could have easily passed through its intended target and had enough energy left to hurt me. But as far as I could tell, I hadn't been hit, and it was a hell of lot quicker than trying to engage the fucker hand-to-hand.

He reached down, dragged the body off me with one hand, still managing to keep his weapon at the ready with the other. "You hit?" he asked.

"I'm okay," I said in a strangled near-whisper. I was still struggling to breathe. "Wind knocked out of me."

He didn't acknowledge the words. Instead, he dropped into a kneeling position, set his shoulder against the remains of the shattered cylinder, and started firing. There wasn't much I could do, not until I could breathe again. I managed to use my legs and one arm to half-push, half-crawl a little deeper into the cover, focusing on trying to force air in and out of my bruised lungs. I took the time to pat myself down, looking for blood. I didn't think I'd been hit, but sometimes shock and adrenaline played weird games with the mind. By the time I'd finished—no new wounds, anyway—I could almost breathe normally again.

Al'awwal had stopped firing, executing a combat reload that was a thing of beauty to watch, pulling out a magazine left handed while using his right to drop the empty magazine. He shoved the new one into the well and had it seated and ready to go without ever bringing his weapon out of battery. But he held his fire.

"How many?" I asked, my voice still a little bit strangled. I cleared my throat. Tried again. "How many?"

"Maybe just a couple," he replied, eyes still trained downrange. The thirty-ought-six sounded and Al'awwal threw me a grin, his perfect white teeth seeming to glow in the dim light. "Maybe just the one." He glanced down at me. "You good to move out?"

I grunted, pushed myself to my feet. My hands were shaking a bit, so my reload wasn't nearly as smooth as Al'awwal's had been, but I slipped a fresh mag in anyway, stuffing the not-quite-empty one into a pouch to reload later. I'd already burned through more than half my combat loadout. "Wait one," I said, dropping down to the bodies at my feet. They were using subguns as well. A quick check revealed theirs to be a sleek-looking Brazilian model that, unfortunately, was chambered in forty-five instead of the nine-millimeter I was using. I thought about it for a moment, then unclipped one, securing it by its tac strap to one of the carabiners on my MOLLE gear. A quick pat down revealed a few extra magazines, which I stuffed into another dump pouch. The extra weight wasn't great, but I'd rather be humping another fifteen pounds than run out of ammo in the middle of a firefight. "Ready," I said.

"We're moving," Al said into the radio.

"I took down another hostile," Thompson's reply came back. "I can't be sure, but I think we've got two more. This room's as bad for thermal visibility as it is normal, but I think they're right near the exit we want."

"Then we go through them," I replied. I clapped Al'awwal on the shoulder as I moved out, resuming my leap-frogging from cylinder to cylinder. The fire from the enemy had flagged off almost completely. If they only had two shooters operational, there really wasn't much they could do but hunker down and wait for a clean shot. But if we got overconfident or sloppy, we'd give them the opportunity they were looking for. Hernandez and Fortier had already been hit. No matter how much I tried to put that thought out of my mind and do the job before me, it kept creeping back in.

We'd almost made our way to the rear wall of the chamber, having continued our wide sweep. The door was set roughly in the middle of the wall we were approaching. We were at most ten yards from it, and maybe twice that from the closest side wall. I saw motion, and immediately ducked into cover, Al close on my heels. The shots rang out a heartbeat later, smashing more glass and showering us with whatever rancid chemical soup filled the watery graveyard through which we traveled. I was long since past the point of being able to smell anything, for which I was eternally grateful. If my brain hadn't decided that it had more important things to deal with, I'd probably be curled into a ball vomiting from the fetid stink.

I leaned out and returned fire, stroking the trigger. I couldn't see much in the sight picture, just muzzle flashes and flickers of movement, but I didn't really need to see anything. I wasn't trying to hit anything, so much as keep the attention of the bad guys directed on me. Al was moving, stalking wider, looking for a better angle. Somewhere, on the other side, Hernandez would be doing the same, provided she was still up. She'd been quiet on the radio, which worried me a bit. And Thompson was out there, rifle ready, looking for the shot. I had no idea where Tia and Fortier were, but I hoped the coroner's assistant was too busy patching up Fortier to put herself in the line of fire.

Thompson's rifle barked and a form behind the barrier rose up. I didn't wait to tell if it was because they had been hit, or if they were trying to move to cover. I just put the reticule on them and squeezed the trigger. Al did the same, and I saw more muzzle flashes from the opposite side of the room. Hernandez was still up. The security guard went down, transfixed by multiple rounds.

In an act of desperation, the final guard rushed from behind his cover. He wasn't screaming. Instead, he had his weapon up and firing, sending a barrage of lead in my direction. I made myself as small as possible as rounds slammed into the glass container and ricocheted off the sturdier metal base. Then the shooter was down, as Al and Hernandez caught him in a crossfire.

They didn't stop to check on me, instead rushing to the position from which the security team had been holed up. I pushed myself to my feet and ran forward to meet them, but it was already over. There were a number of bodies, and the pair had kicked weapons clear from dead hands, but it looked like we were alone.

Then I really looked at Hernandez.

Her face was ashen, and her left arm hung limply at her side. Blood oozed from a wound high on her biceps and flowed down the arm, until it dripped from the fingers of her hands. "Dammit," I snarled. I keyed the mic. "We need Tia up here, now."

"It's okay, *hermano*," she insisted. She threw me a wan grin. "If it hit anything really important, I'd be dead by now."

"Shut up, Hernandez," I said. I was vaguely aware of Al'awwal securing the area, making sure there weren't any hidden bad guys waiting for the opportune time to strike. Which was probably what I should have been doing. Instead, I moved to Hernandez's side, and shined a flashlight into the wound. She winced as I manipulated her arm, turning her to check for an exit wound. I found one—a nasty, ragged tear from which more blood oozed. I said a silent prayer, thanking whatever gods might be listening that the bullet had missed the brachial artery.

Then Tia was there, pushing me out of the way. "Keep the light on her," she said as I gave way before her professional brusqueness. "Through and through. You'll be okay." She opened her medkit and started pulling out bandages, disinfectants, and god-alone knew what else. I did my best to keep the light steady as she worked, but was distracted as the rest of the team arrived. Thompson had slung his rifle and had his pistol—a big revolver—in hand. Silas and LaSorte were carrying Fortier between them, a situation none of the three looked particularly comfortable with.

The detective had his right pant leg cut away halfway down his thigh. A tightly wound bandage—already showing some seeping red against the white—wrapped tightly around his leg, covering from his kneecap up beneath the ragged hem of his shortened pants. He was sweatier than usual, and a grimace of pain twisted his face, but his subgun looked like it had been put to use. "This sucks, Campbell," he said. "Why couldn't you find a base guarded by geriatric Girl Scouts or something?"

"They'd probably kick your ass, too," I shot back, but without any real heat.

He made a sound that was half-grunt, half-chuckle as the synthetics lowered him to the ground. If he was disturbed by resting so close to so many corpses, it didn't show on his face. "What now?" he asked, rubbing gently at his leg.

"We keep going," I said at once. I glanced at my watch—the entire fire fight from the first rounds to now had taken less than four minutes. "Hopefully this was their ready team, and any other security is still gearing up. We've got a small window to get this shit done."

"Lead on, oh Captain," Fortier said with another snort. "I'll be sure to hop along behind you." There wasn't any sarcasm in the words, just a sort of comic fatalism. I felt my stomach twist a bit. Maybe it was from the stench of my own kit—now that the adrenaline was calming down, my sense of smell was returning, and it smelled like I'd rolled around on a slaughterhouse floor before taking a nice long swim through a chemical tank. But maybe it was the fact that, for a second there, I could almost like the fat detective.

I shook that thought from my head. "You good, Hernandez?" Tia was tying off a bandage. I noticed an expended syringe on the floor, probably a pain killer.

"The doc's worked her magic," Hernandez responded. She tucked her nine-millimeter barrel first under the armpit of her wounded arm, wincing as she did so. It allowed her to drop the mag, then pull a fresh one from her own dump pouch, and slam it back into the gun. She gritted her teeth and racked the slide by shoving forward with her right hand while clamping down on the frame with her left arm. It had to be excruciating with the bullet wound, but she bared her teeth in something akin to a grin. "Might need some ammo, though."

"Two minutes to reload mags and re-kit as best we can," I said. I pulled some nine-millimeter subgun mags from my pouch. "Use these to reload, Hernandez. I'll switch to this." I patted the Brazilian weapon. "Everyone else, find whatever you can use and let's get locked and loaded. We've still got a job to do."

Chapter 20

We made our way through the underground Walton Biogenics facility. Maybe my prediction was right, and the guards we'd taken down were the Walton equivalent of a rapid response team and the rest were gearing up to come finish our little operation. Maybe we were luckier than we had any right to expect, and that had been *all* the security force, dropped in the charnel chamber that housed the remains of so many synthetics. Whatever the reason, we made our way through the halls until at last we were in front of another unlabeled door. Well, not entirely unlabeled. There was nothing to indicate who worked here or what the specific function of the room was, but the plain metal door did bear a single sign.

It had the black circle and three crescents on a field of bright yellow that anyone over the age of about ten years old would instantly recognize. But in case someone lived in a cage, the word "Biohazard" was painted in block letters beneath the symbol.

"Seems like we're in the right place," Al'awwal noted.

"To bad we don't have any MOPP gear," I said. "I guess we just open the door and go in."

"A moment, Jason," Silas said, voice strained. The synthetic looked… bad. As bad as when he'd been in the mask. His breathing was strained, his face sweaty. His frame, always intimidating, seemed somehow shrunken. But the determination in his eyes burned as bright as ever. "We can verify if there are any warnings on the network. If LaSorte can take care of Detective Fortier on his own for a moment?" LaSorte nodded, shifted his stance a bit, and took the full weight of the injured detective. Fortier, for his part, tried to keep as much of his weight as possible on his uninjured leg and off the synthetic. Despite Silas's illness and Fortier's injury, the three working together had managed to slow us only a little bit, while keeping the shooters free to engage any combatants that popped up.

Silas's fingers swiped over his screen. "Everything seems to be intact. Or, rather, shut down. There is no indication of any contaminants." Another swipe. "And the door should be unlocked." A strange expression crossed his face, and he swallowed numerous times, as if trying to get down a mouthful of food that was sticking in his throat. "And, Ms. Morita, it may be time for more of the numbing agent."

Tia moved to his side, administering another dose of the mild paralytic that kept Silas from giving our position away with the racking coughs the Walton virus had left him with. I waved at the others, and they stacked up, moving now like a well-oiled machine. We weren't exactly expecting armed resistance on the other side of the door, but practice and preparation now might save lives later. I nodded to Al, on the opposite side of the doorway from me. He reached out, pulled the latch, and gave the door a shove.

I was the first one through, the unfamiliar subgun up and at the ready, flashlight sweeping across the room. My first impression was of a hospital, or maybe a morgue. Clean, white tile. Stainless-steel tables. Lots of glassware. A bank of indefinable machines and equipment that reminded me vaguely of the forensics lab. The back wall wasn't really a wall at all, but rather a giant sheet of glass or translucent plastic. I could see behind it to a number of smaller chambers—labs, maybe—isolated from the rest of the area. The room was large— not half as big as the synthetic graveyard we'd had the firefight in, but still huge. Thirty people could have comfortably worked in the space. Fortunately for us, it was empty.

The entire team made their way inside. Silas and LaSorte found a rolling office chair, and deposited Fortier in it while the rest of us spread out. Al stayed at the door, covering our six in case security showed up. "Is this it?" I asked. The question wasn't directed at anyone in particular, but all eyes turned to Tia.

"Someone find a light switch," she said.

"I've got it," LaSorte replied, tapping at his screen. The overhead lights, bright white LEDs, burned to life, banishing the shadows and filling the room with an almost sterile glow.

"What are we looking for?" Hernandez asked. Tia had fashioned her a sling out of an elastic bandage, securing Hernandez's left arm in a more comfortable position. She'd holstered her sidearm, leaving her right arm free to poke and prod at the various vials and test tubes scattered across the tables.

"I'm not sure," Tia admitted. "I need to get into one of their screens. LaSorte? Silas?" The pair nodded and moved to one of the desk-mounted screens, powering it on and starting to work their magic. "The rest of you... Try to find any handwritten notes. It's a long shot, but maybe there's something they wrote down. And anything in a sealed vial, like the kind that holds drugs to be administered via hypodermic needle." She rummaged around in her medkit, pulling out a small glass tube sealed with plastic or rubber at the top. "Like this. But don't open *anything*," she warned. "We don't know what might be cure and what might be plague. So, look, don't touch. Okay?"

We all responded in the affirmative, and set about our tasks. It took me about thirty seconds to realize it was futile. I had no fucking idea what I was looking at. I was afraid to reach out and touch any of the assorted glassware—though none of it looked to have anything in it, anyway. It reminded me of any time I walked through one of the few brick-and-mortar stores that clung desperately to existence, the kind where every available inch of space seemed to be packed with shelf upon shelf of breakable shit. It always felt like one wrong turn, one misstep, and I'd find myself shattering thousands of dollars' worth of merchandise. Maybe that's how they stayed in business.

Still, I did my best. Opening drawers, poking around racks of test tubes and flasks and shit I couldn't even name. Looking for anything sealed, or, a treasure beyond worth, a fucking notebook. Anything.

No one else seemed to be having any luck, either. Fortier had rolled his chair one-legged over to the individual labs at the back and was studying the control panels to the airlock-like doors. I hoped to god he wasn't dumb enough to open one, not without clearing it with Tia first. The others were pretty much doing the same thing I was. Wandering about, poking their noses into whatever bit of lab tackle looked interesting. Except for Silas, LaSorte, and Tia, who all three had their faces close to one of the screens. They were our real hope at finding a cure. The rest of us were just the mooks who had to deliver them to this room and get them back out again. It was humbling to think that, despite being the "face" of the revolution, when it came down to it, I was just a monkey with a gun.

"No!" The cry came from Tia, and it had me spinning about, bringing my weapon to my shoulder and scanning for targets. My eyes found her, and I had to scan again, she looked so distraught. Silas and LaSorte weren't looking much better. Or rather, LaSorte was looking almost as bad as Silas who, generally, looked like shit. All of their eyes were locked onto the screen before them.

"What is it?" I asked, moving that direction. The others were gathering as well, even Fortier, rolling his way toward us. I noticed that his bandages had darkened. The wound wasn't gushing, but he was still bleeding. Bad sign, and something I should point out to Tia.

"It's gone. It's all gone," she wailed, glaring at the screen.

"What's all gone?" I asked, trying to keep my voice calm and soothing against her despair.

"The cure."

Those two words hit me like a fifty-caliber bullet. Had we really come all this way, fought through the security, taken casualties, just to fail? "How?" was the only thing I managed to get out.

Silas answered, voice strained from the paralytic, but lacking the despair that filled Tia's voice. He sounded almost resigned somehow. "It was part of the decommissioning process, Jason," he said. "They had not produced much of the...cure."

"Targeted virus," Tia corrected absently, her eyes, tears leaking from the corners, staring blankly at the screen. I wasn't about to ask for the difference between the two.

Silas shrugged his acknowledgement. "Targeted virus. What they did make, it seems they did only for use of their soldiers. Who, it seems, are not genetically immune. They require the vaccine, the same as any of us would. According to the records we were able to find, all of the cure they produced was used. There is none stored, and it seems they destroyed all the samples. There is nothing left."

"No," I said flatly. "I don't accept that. It can't just be gone. We're in their fucking lab for Christ's sake. Can't we just make more?"

"From what?" Tia asked, and I winced at the bitterness in her voice. "You can't just push a button and make a cure out of thin air. Even if we could figure out which of this equipment they used, or what the process was, we'd need..." She trailed off. A strange expression flashed across her face. It was half the "eureka moment" of an idea and half a flash of horror.

"Need what?" I demanded.

"Shut up, Campbell," she snapped. "I'm thinking."

I'd never seen her like this before. I looked at the others, who exchanged shrugs with me. We backed off, even the two synthetics, giving her space to work. I was conscious of the time ticking by. If there was any security force left in the facility, they'd have gathered in strength, maybe even put out a call for reinforcements. We were far enough from anything that we probably didn't have to worry about outside reinforcements getting here, even by chopper, before the whole thing was done, but that might not matter.

I worked the problem in my head, forgetting about searching for anything in the lab. I'm not sure how much time had passed while I was considering options and working my way through tactics, but my reverie was shattered when Tia said, quite distinctly, "Well, fuck me." Hearing Tia say those words, whatever the context, could probably have woken me from the dead. In this case, though, it got everybody's attention.

"Did you find anything?" Hernandez asked.

Tia looked up from the screen and around the room. She seemed to be searching for something. Her eyes found Fortier, who was sitting, slumped in his chair, by the glass wall leading back to the working labs. "Fortier," she said, raising her voice nearly to a shout. "Check those labs. You're looking for a…" She trailed off. Thought about it for a moment. "You won't know what it's called. You're looking for something that looks like the offspring between Frankenstein's lab and Satan's juicer. It should be in one of those labs."

That description certainly got all our attention, and Fortier uttered a weak laugh and after apparently dismissing the lab he was right outside of, starting slowly rolling toward the next one. The rest of us started moving that way, all except Tia. There was something…off…about her posture. Like she was both excited for, and at the same time dreading, whatever it was that Fortier might find.

"Got it," Fortier shouted. "Ha! Satan's juicer. What the fuck am I looking at?" he demanded.

"A chance," Tia said. But there were tears in her eyes again.

"What is it?" I asked, turning back and moving to her side.

There weren't just tears in her eyes. She was crying. No. *Sobbing.* Deep, wracking sobs that she was somehow holding most of the way in, making her body shudder with suppressed emotion. "Oh, Jason," she whispered and threw herself at me. Her arms locked around me, and I was suddenly juggling my subgun and Tia. "I wish there *wasn't* a way." Her words were said with such savage intensity that I pushed her momentarily away, so that I could stare into her tear-stained eyes.

"Jesus, Tia," I said. "What is it?"

The others had gathered now, forming a loose semi-circle around us. No one said anything, aware that Tia wasn't exactly in a place to have questions shouted out her. But the look in all their eyes shouted the questions anyway. What had she found? And why was she reacting this way?

She pushed herself away from me and collapsed into the chair again. For a few heartbeats, she just sat there, staring into her hands. Then she drew a deep breath and scrubbed her palms over her face, wiping away the tears. When she looked back up, her features were calm, though her eyes were still deep wells of pain. "There's a way," she said.

Everybody opened their mouths to speak at once, but she held up one hand. I wasn't sure if it was the professional authority or the raw emotion, but we all obeyed that outstretched hand and kept our mouths shut. "Listen first," she said. "The machine that Fortier found... We can use it to make more of the targeted virus... The cure. Enough to start LaSorte, Al'awwal, some of the others on it. And, more importantly, enough to reverse engineer the process. Hopefully enough that any halfway competent bio-chem student or hospital can make more."

"That's fantastic," Hernandez exclaimed. Her next words died on her lips as Tia turned a hopeless stare on her.

"But we can't make it out of thin air. Walton built a machine to expedite the process. It's complicated," she said, rubbing her face again, "but the short version is that it takes the original virus, breaks it up, and reassembles it into a sort of engineered retrovirus that seeks out and neutralizes the original agent." She paused. Opened her mouth. Faltered. Look back down at her hands.

"But it cannot make the retrovirus out of nothing," Silas said. An understanding smile stretched his lips, the first I'd seen in a long time. He stepped forward and placed one hand comfortingly on Tia's shoulder. "It is quite all right, Ms. Morita. Please. Tell them the rest."

She gazed up at him and the tears started again. But her voice was steady as she continued. "To have any chance of reverse engineering things, we're going to have to get a lot of different labs involved. We're going to need a hell of a lot of the retrovirus, of the vaccine, if we're to have any hope of saving more than a few dozen synthetics."

I still wasn't getting it. "So?"

"So, we need a lot of the virus to make a lot of the retrovirus, *hermano*," Hernandez, said. Her voice had dropped to a whisper and she was looking back and forth from Tia to Silas.

It hit me then. We needed a lot of the virus. And the only virus we knew we had was currently coursing through Silas's veins. Satan's juicer. Motherfucker. "How much?" I demanded. Tia visibly flinched at my tone, and I wanted to reach out to her, but I couldn't. She was just the messenger, but damn it. Just. Damn it. "Sorry. How much?"

"Too much," she replied.

"What's going on?" Thompson asked. The rookie looked completely poleaxed, he was so lost in the conversation. "Can someone please spell this out for me?"

"They need the virus that is in my system," Silas said. That smile was still on his face. "And to get it, they will need my blood. In my weakened state, I imagine there could be serious consequences from even a moderate amount of blood loss." He chuckled. Actually fucking chuckled. "I imagine a moderate amount is not what we are needing, here. Correct?"

Tia just nodded.

"And so," Silas said, "I find myself with the opportunity to save my entire race, and all it will cost me is my life. Tell me, would any of you hesitate, if faced with such a decision?" He laughed, softly, strained by the paralytic, but with genuine mirth. "Of course you would not." He raised his hands to stave off our objections to his high opinion. "You can tell yourself otherwise, but the fact that you are here, putting your lives at risk to save the synthetics, gives away the lie." He stared at each of us in turn and his shrunken, plague-ridden body seemed to swell. He stood straighter, as if a great weight had dropped from his shoulders. He drew a deep breath. "Thank you," he said, to each of us in turn. "Each of you has done more for the synthetic cause than I can possibly say."

Fortier was trying to turn away, and I swear to fucking god, I saw tears of shame and denial on the fat man's cheeks. "Even you, Francois Fortier," Silas said. "Perhaps especially you, since if we are successful, you can be held up as an example of how humanity can change. How humanity *must* change. But you all have offered up your lives to make the lives of the synthetics better. Now"—the smile broadened—"Now it is simply my turn."

LaSorte was openly and unashamedly weeping, and I saw tears in Hernandez's eyes as well. Hell, I felt them, like little hot suns burning at the back of my own eyes. Tia stood back up, locked her arms around Silas's waist, and buried her face against his chest. He leaned down, and whispered something into her ear. Shudders passed through her body, but then she was pushing herself away, attempting to straighten out her tactical gear with the sharp little tugs that women often used with suits or dresses. Silas gave each of us another smile, and then said, "I believe the detective would say that it is time to get to work."

I damn near lost it at that. I felt the tears spilling over, but I drew a ragged breath of my own and did my level best to will them back into my body. It didn't work, but the concentration kept me from devolving into a blubbering mess. "There is no other way?" I asked.

"No," Tia said in a voice so soft I had to strain to hear it.

"You are sure, Silas?" His arguments all made sense, and I knew beyond a doubt that I'd make the same choice. Even so, I had to be certain.

In answer, he started walking off to the lab with the machine Tia had so eloquently described as Satan's juicer. "I got the door," Al'awwal said. There was a hitch in his voice, and I turned to see that even he had tears in his eyes. He met my gaze briefly, then turned away, shouldering his weapon and taking up a post just inside the doorway. It gave him a perfectly legitimate reason to turn his back on us, hiding his own tears.

Silas moved with the same implacable determination that had always been his hallmark. I knew then that not only would trying to stop him from doing this be wrong, it would also be impossible. As soon try to stop an avalanche. The thought brought a smile to my face, even through my tears, and I took two long strides to catch up with the albino synthetic. He might be walking to his death, but he sure as shit wasn't going to walk alone.

He glanced up at me and gave me a slight nod, that single gesture saying more than we could have said with words. It, and the gratitude and contentment I read on his normally expressionless face, somehow encapsulated everything we'd been through together, everything we'd done to get to this point. What had Sanjay, the first victim of the plague, said?—"*If I die, I die free.*" I saw that in Silas's gaze, felt it in the sureness of his stride. If he died, he died free.

The others seemed to understand that we needed to do this part alone. They held back—not far, just a few paces, giving us a little space, a little privacy. LaSorte must have been working his magic, because as we approached the airlock-style door into the lab, it cycled and opened. We didn't even have to break stride. I felt my steps flag a little as I saw the machine. It wasn't quite as bad as I was expecting from Tia's description. More than anything, it looked like the big brother of the cell separators used for plasmapheresis. A comfortable-looking chair. A number of tubes and wires. A big blocky machine that, yes, had a cylindrical shape reminiscent of a juicer, particularly with the nozzles and hoses. But that was it. Still, I felt myself hesitate.

Silas had no such hesitation. He walked up to the machine, gave it a quick once-over and then, smooth as if he'd done it a thousand times before, slid into the chair. Tia appeared at our side, and started doing something with the machine. While she worked, Silas looked up at me. "Do not worry, Jason," he said. "I truly am ready for this. And I know that if you could trade places with me, you would." He reached out a hand, grabbing my forearm. "In all my years, I have never had a friend. Friendship, real friendship, among synthetics is—no, *was*—a path that could only end in pain. These last few months…" He trailed off, and I looked up toward the ceiling blinking rapidly as I felt fresh tears spilling from eyes. "No matter what happens, Jason, I would not trade them."

I took his hand in mine, squeezed. I couldn't get any words out. I was afraid if I tried, I'd lose it. So, I just squeezed his hand. It was enough.

"You'll feel a little pinch now," Tia said. She was holding some plastic tubing that ended in a large gauge needle. She hadn't bothered swabbing the injection site or anything like that. What was the point?

"Do it," Silas said. She inserted the needle into his veins, right near the elbow joint. Aiming, I realized, for the brachial artery. The only indication of pain or fear was the tightening of his grip on my hand. "Make sure Evelyn and Jacinda get dosed as soon as possible. They have to live, Jason. Promise that you will keep them safe."

I nodded, tears falling from my eyes onto his brow. He didn't seem to notice. "Good. You are a man of your word." He smiled, though it seemed weaker. I was aware of the machine humming, of Tia stepping away from the bedside to monitor the progress. How long would it take? "Al'awwal and LaSorte, too," Silas said. "They will both try to refuse. To insist that there are others more important or more deserving. But they are the ones who will have to carry things to completion. LaSorte has all the keys."

I didn't quite understand that last bit, but I just nodded. If nothing else, I could make sure that they got the cure. Silas's grip was weakening, and his hand was growing colder. His body had been ravaged by the plague. Only his enhanced constitution and iron will had kept him upright for the infiltration of the Walton Biogenics facility. Now, with his blood being rapidly drained, he was losing the ability to fight.

"Thank you, Jason," he whispered. And then his eyes closed. His grip eased. I could still see the slightest rise and fall of his chest, and I looked over at Tia, my eyes wide. She just shook her head. He'd lost consciousness, but that shake told me what I needed to know. He wouldn't wake up again.

I held his hand, kept it clutched tight in my own. Conscious or not, I couldn't let him face this last part alone. It didn't take long. No more than a minute later, his chest rose and fell for the last time. A brief shudder passed through him. And then he was still.

Chapter 21

"He's gone," Tia said. She looked at me over Silas's body, the tears running freely down her face. They mirrored my own. The others, all excepting Al'awwal, came forward then, to pay their last respects. I had to turn away from their pain, lest it reinforce my own. Tia was still busy. Still working the problem. Still getting what we came for.

"How long?" I asked her.

She knew what I was asking without having to explain. "Not long. This is better tech than anything I've seen before. If we could take it with us…" She shrugged. "But we can't. Maybe we can force Walton to share the technology." We both snorted at that thought. "It would save lives, Campbell. We'll have enough to do as Silas wished, to take care of Evelyn, Jacinda, LaSorte, and Al'awwal. With enough left over to synthesize more. But if we had these machines? We could do it so much faster. Save so many more lives."

I looked over my shoulder, to see LaSorte bent double over Silas's body, head down on his folded arms, weeping. "We can only do so much, Tia. But, and I hate myself for this, we have to do it *now*. We have to get out of here, and every second we wait, it gets harder."

She glanced at the screen. "Two minutes," she said.

I nodded. Turned to the others. "I need everyone in the next room in thirty seconds." They looked at me, shocked by the steel in my voice. LaSorte looked more than shocked. He looked hurt. And pissed. I didn't care. "Do it," I said, and walked out.

No one looked happy, but thirty seconds later, everyone but Tia—who was still finishing up with the cell separator or gene splicer or whatever the fuck the machine was—was standing in a loose semi-circle around me. Everyone looked beat, emotionally and physically drained. LaSorte still looked pissed, and Al... the only thing I could call the look on his face was...murderous. At least I didn't think that one was directed at me.

"We're all tired. We're all hurt. And most of us just lost someone we loved." LaSorte started to speak, but I cut him off. "I know, LaSorte. I know I'm not giving you time to mourn. I know it's not right. I know it's not fair. Too fucking bad," I damn near shouted. "Every second we sit here, Walton is gathering their forces. Do you think that one paltry security team is all they left behind? No. They're out there. And they're going to do everything in their power to make sure that we die here. And if we don't get out of here, if we don't get the cure back to revolution central, that means we did all this for nothing. That means Silas sacrificed himself for *nothing.*" I was glaring at them, practically growling the words, but I didn't care. "I'm not going to let that happen. Do you understand?" They growled back their affirmatives, and in that moment, I thought that maybe even LaSorte would be capable of pulling a trigger.

Tia came up to me. Her pack looked much fuller than it had, and I didn't want to think about the contents. I doubted it was literal bags of Silas's blood, but that was the image in my head. In her hands, she held two syringes. "LaSorte. Al'awwal. You get the first doses of the cure."

"I'm not even sick," LaSorte objected, even as Al'awwal was saying, "Not necessary."

"Shut. The. Fuck. Up," I snarled. "Not my call. Not your call. Silas's wishes, and if I have to beat you down and inject you myself, I will." In that moment, I meant it. I was on the very edge of losing control, feeling the kind of unbound violence that hadn't surfaced in me since the night I killed Annabelle's parents. I needed to get a grip, to get control.

But at least it was working. Both synthetics looked at me, the shock of my threat breaking through their reticence. Tia didn't hesitate, just stepped up and took advantage of the situation to inject each of them. "Good," I said. "Now, we're getting out of here. By now, they've figured out how we got in. Trying to get out the same way would be suicide. We know the facility is decommissioned, so we're going out through the main building. LaSorte, you need to find us the shortest path to the surface, and from there out to the parking lot. There's security here, so they'll have vehicles. We'll be commandeering a couple."

"On it," he said. His anger had dissipated, and while his eyes were still dark with grief, his voice was determined.

"Good. You're also going to have to help Fortier on your own." I glanced at the detective. It looked like the bleeding had stopped again. He looked like I felt—tired, wrung out, in a shitload of pain, though, in his case, physical. "You gonna be able to fight?" I asked.

"As long as someone can hold me more or less upright and point me in the right direction," he replied.

"Good. Thompson."

"Sir?" Thompson barked, falling, perhaps unconsciously, back into his training.

"Your job is to make sure that Tia stays safe. She's got the knowledge and the cure. She's the one who has to get out. Her survival is paramount. You kill anything that tries to get to her. Got it?" He threw me a salute and stepped close to Tia, who, for once, didn't bother objecting.

"Me and Al are taking point. We kill anything that gets in the way." I looked at the First. "Any issues with that?"

The smile that creased his face was more like a snarl. "None whatsoever."

"Hernandez, you're tail-end-Charlie and what passes for our reserve. Go wherever you think you're needed."

"Roger that, Campbell," she said crisply. Even with her arm in a sling and tearstains on her face, she looked ready to kick ass and not bother taking down the names.

"Good." I looked back toward the chamber where Silas's remains would rest. It was foolish to think that we'd be able to reclaim them, more foolish to try and take them with us. This underground facility would be his graveyard, at least until Walton Biogenics or their successors did something with the remains. It saddened me, but I knew that the part of Silas that made him Silas wasn't with the flesh. He'd shuffled off his mortal coil, and I prayed to god that he was finally free and at peace.

"Section," Thompson suddenly barked, turning on his heel to face the chamber. "Atten-*shun*!" I found myself bracing automatically to the rigid stance of attention and was aware of Hernandez doing the same at my side. Fortier pulled on LaSorte's sleeve, and the synthetic helped him up, so that he, too, could stand in an approximation of the position. Tia came up on one side, Al'awwal on the other. Tia just stood straight, making no effort to truly emulate the military pose, but Al'awwal slipped into it so easy that I suddenly wondered if he had actually managed to serve at some point in his lengthy years. "Pre-sent," Thompson said, "arms!"

I snapped out a salute, conscious of the other officers and Al'awwal following suit. Tia placed her hand over her heart, and LaSorte did the same. It wasn't much as far as funeral rites went, but it was the best we could do with the time we had. We held it for a few seconds, and then

Thompson barked, "Order arms!" My hand snapped back down to my side, ending the salute.

"Rest in peace, friend," I said, dashing fresh tears from my eyes. "Thank you for that, Thompson," I added. Then I drew a long breath, released it as a sigh. "All right, everyone. Time to get to work."

* * * *

Al eased open the door and I reached out into the corridor, using a shard of a broken mirror to survey the hallway in both directions. As expected, I caught faint flickers of motion from either end, where the hallway bent. Walton Security knew where we were, and they'd set up a nice, lethal abattoir for us to walk into.

"They're out there," I informed the others. "But it looks like they're content to wait for us to walk into the kill box. They know we aren't going anywhere right now."

"Flashbangs?" Hernandez asked. Among the gear they'd smuggled out of the station were a few flashbangs—nonlethal grenades that produced a brilliant flash of light and a massive detonation without any of the fiery explosion or shrapnel of their deadly cousins. We hadn't had the time to deploy them earlier.

"Might as well," I agreed. "But they're at both ends of the hallway. We're going to have to toss 'em, and then split up and try to take down whoever's out there before they get their senses back. If they've got defense in depth…" I shrugged. If they were smart enough to set up a layered defense, with one position covering the next, we were screwed. But even if we were dealing with some of Walton's elite bully boys, they couldn't have an endless supply of bodies, and I doubted they'd have wasted them all here. Even if it was the better strategy, corporate types always wanted a reserve, a fallback plan. No. They'd have broken their teams up, left some to guard the exits or have some kind of "omega plan" to deal with us if we broke through. "Al, we're the most mobile. I go left. You go right. Hernandez, you're with me. Thompson, you go with Al. Tia, take his rifle and give him the riot gun." They swapped weapons, Tia looking surprisingly comfortable with the long gun. "Fortier, Tia, you're our reserve. Something goes wrong, you guys need to come to the rescue." I got a nod from both, though with Fortier reliant on LaSorte to get anywhere, I wasn't sure how much help he'd be in a charge. "All right. Pass up the flashbangs and get ready."

The ordinance was passed forward and I gave everyone a ten count to get the last of the jitters out. Then I pulled the pins, leaned out fast and tossed a grenade each direction. I was already leaning back in before the first rounds started firing as the enemy positions reacted a touch too slow. I turned my back to the door, clamped my hands over my ears, shut my eyes, and let my mouth hang open. We were far enough away that it might not be necessary, but better safe than sorry. The other detectives and Al both had enough training to respond accordingly. I hoped Tia and LaSorte saw us and copied the pose.

A few seconds later, there was the earth-shattering *kaboom*. Okay, not quite that loud, but I sure as fuck was glad I'd covered my ears. The flash wasn't so bad, distance and corners being what they were, but the concrete hallways did a hell of good job of amplifying and carrying the noise. I was up and moving, my ears still ringing, the second the blast had past. I was conscious of Hernandez on my heels and Al'awwal and Thompson sprinting down the corridor in the other direction.

We had the shorter dash, about thirty feet of hallway before a new hallway crossed its path and the first one terminated. I slid into the intersection, turning right, Hernandez at my six turning left. Her nine-millimeter started barking a heartbeat before my forty-five. The flashbang had done its job. There were four bad guys on my side of the hallway, all of them disoriented. The one at the back, farthest from the blast, had at least some sense about him still as he was clawing for his weapon. I shot him first, three quick trigger pulls that started center mass but rode upward on the recoil so that the third round drilled a half-inch hole into his forehead. I walked my fire closer, putting rounds into each of the guards. It was cold-blooded. But we didn't have time to play cop and break out the restraints, even if we'd had any. And we couldn't afford to leave live enemies at our backs.

When I'd executed the last guard—no sense in sugar coating it—I turned to find that Hernandez had dealt with hers. Three security guards on her side. Three bodies on the floor. She was executing another combat reload, all with one arm tied behind her back. Okay. In front of, but still. I did a quick mag swap and started moving out, going to support Al'awwal and Thompson, but there was no need. I hadn't registered their battle, not in the intensity of the moment, but as I turned their way, they were already heading for us.

"We need to move out," Al'awwal shouted. "Our guys got a radio message out. They know we've broken through this position."

Not ideal, but not something we were likely to have been able to prevent, either. Thompson and Tia did another weapon swap, this time on the move as we got the entire group in motion. I felt a little guilty as we swept past the bodies I'd dropped—it was clear they hadn't made any effort to defend themselves. But only a little. It wasn't just kill-or-be-killed. It was kill-or-millions-would-die-and-everything-you've-done-will-be-for-nothing.

"Left," LaSorte called as we reached another intersection. I moved into it, subgun up and ready. We kept moving that way, heads up and on a swivel, following LaSorte's shouted directions as he guided us through the labyrinth of the underground facility and toward the upper floors and freedom. We weren't able to move at a sprint, or even a run. With Fortier lamed, the best we could do was a sort of half-jog. Even that was wearing on LaSorte, Fortier, and even Hernandez, whose wound had to be paining her.

"Right," LaSorte said as we approached another intersection.

I hugged the wall and popped around the corner and ran full tilt into the enemy. They'd been running as well, clearly trying to get to some position, somewhere. We were intermixed before I could even shout a warning, and the hall erupted into chaos and gunfire.

For a frantic moment it was all assholes and elbows, as both teams intermingled and tried to separate the good guys from bad. I punched the barrel of the subgun forward, slamming it hard into the chest of a security guard, and pulled the trigger at contact range. Then I twisted to the side, letting the falling corpse past. That gave me line of sight to another security guard, who was posting up, bringing his weapon to bear and training it on Tia. Fuck that. I dropped him with three quick shots and then the roar of Tia's shotgun momentarily deafened me. I felt something slam into my plate carrier, heard someone else cry out in pain. The staccato pops of Al'awwal's bullpup sounded, and two more bad guys dropped.

Then it was over. I did a quick count. Counted again. Ten bad guys down.

But only five of us standing.

LaSorte and Fortier were both on the ground. Fortier didn't look like he'd been hit, just dropped when LaSorte fell. But the synthetic had one hand clenched tight to his side, and I could see the blood welling out from between his fingers. "Medic," I shouted, mostly by force of habit, before turning my gaze on Tia.

She was white as a sheet, fingers trembling on the shotgun she held. Her eyes were locked on one of the security guards. Or what was left of him. The shotty was loaded with solid slugs, and a full ounce of lead did very bad things to the human head. Odds were, she hadn't been going for a headshot, but the top half of the security guard's nugget had disintegrated, painting the wall behind him. "Be sick about it later," I snapped, grabbing her arm and pushing her toward Fortier and LaSorte. I hated to do it, but we didn't have time to coddle anyone. "Anyone else hit?"

"You are," Hernandez said, leaning against the wall as she did another one-handed reload. Everyone else was doing the same, making sure their weapons were ready for the next engagement. I was about to follow suit, when Hernandez's comment reminded me of the impact on my plate carrier. I reached down, felt for the wound. It was right over my solar plexus.

"Fuck," I whispered, as I pulled out chunks of the shattered ceramic plate. "Too close."

"You okay?" Al asked, looking back down the hallway rather than in my direction.

"No blood," I said. "Hurts a little to breathe." I didn't realize it until I'd said it, but it was true. "I'll be fine. Tia? How are LaSorte and Fortier?"

Fortier beat her to the answer. "I'm fine. Wish this fucking leg would stop bleeding, but if someone can lend me an arm, I'm ready."

"LaSorte will be okay, too," Tia said, voice quiet. She still looked shaky, but tending to the wounded seemed to have centered her. "Just a crease. Painful, but no real risk."

"Can you still help Fortier?" I asked the synthetic who was being pulled to his feet by Tia.

"I think so," he replied.

"Good. We can't afford to take shooters off the line. Are we ready to move?" I got thumbs up all around and nodded. "Let's do it, then." We shuffled to our feet, but before we could start moving, one of the hallway doors sprang open. A team of three Walton personnel emptied into the hallway, already firing.

I felt two hits on my back, and they threw me to the ground. I managed to spin as I fell, landing on my knees facing the shooters, and I saw LaSorte, Fortier, and Tia all drop before the barrage.

"Mother fucker!" I screamed. My vision went red and I was aware, tangentially, of my finger working the trigger as I used my legs and one arm to half crawl, half throw myself forward. I got the first one with three or four rounds, and put a few more into the second. The third was too close, the barrel of his Brazilian subgun swiveling down to meet me, so I dropped my own weapon and grabbed the barrel. It was hot as shit, but I didn't feel it, yanking it past me and down as he fired, the rounds going off so close to my head that my hearing was replaced with a loud whine.

The unexpected tug cost the shooter his balance though, and he hit the ground hard. I was on him, straddling his back, before he'd had the chance to bounce. I sent elbow after elbow into the exposed bit of neck between his ballistic helmet and his vest. I heard something crack. Maybe from him, maybe me, but I didn't care. It was Annabelle all over again. I wasn't going to stop until I took his fucking head off.

"Campbell! Campbell! Jason!"

Tia was screaming at me. Tia. *Tia* was screaming at me. Annabelle was dead. Tia was dead. Dead like Annabelle. I'd seen the shooters drop her. But the dead didn't scream. My vision cleared.

She was standing over me, shaking me, trying to get me to come back to myself. I scanned her, looking for injuries. Her nose and mouth were bleeding, probably impact from hitting the floor. But I didn't see any other blood. No other injuries.

"Jason, stop," she said, her voice pleading.

For a second, I didn't understand. Then I looked down at the man I'd tackled. Or what was left of him. Sometime during the barrage of blows, his helmet had come loose. Sometime later, his skull had split. I'd been pounding my elbow repeatedly down into a pulpy mass of shattered bone and liquifying brain tissue. It was…unpleasant. I could feel the pain shooting through my elbow, knew that I probably had fragments of the guard's skull lodged in it. I didn't care.

Tia was alive.

I scanned the hall. Al and Thompson had taken up guard positions, watching all avenues, alert for the possibility of more attackers. Stupid. Not them. Me. Should have ordered that to begin with. "How?" I asked, not sure what I was asking.

"A couple of rounds hit my pack," she explained. "I got lucky. We all got lucky. They didn't penetrate the pack, and they missed most of the retrovirus."

"Fortier? LaSorte?"

"It's bad," Tia acknowledged. "But let me look at you, first. You're bleeding." She looked at the corpse I was riding with disgust, but still said, "Don't move, okay? I need to look at your back."

At that point, the pain hit. It hurt most right over my kidney. I remembered now, getting hit again, but there should have been a plate there. The vital organs all had plates over them. So why the hell did it hurt so bad?

"The plate shattered," Tia said as if reading my mind. "A good chunk of a ceramic shard broke off. It looks like it's pierced your back. I can't tell how deep."

"Pull it," I said.

"That's incredibly dangerous," she replied. "It's better to leave it—"

I cut her off. "No. I know. It's better to leave it in. If you can get to a hospital. Or immobilize the patient. We can't do either. Yank the fucker and let's see what happens. It's move or die, Tia, and I can't move with a knife in the back."

"Fine, you stubborn ass." I didn't think that was particularly fair, and neither was the sharp, sudden pain as she pulled the shard free. For a second, I thought the pain was going to make me vomit, but then it eased. Which is to say, it hurt like hell, but I could move.

"Thanks," I said. "Help me up?"

She grunted and pulled me to my feet. My back hurt. My chest hurt. Hell, my everything hurt, but I was still operational. Maybe we had a chance.

Then I saw Fortier. And LaSorte.

Both were leaning up against a wall, next to each other. Fortier's already injured leg was red with new blood; he had torn the wound open somewhere along the way. But his left arm was also shredded, hanging limply below a tourniquet that crossed his biceps. I could see the bones of his arm, so mangled was the wound. His face was paper white, but his eyes were open, somehow holding on to consciousness.

LaSorte didn't look much better. He was hunched forward, head in his hands. His side was still bleeding, adding its own red stain to the pool collecting around Fortier. I couldn't see any new wounds on him.

"He saved me," LaSorte whispered as I limped over to them. "Shoved me out of the way. He took bullets meant for me."

I looked at Fortier with a new appreciation and an arched eyebrow. Tia had rematerialized at his side, and was administering something from a syringe. I wasn't sure how deep her medkit ran, but I was damn glad she had it. Now that she'd mentioned it, I could see the bullet holes in the pack on her back. Which reminded me of the gash in mine.

Fortier gave a wan smile and a one-armed shrug. "Seemed like I owed synthetics something," he grated.

I was eying him appraisingly. "We have to move out," I said.

He snorted. "Fuck you, Campbell. I'm done following you around. I've finally found a nice comfortable bit of hallway. Think I'll just stay here." The words were flippant, but his eyes were somber. He knew that there was no way he was going to walk. Getting him out would require a stretcher and a couple of bodies. And even then... I looked at the blood, at his color. At Tia's expression. They told a clear story. Fortier wasn't going to make it. The grin on his face told me he knew it, too.

"What?" LaSorte demanded, turning on Fortier. "You can't. Campbell. He saved my life. We can't just leave him."

"Got to, kid," Fortier growled. I wondered if Fortier had any idea that LaSorte, despite all appearances, may well have been older than him. "Try to drag me with you, and I'll slow you down. Plus, if I move much, it'll probably kill me. Right, doc?" he asked, looking at Tia, who was securing the remnants of his lower arm as much as possible. The fact that Fortier wasn't reacting at all to her ministration of the grievous wound was either a testament to the power of the drugs Tia had given him or, more likely, a combination of the tightness of the tourniquet and the onset of shock.

"Contact left," Al snapped, following the words with a salvo from his bull pup.

Thompson's sidearm, a .357 revolver, also roared. "Contact rear," he added as he pulled a speed loader out of a dump pouch to make a quick reload if the need arose.

"You gotta move, Campbell," Fortier said. "Wish I could say it's been fun. But you're a fucker and I never did like you. "Even if you turned out to be right." A faint flush managed to suffuse his face, despite the blood loss. "Tell my girls how I died." Then he pulled the quick release strap on his subgun, letting it fall to the ground, and unholstered his pistol. He pulled a couple of extra mags from his dump pouches and set them in his lap. "Anyone got a real grenade?" he asked.

"We only managed to smuggle out two," Hernandez said as she approached. She pulled the ordinance from her pack, and passed them over.

"I'll buy you as much time as I can. But you better get the fuck out now." He pulled the pin from one grenade with his teeth, but didn't release the spoon. Instead, he stuck the grenade under his good leg, using the weight to keep the spoon from ejecting and priming the trigger. He pulled the pin on the next grenade and held it in his hand. With the pistol in his lap, a grenade in hand, another ready to blow if he so much as moved, he was ready to put up a hell of a last stand.

I reached down and gave his good shoulder a squeeze. "Wish I'd had the chance to get to know this Fortier," I said.

"Fuck you," he replied. But he said it with a smile.

LaSorte was still looking poleaxed, but I dragged him to his feet. "Get it together, LaSorte," I barked, my face inches from his, trying to snap him out of it. "You're the only one that can get us out of this shithole. And according to Silas, you're the one that has all the keys to keep the revolution running. So, we don't have fucking time to coddle you."

He licked his lips, looked from me to Fortier. Winced as more gunshots rattled off from Al and Thompson.

"We gotta move!" Thompson shouted.

"Understood, Detective," LaSorte said. The words were shaky, and he couldn't stop looking at Fortier, but he said them. Something in his tone, or maybe the words themselves, reminded me, just a little, of Silas.

"Good. Hernandez, me and you got point. Al, Thompson, keep up your fire from the rear. Make sure you don't hit Fortier. Tia, LaSorte. In the middle. Let's move out."

I saw Tia pull one more syringe from her pouch and inject Fortier before standing up and joining us. Fortier looked immediately better, sighing a bit and taking a firmer grip on the grenade he held. The pain had eased from his face.

We moved quickly down the hallway, leaving Fortier leaning against the wall, staring intently in the direction of the enemy.

"What was that?" I asked.

"Powerful narcotic," she replied. Then frowned. "Related to heroin. All the rage on the streets. It will probably kill him, especially with everything else I pumped him full of. But not for a few minutes."

I nodded. Fortier wasn't going to last a few minutes, anyway. "Got any more?"

"A couple."

That was comforting.

We moved out. I trusted Al and Thompson to make sure the security behind us kept their heads down. Then we rounded another corner, breaking line of sight. Thompson and Al stopped shooting, but even through the ringing in my ears I heard the faint sounds of a heavy metal object striking concrete. A second later a thunderous explosion rocked the halls. Then the sound of smaller caliber fire—Fortier's pistol—took up the cadence, counterpointed by fire from the security subguns. I shook my head. The universe was upside down. Silas was dead and Francois fucking Fortier was making an honest-to-god heroic last stand so that we could get away. They awarded the Medal of Honor—posthumously—for that sort of thing in the green machine.

We went another fifteen, twenty seconds, and then the second grenade went off. I had no doubt that it went off underneath Fortier, as the bad guys charged his position. Everyone winced when they heard it. Everyone, even the noncombatants, knew what it meant. But we were past the time for tears. Past the time for regrets. That would come later. Now, we just had to hope that Fortier's sacrifice, that Silas's sacrifice had been worth it.

"Stairs on the left," LaSorte said. His voice was tight with pain, and he kept one hand pressed tight against the bullet crease in his side. The other held his screen, out and at the ready, and the directions kept coming.

We stormed the stairwell, half-expecting to find another security team waiting for us. Stairs were almost as bad as hallways from the shooting gallery perspective. But it was clear. The steps themselves were metal, zigzagging up a square concrete tube, lit by dim LEDs. "Five flights to the surface," LaSorte said.

We moved as fast as we could, given our state. At each landing we slowed, and either me or Al'awwal stopped to cover the door until the rest of the team was past, essentially switching spots at point and tail on every floor we passed. It was exhausting, sprinting up a flight of stairs, waiting in tense silence while everyone else passed you by, wondering if the door your weapon was trained on was going to be kicked in. Wondering if you'd hear booted feet rushing down from above or up from below. And then having to sprint back up to the others to catch up. By the time we'd cleared all five flights, we were all panting. Even Al'awwal, who had the stamina of an Olympic athlete crossbred with a horse, was sweating and short of breath. That did shitty things to marksmanship, but the odds of us surviving another firefight were getting longer with each passing minute, anyway. We couldn't do much but hope that LaSorte had found a clear road out.

"One hundred feet," LaSorte said between gasps for air. "Straight shot. Emergency exit. Empties into an employee parking lot. Should be multiple vehicles in the lot. Even with the place being decommissioned, we know there's security. Probably other employees, too."

We were risking a lot on a probably, but it was our only chance. I found myself missing Silas and his seemingly endless supply of battered cars that showed up when you needed them. I wondered if one of the "keys" LaSorte had was to that whole operation. Not that it was going to help us here, even if he did.

"It's going to be guarded," Al'awwal noted. "Do we have any ordinance left?"

"Help me with the pack," Hernandez replied. Tia moved over and helped her get the straps off her good shoulder and then past her sling. "We probably should all ditch the packs, or at least get them down to bare necessities." While she spoke she was tearing open the Velcro top and rummaging around. In the end, she came up with two tear gas grenades and one smoke.

"We don't have enough masks to get us all through the tear gas," I said. "I wish we did, but it won't do a lot of good if we incapacitate ourselves."

"Smoke?" Al'awwal asked.

It was a tough question. Again, we didn't have gear to see through the smoke. Only Thompson's rifle had a thermographic scope. The rest of us would be just as hindered as the enemy. If they blindly opened fire once the smoke started, we'd be in trouble. But if they waited, we might be able to get the drop on them.

I studied the map on LaSorte's screen. It looked like a hallway lined with offices dead-ending at the emergency exit. If I was the bad guys, I'd have people posted in the doorways of the last couple of offices. I tried to remember how many of the bastards we'd dropped already. A dozen in the chamber of horrors. Another ten or so in the first guarded position. Three more in the ambush where Fortier had been hit. Plus however many Fortier had managed to catch in his last stand. Jesus. We'd dropped most of a platoon. How many guards could they have running this decommissioned nightmare?

"Fuck it. Worth a shot," I said. "We'll pop smoke, then charge in two teams down the walls of the hallway. I'd put money on these last four offices," I tapped the screen, "being where any shooters are, so focus there. But don't ignore the other doors. We don't have time to clear each one, so watch your ass."

I'd shrugged out of my own pack while talking, and made sure to top off my magazines. I had a few loose rounds, but I left them, along with the rest of the contents of the pack. I wished I'd had the foresight to bring some extra plates. As it stood, my carrier was next to useless. I dropped it too, pulling the lighter Kevlar from the pack and donning it instead. It wasn't as good as the plate carrier, but it was better than nothing.

"Okay," I said as the others made their final preparations. "They can't know we're here, but they know something's going on. Al, you've got the best arm. You throw the grenade. Hopefully, they'll be enough on edge to think it's the real deal and dive for cover. Once the smoke starts, we haul ass. If we're lucky, we'll take them like we did the guards we hit with flashbangs. If not…" I shrugged. "If not, we take them anyway. Questions?"

The only response was some checking of weapons, and Al reaching out a hand to Hernandez for the smoke grenade.

"Ready," he said, holding the explosive in both hands, one on the body, one on the pin.

I looked at each person in turn, got answering nods. I moved up to the doorway, grabbed hold of the handle. "Now!" I barked, yanking the door open.

Al'awwal hurled the grenade down the hallway. I heard it hit the tile floor, bounce, slide. A few rounds rattled off as I slammed the door shut. They didn't seem to be aimed in our direction. More like panic fire. Then I heard someone shout, "Grenade!"

Good. Maybe that would slow them down. There was a sharp *bang* followed by a hissing sound. I opened the door once more and Al sprinted through it. I was on his heels, the others following close behind. I went down the left side of the hallway, Al down the right. Thompson was on Al's six, then Tia. Hernandez and LaSorte followed me.

Smoke had filled the hallway, thickest down near the end where the grenade had landed, but already drifting toward us. I heard coughing ahead, which was a good thing. Meant the security guards didn't have masks and would be hampered by the smoke. So would we, but at least we had surprise on our side.

The first shots started sounding from the enemy, but I didn't hear any ricochets. I hoped that meant they were firing down the middle of the corridor, thinking we were charging right into the teeth of their guns. The muzzle flashes illuminated the white smoke in odd ways, casting orangish shadows, but it also helped give away the enemy position. They weren't in the last four offices, but rather, only in the last two, one on each side of the hall.

I opened up with the subgun, stroking the trigger as fast as recoil control would allow. I wasn't aiming at the muzzle flashes on my side of the hallway. The angles were all wrong to do any damage there. Instead, I focused my fire on Al's side, and by the sounds of surprise and the screaming, I found at least one target. Al's team opened up as well, doing the same thing, spraying across the hallway at my door. They had a hell of a lot more firepower, between Al's .556 and the twelve gauge Tia was operating. Even Thompson's .357 packed a powerful wallop, and the fire from that side of the hall suddenly slacked. Then there was a scream behind me, and Hernandez dropped. LaSorte was on her in a heartbeat, and though every part of me wanted to check on her, I kept moving, kept shooting. I executed a combat reload, dropping the magazine and ramming in a new one so quickly that it barely broke my pattern of fire. I continued slamming round after round into the best approximation of the doorway I could picture, given the thick smoke.

I saw the silhouettes of Al's team closing on my point of fire, popped off a couple more rounds, then stopped shooting. The moment I did, they charged forward, breaching the room. I did the same, sprinting the last dozen feet or so, one hand training on the left wall until it found the doorway. I came in shooting, putting rounds into the forms lying in the room. I needn't have bothered. Between the slugs, the bullpup, and the heavy revolver, the place had been shredded. Three bodies were on the ground. All three dead. "Clear," I shouted.

"Clear," came the response from Al.

"Tia!" that was LaSorte, calling from somewhere up the hallway, where Hernandez had gone down.

"Fuck!"

I rushed back that way, coughing and choking on the smoke. I could see Hernandez on the ground, teeth gritted in pain and a low, steady stream of Spanish expletives falling from her lips. At least she was alive. Blood was pouring from a wound in her hip, and I winced in sympathy. From the angle, it had to have hit bone, which meant, at best, a long and painful recovery.

Tia arrived. Took one look at the wound and pulled out a syringe. "This is going to feel really, really good," she said. "We'll get you up and moving, but I need you to stay as calm as possible. I don't want you to have a heart attack on me, okay?"

"Hurry the fuck up," Hernandez snarled. "Just drug me already. And let's get the fuck out." At least she wasn't spouting some nonsense about staying behind. Not when we were this close.

"Al, take LaSorte and Thompson. See if you can find us a vehicle," I ordered.

"Roger that," Al'awwal replied.

They disappeared out the door as I put one arm under Hernandez's good shoulder. "Up we go," I said, lifting her by main strength. We both gasped as our respective wounds rebelled against the strain, but I managed to get her on her one good leg without us both falling over. Tia was dropping the syringe, and getting her weapon back in battery.

"I thought you said I'd feel good..." Hernandez started to say. Then her eyes widened, glazed over a bit. "Never mind. You're a nice lady. You should marry her, Campbell."

That took both of us by surprise and we shared a startled glance. "Gotta move," I said, lurching forward in the world's most awkward three-legged race. We hadn't had time to bandage Hernandez, and she was leaving a fair amount of blood behind, but that could wait.

A van with Walton's logo plastered on the side pulled up to the door. I raised the subgun left-handed, ready to fire—and single-handed from my off hand, definitely miss by a mile—when I realized that LaSorte was sitting in the driver's seat. The doors slid open, and we piled in. Before they had even started to close the van was in motion, sending us tumbling to the floor. Hernandez didn't even scream, so good were the drugs Tia had given her.

I did. Like a school girl.

Back injuries sucked.

Epilogue

The three women could have been sisters.

They didn't look particularly alike, one being tall, lithe, blonde, another petite, dark-haired, and the third, red-haired and built with the compact muscles of a gymnast, but they shared similar mannerisms. They shared a familiarity with one another that was generally reserved for siblings. They sat, one next to the other, on a small couch, too small for three people. They touched hip-to-hip and shoulder-to-shoulder, but seemed to take comfort in the contact. All three had been among the first inoculated against what was now being called Synthetic Flu.

They watched the screen in front of them as the news unfolded. It had been nearly three months since the assault on the Walton Biogenics facility now widely known as the Potato Farm. The names of those who had gone in, and the names of those who had not come back out, were widely known. Some hailed them as heroes. Some as villains. For others, like the three women, the relationship was even more complex.

They had belonged, until very recently, to an NLPD detective by the name of Francois Fortier. He had not, in their estimation, been a good man. He had certainly not been a kind man. They had been subjected to degradation, humiliation, pain. And then, as they had watched from hidden places and secret screens the revolution spread, he had changed. Changed to the point where he had, according to a long message from none other than Jason Campbell himself, given his life to save a synthetic, a Toy.

They had shared many a long conversation around that. It didn't undo what had been done to them. There was no balancing of some cosmic scale where they could simply forgive and forget. But, they had concluded that, perhaps, a person, human or synthetic, man or woman or anything else, could be more than just one thing. Could be defined, *should* be defined not just by the bad they had done, or by the good they had done, but by *all* they had done, by the sum totality of their lives. Maybe, just maybe, a person could be an asshole and a hero.

Certainly, people seemed to think as much about former detective Jason Campbell. While those who had helped him had been pardoned, the man himself was still wanted by several agencies for, if, no other reason, having orchestrated a jail break. There were those who called him a murderer. Others who felt he was an anarchist, seeking to tear down the fabric of society. Others still, who while they mouthed support for his cause, felt *someone* had to be held responsible for inciting riots and protests and countless atrocities. And so he was still wanted, still a fugitive, sought after by law enforcement agencies across the world.

But the consensus among the vid reports and bloggers was that no one was looking very hard. The focus, instead, was firmly on Walton Biogenics and the empire they had built on the backs of their slaves. The women—they still hadn't chosen names for themselves, but refused to think of themselves by the names *he* had given them—found it both sad and amusing that as much outrage, perhaps even more, was directed at the fact that Walton Biogenics had *also* suppressed medical research that could extend the lives of people, cure numerous illnesses, and generally lead to better health for all. While that was certainly criminal, from their perspective, it paled in comparison to what had been done to synthetics.

Had been, being the operative words.

In the wake of the revelation of the plague and the sudden appearance of samples of the retroviral cure at medical centers across the nation, country after country had passed emergency measures granting full citizenship to the synthetic population. The road to freedom had not been smooth, but it had not been quite as rough as some had feared. The attempted genocide by Walton officials had been a bucket of cold water on the anger of those who might object too strenuously.

Walton was in the process of being dismantled. As was so often the case, it looked like only a few of the employees would see any real consequence beyond the seizure of their assets. The blame game had been played to perfection, and, miraculously, only a dozen or so people in an organization spanning tens of thousands of employees could be shown to have any true culpability. Those dozen would be sentenced. The rest would go free.

But Walton was done. Every dollar of their assets and stock had been seized, every penny that could be shown to have come from their dealings, forfeited. That pool of money had been earmarked to be partitioned out among the synthetics, among the survivors. They had already seen some of it, in the form of a monthly endowment that, in addition to the BSL, would provide a relatively comfortable life, even if none of the three chose to seek other employment.

The growth of synthetics had been outlawed, unanimously and universally. And some ground had already been taken in reversing the engineered sterility that had been built into them. No synthetics would be grown, but in the future, they could be born. The little baby Jacinda had been the first natural-born synthetic, but she would not be the last.

This was all good news to the three women, the three former Toys. But it came with new burdens. They had never been free. They had never had the agency to act of their own free will. Quite simply, they didn't know where they fit in society, didn't know what to do with themselves. Programs were being set up, funded from the massive trust provided by the liquidation of Walton Biogenics. Counseling was available. Perhaps soon they would avail themselves of those services.

But for the moment, they were content to sit here, watching the world change on the screens, in the company of women who were closer, each to the next, than genetic sisters could ever be. They were content to walk slowly into their newfound freedom, and let others, like this LaSorte who was driving so many of the changes, plow the road.

They would walk it, too.

In due time.

About the Author

J.T. Nicholas was born in Lexington, Virginia, though within six months he moved (or was moved, rather) to Stuttgart, Germany. Thus began the long journey of the military brat, hopping from state to state and country to country until, at present, he has accumulated nearly thirty relocations. This experience taught him that, regardless of where one found oneself, people were largely the same. When not writing, Nick spends his time practicing a variety of martial arts, playing games (video, tabletop, and otherwise), and reading everything he can get his hands on. Nick currently resides in Louisville, Kentucky, with his wife, a pair of indifferent cats, a neurotic Papillion, and an Australian Shepherd who (rightly) believes he is in charge of the day-to-day affairs.

For more info please visit www.jtnicholas.com, or find him on Facebook and Twitter @JamesTNicholas.

SINdicate

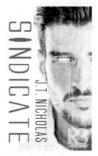

Don't miss this thrilling installment of
J.T. Nicholas's New Lyons Sequence series!

The Post-Modern Prometheus

Synths were manufactured to look human and perform physical labor, but they were still only machines. That's what the people who used—and abused—them believed, until the truth was revealed: Synths are independent, sentient beings. Now, the governments of the world must either recognize their human nature and grant them their rightful freedom, or brace for a revolution.

Former New Lyons Detective Jason Campbell has committed himself to the Synths' cause, willing to fight every army the human race marches against them. But they have an even greater enemy in Walton Biogenics, the syndicate behind the creation and distribution of the "artificial" humans. The company will stop at nothing to protect their secrets—and the near-mythological figure known to Synths as "The First," whose very existence threatens the balance of power across the world . . .

Chapter 1

There was a body on my doorstep.

I don't know what woke me, or what drove me to climb so early from the narrow cot that served as my bed. Maybe it was some lingering cop instinct from my time with the NLPD, that nagging sense that something was wrong. It was that instinct that had me tucking the paddle holster of my forty-five into the waistband of the ratty jeans I had fallen asleep in.

I slid open the door of the eight-by-eight walled office cubicle that served as my bedroom and stepped out onto the cavernous floor of what had once been a call center. The first rays of dawn were peeking over the eastern horizon, filtering through what remained of the call center's windows, casting the interior in monochromatic grays accented with darker pools of shadow.

The broad floor was filled with sleeping people. Sleeping synthetics. The genetically engineered clones that had served as an underclass of slave labor for decades and, with a small amount of help from me and a whole lot of work and planning from a synthetic named Silas, had begun a de facto rebellion.

I padded among them on bare feet, stepping as silently as possible, and yet, without exception, the eyes of each synthetic I passed popped open. They stared at me, stark white against the gray, eyes wide, searching, and somehow fearful. Not one of them moved. They waited in statue-like rigidity, a coiled-spring tension resonating from their stillness. It lasted only a moment, until they realized where they were; until they realized who I was. I couldn't begrudge them that moment of fear, but it still hit me like a punch to the gut.

Such was life in revolution central. Nearly a month since we had taken over the air and net waves. Nearly a month since we had ripped off the veil covering the ugly truth that synthetics were not unthinking, unfeeling things, but as much people as any of the naturally born. Nearly a month, and for synthetics, things had gotten worse.

Much worse.

It wasn't unexpected. Silas had predicted the reaction from society at large when we shone a spotlight on the truth that everyone suspected but no one seemed willing to admit. It had started with protests. Angry people marching with signs about respecting their rights and not dictating what they could do with their bought-and-paid-for property. The protests should have collapsed under the weight of irony alone, but instead they had given way to violence—violence directed almost entirely against synthetics. Viral videos of synthetic beatings—always popular—had hit unprecedented highs, as had videos depicting darker, more depraved "punishments" for those who dared to think they might one day be "real" people. The violence, in turn, had given way to death. Not on a widespread scale—not yet. Whatever else they might be, synthetics were, after all, expensive. Only the very wealthy could afford to dispose of them wantonly.

We'd given the world an ultimatum: give synthetics rights, or be prepared to have all the little secrets that they had gathered in their decades of near-invisible servitude released to the public. Silas had managed to bring together and weaponize secrets that could topple governments and destroy lives. The plan was simple enough—release a wave of compromising information on a number of politicians and public figures. The first wave was embarrassing, but not damning, not actively criminal. If that failed to spark action, then a second, more catastrophic wave would be released. And so on, until the governments either acceded to our demands or toppled from the sheer weight of skeletons tumbling out of closets.

But as that deadline crept closer—now just over a week away—the bodies were beginning to pile up. The richest among society—individuals and corporations alike—could afford to throw away a synthetic here, a synthetic there, and as the dawn of revolution approached, they made their position clear. One billionaire businessman had gone so far as to cobble together a reality livestream. Every day, contestants undertook a series of challenges, and the winner got to kill a synthetic in any way they chose, all during a livestream that, last I checked, had viewership measured in the millions.

And yet, there was hope out there.

That hope was part of the reason the floor I moved across was filled with synthetics, crowded in here and there in clusters amidst the cavernous call center. They would trickle in by ones and twos, somehow always finding us, despite our having changed locations four times in the past month. Most told the same story—their nominal owners, horrified by the revelation that they had, in essence, been keeping slaves, but terrified of the possible reprisals from those who thought differently, had simply set them free. Turned them out. Part kindness, part assuaging of guilt...and part washing your hands of a problem you wanted no part of.

I didn't know how they found us. They trusted me enough to share some pieces of their stories. The part I played in the rescue of Evelyn, what I had sacrificed to get the truth out, had earned me that much.

That didn't stop a young synthetic girl, maybe seventeen, from rolling into a half crouch as I neared. Her hands were extended in front of her, a gesture half defense, half supplication. Her look of horror and shame and guilt and fear reminded me so suddenly and sharply of Annabelle that it was like a knife twisting in my intestines. Her mouth opened and formed a single word, not spoken, but clear as a gunshot nonetheless.

"No."

What could I do? I wasn't the one who had hurt her, but she'd been hurt, badly. I offered a smile and kept my distance. It took a moment for the recognition to dawn, for the panic to quiet. Quiet, but not fall silent.

I was still an outsider. I belonged to a different class, a class that had long subjugated and tormented them. A human. Trust only extended so far. But I had my suspicions as to how they found me, and my suspicions had a name.

Silas.

The albino synthetic who had started my feet on this path remained elusive. We received messages from him on a regular basis, and he made brief appearances a couple of times a week, mostly to check in on Evelyn and make sure she was receiving the medical care she needed so late in her pregnancy. But after only a short visit, he would vanish with the ease that had made him so damn hard to track down in the first place. He, or rather his messages, told us when to move, and where to move. That let us know when my former brothers and sisters in blue were getting too close. I had no doubt that it was his network that funneled the turned-out synthetics to our door.

I just didn't know what in the hell he expected me to *do* with them.

Whatever Silas might hope—whatever I might hope—when February 1 rolled around, the governments of the world would not simply roll over, pass some new laws, sprinkle a shit-ton of fairy dust, and declare that synthetics were now all full-fledged citizens. And by the way, sorry about all the assaults, rapes, and murders suffered in the interim. No. The months ahead would be steeped in blood.

And not one of the synthetics that were beginning to stir with the rising sun would be able to spill a single drop of it. Call it conditioning. Call it brainwashing, but synthetics were engineered to be incapable of violence, even in self-defense. Which was going to make fighting a war pretty fucking hard.

* * * *

I had nearly reached the main door of the call center. The entire front of the building—once a shining wall of steel and glass—had been boarded up, long sheets of plywood secured to the frame. Thin cracks of light filtered in where the boards fit imperfectly, and more came from openings higher up, where other windows had been spared the fortification. I had moved through that fractured light, my unease growing with each step. I dropped my hand to the butt of my pistol, thumb finding the retention lock and easing it forward.

A four-by-four rested in a pair of brackets across the door, barring it more effectively than any lock. I had eased it off with my left hand, straining slightly with the effort, and lowered it to the floor. I had pulled the door open, reflexively scanning left and right, searching for threats. Nothing. The tension I'd felt since awakening had started to ease.

Until I had looked down.

And saw the body.

Printed in the United States
by Baker & Taylor Publisher Services